He could make any bargain he wished, because he held all the power.

She believed he possessed what she wanted, and she had no idea that it was, indeed, she who had what he so desperately needed.

He made the logical decision.

"Are you willing to submit yourself to me? To become the vessel of my sacrifice?" Seth asked.

The color drained from her face. Her eyes grew wide as saucers. "Wait. *Sacrifice?* What kind of sacrifice?"

Seth's lips curved in a humorless smile, showing her the tips of his long, lethal fangs.

"My dear, I am vampire. And my need? It can be slaked only with your blood."

Books by Nina Bruhns

Harlequin Nocturne

*Night Mischief #25
**Lord of the Desert #93
**Shadow of the Sheikh #100
**Vampire Sheikh #105

*Dark Enchantments
**Immortal Sheikhs

NINA BRUHNS

credits her Gypsy great-grandfather for her love of adventure. She has lived and traveled all over the world, including a six-year stint in Sweden. She has two graduate degrees in archaeology (with a specialty in Egyptology) and has been on scientific expeditions from California to Spain to Egypt and the Sudan. She speaks four languages and writes a mean hieroglyphics!

But Nina's first love has always been writing. For her, writing for Harlequin Books is the ultimate adventure! Her many experiences give her stories a colorful dimension and allow her to create settings and characters that are out of the ordinary. She has garnered numerous awards for her novels, including a prestigious National Readers' Choice Award, three Daphne du Maurier Awards of Excellence for Overall Best Mystery-Suspense of the year, five Dorothy Parker Awards and two RITA® Award nominations, among many others.

A native of Canada, Nina grew up in California and currently resides in Charleston, South Carolina.

She loves to hear from readers, and can be reached at P.O. Box 2216, Summerville, SC 29484-2216, or by email via her website at www.NinaBruhns.com or via Harlequin Books, www.eHarlequin.com.

VAMPIRE SHEIKH

NINA BRUHNS

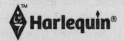

TORONTO NEW YORK LONDON
AMSTERDAM PARIS SYDNEY HAMBURG
STOCKHOLM ATHENS TOKYO MILAN MADRID
PRAGUE WARSAW BUDAPEST AUCKLAND

Recycling programs
for this product may
not exist in your area.

ISBN-13: 978-0-373-61852-1

VAMPIRE SHEIKH

Copyright © 2011 by Nina Bruhns

Dear Reader,

And so we come to book three of the Immortal Sheikhs trilogy. What an incredible journey it has been! This has hands down been one of my very favorite series. Being able to reimmerse myself in my love for all things ancient Egyptian has been an absolute treat!

Have I saved the best for last? Perhaps…

The hero of *Vampire Sheikh*, demigod Seth-Aziz, has truly captured my imagination. From the beginning, he reminded me of a twelfth dynasty poem that is a classic among Egyptologists and philosophers alike: "The Discourse of a Man with His Ba," also known as "The Man Who Was Weary of Life." Imagine my surprise when Seth actually started quoting passages from the poem. Surely, I had found the composer of this amazing piece from so long ago.

Cast in the mold of the brooding philosopher-king that we romance readers love so well, Seth-Aziz has sacrificed his personal happiness for the sake of his people. But like all people, modern and ancient, what he really yearns for is love. The love of a woman who truly understands him. The love of someone who can share his burden of leadership.

I hope you have loved immersing yourself in the mysterious, exotic world of Egyptian gods and shape-shifters as much as I did. And if you'd like to read the full text of Seth's poem, please check out the *Vampire Sheikh* page on my website, www.NinaBruhns.com.

Good reading!

Nina

For all the anonymous poets and philosophers of the past and the future, whose amazing words and universal truths will continue to inspire us all through the ages.

Stanzas from an Egyptian XII Dynasty Poem

The Man Who Was Tired of Life:
The Discourse of a Man with His Soul

O my Ba, so foolish to belittle the sorrows of life.
Lead me toward death... For my suffering is pressing,
A burden too heavy to be borne.
O sweet relief, if the gods would but scatter
The secrets of my body.

Lo, my name is reviled,
More than the smell of carrion
On a summer's day when the sun burns hot.

Lo, my name is reviled,
More than that of a woman
About whom lies are told to her husband.

Lo, my name is reviled,
More than the town of a monarch
Which utters sedition behind his back.

To whom shall I speak today?
Gentleness has perished
And violence rules the day.

To whom shall I speak today?
Men are contented with evil
And goodness is neglected.

To whom shall I speak today?
The past is forgotten,
And the need of yesterday's hero ignored.

To whom shall I speak today?
My heart is burdened
For lack of a soul companion.

Death is within my sight today
Like the scent of myrrh,
Like shelter on a windy day.

Death is within my sight today
Like a childhood path,
When a man returns home from war…

Chapter 1

Present day
Winter Palace Hotel
Luxor, Egypt

There was someone in her hotel room.

Josslyn Haliday bolted upright in bed, listening intently in the midnight darkness. She heard nothing. But she felt a presence—a thick, almost physical energy creeping over her bare skin. *Dark. Ominous. Threatening.*

"Who's there?" she called into the black void of the room.

No reply.

Unbidden, her sister Gemma's last warning echoed through her mind….

Beware the vampire.

Despite the heat of the Egyptian desert pressing in

through the open balcony door, a chill of goosebumps spilled down Joss's arms.

Slowly, she eased her hand toward the shotgun she'd hidden under the hotel's luxurious bed linens. Her fingers clasped the familiar wooden stock and eased it upward.

"Show yourself or you'll live to regret it," she called out in Arabic, and she snapped the gun up, sweeping it in a half-circle, seeking the unseen intruder.

Joss did not believe in vampires.

Or shape-shifters or mummies or any of the other fantastical creatures of the myths and legends her ethnographer sister Gemma seemed to take at face value when listening to the stories of the local villagers. Josslyn was an archaeologist, a scientist, and she needed to see hard evidence to instill belief.

This prowler was a common thief, nothing more. Josslyn's few possessions and those of her two sisters which she had managed to grab on her way out the door of the villa after reading Gemma's dire warning note were all stashed in this room. Their money. Their research. Their passports. Someone was obviously hoping to steal those.

Clearly, it had been a mistake leaving the balcony door wide open. But when she'd gone to bed earlier, the hotel had been in the midst of one of the ubiquitous Egyptian electrical brownouts, and she would have melted into a puddle of sweat if she'd left it closed and locked.

No problem. She'd deal with this thief. She racked the gun. The loud *ka-chunk* ricocheted comfortingly off the plaster walls, bolstering her courage.

Just outside the French door there was an almost imperceptible scratching noise. Then suddenly a tiny flame flashed red. The silhouette of a large hand cupped it, and the tip of a black Egyptian cigarette flared to life. The rich, acrid smell of tobacco wafted to her nose in the hot stillness.

"What are you planning to do, shoot me?" a deep masculine voice asked. His English was cultured, his tone unsettlingly unperturbed by her threat.

She narrowed her eyes. Not exactly what she'd expected. "Stay on my balcony one minute longer and you'll find out," she returned.

A thin drift of smoke was caught in a golden luminescence, reflected by some unseen light below.

"This is, in fact, my balcony as well," the man said silkily. "I believe we share it."

She frowned and searched her memory of the verandah's setup.

Damn. He was right.

Still… "That hardly gives you license to intrude on my privacy."

"I do beg your pardon. That wasn't my intent. I couldn't sleep and found myself wandering."

Another puff of smoke oozed into the room. Normally she hated the smell of cigarettes, but there was something almost…alluring about the spicy fragrance of his blend. A shiver raced over her arms. Along with the heavier brush of an indefinable sense of unease. The air was electric with it, like a touch of foreboding.

She didn't believe his assertion of innocence. His presence on her balcony had a purpose, and she'd bet her last dollar it wasn't insomnia. She was also beginning to fear it wasn't to steal passports, either.

"Get away from my room," she ordered. "Or I *will* shoot you."

He chuckled softly and took a half step closer to the open door. Her pulse leapt. A roll of weird energy, like the electric crackle of an approaching storm, raised the fine hairs on her arms. He halted at her threshold, framed by the French doors. She could just make out his body silhouetted against the backdrop of the night sky. He was big and broad.

She really wished she could see his face.

"Your sister sends her greetings," he said conversationally.

Joss faltered. *What?* The gun wavered in her hands. "Gemma?" Scrambling up to her knees on the bed, she raised the gun again. "Where is she?" she demanded harshly. "What have you done with her?"

At least she assumed he'd meant Gemma. Both her sisters, Gemma and Gillian, had disappeared over the past two weeks. Gillian with a man claiming to be a British lord, an expatriate living on an unlikely estate somewhere on the west bank of the Nile River. Gillian had sent a note saying she was with him, and not to worry, but Joss and Gemma became skeptical when she didn't come home after a week. Then a few days ago Gemma had been following a clue to Gillian's whereabouts, and was abducted by a mysterious band of fierce desert warriors and their sheikh leader. Gemma had also been able to smuggle a note to Josslyn, parts of which were burned in her memory.

Pack a suitcase...quit the villa.... Those men from

*yesterday are coming back to kidnap you…. Go! Now!…
Beware the vampire! Do not trust him….*

Of course, that last part was crazy. If Joss weren't
so desperately worried, she'd think Gemma had gone
totally off the deep end. Could she have been drugged?
Possibly by the very man on Joss's balcony? He didn't
look like a desert warrior…but he did look fierce.

The shadowed figure at the French door took another
drag on his cigarette, dropped it and ground it out under
his shoe. "Actually," he said, "it is of your other sister I
bring word."

"Gillian? But—" Joss finally unfroze and reached
for the lamp on the nightstand. She needed to see this
guy.

The light snapped on, dimly illuminating the features
of the man. He really was big. Tall. His handsome
features were Middle Eastern, but he was dressed as
a Westerner, in an elegant white linen suit with stylish
European leather shoes. Not menacing, exactly. But
arrogant and… Okay. Yes. Menacing. An unpleasant
shiver crawled down her spine.

"Who are you?" she demanded. "Are you Gillian's
new—" *Lord, how to put it? And please, God, no*
"—gentleman?"

His lips curved. "Lord Rhys? No, I'm not. My name
is Harold Ray and I'm…an acquaintance of his. Please,
call me Ray."

Lord Rhys? Obviously Gillian's expat boyfriend.
But the name rang a bell somewhere else in her mind.
Though she couldn't put her finger on it. "What do you
want?" she asked Ray. "Tell me what Gillian said."

Harold Ray tilted his head. "Wouldn't you like to put down that gun first?"

Was he kidding? "No. Talk to me. Now."

He tsked. "I must say, your sister has much better manners." He took another step forward, this one bringing him across her threshold.

"Hey! Stop where you are!"

The absurd thought came to her that at least the intruder couldn't possibly be a vampire. Didn't they need an invitation to enter one's abode? And she could clearly see his reflection in the glass of the French door.

Good freaking grief. Not that she believed *any* of that bullcrap.

It was a testament to her completely frazzled nerves over her missing sisters that the thought had even entered her desperate mind.

Ray gave her a little knowing smile and brazenly wandered into the room, casting a casual glance around. The storm brewing in the air stirred ominously. He extended a finger and touched the head of a bronze statue of Sekhmet that decorated a reading table. It seemed to light up.

Along with her nerves. Jesus. Was he really going to make her *shoot* him?

"Gillian is fine," he said, temporarily delaying her itchy trigger finger. "And very much in love with Rhys Kilpatrick."

The name finally hit her like an icy dash of hard evidence. Now she *knew* this guy was lying. Lord Rhys Kilpatrick was a dead man. *Long* dead. A British officer in General Gordon's infamous 19th Hussars, he'd been killed in 1885. It was his grave marker her historian sister had been searching for when she went missing.

"I don't doubt Gillian is in love," Joss drawled. But not with anyone in *this* jerk's acquaintance. Time to get rid of this Harold Ray character, whoever he was. He was giving her the creeps, big time. His body actually seemed to be getting bigger, shimmering in the golden glow of the nightstand lamp.

She slid gingerly off the bed, keeping the gun carefully trained on him. And did her best to ignore the way his lascivious gaze slid over her body, which she realized must be all too visible in the lamplight through the opaque fabric of her thin summer pajamas.

"Get out," she told him firmly. "Get out now, or I swear I *will* pull this trigger."

His gaze strayed to the gun, slid up her arm and paused on her neck, then went to her eyes. "You are a brave thing, I'll give you that, Miss Haliday. I can see why Seth wants you."

Seth? Who…? He must be talking about Gemma's kidnapper. *And the lying bastard in her room was obviously in league with him.* Oh, my God. They must be holding both Gemma and Gillian captive!

"You and your buddy Seth can go straight to hell," she ground out, fighting a wave of nausea at the thought. "I'll get my sisters back if it's the last thing—"

She didn't see him move. One second he was across the room, the next he was standing in front of her, his hand reaching for her gun. Her pulse surged. *Not a chance!*

She pulled the trigger.

Nothing happened. A harmless click echoed through the room.

Oh, shit. Shitshitshit.

"Believe me, Seth is *not* my buddy," Ray returned as though he hadn't even noticed he'd just been meant to die. He smiled down at her. Now he looked *really* menacing. Downright sinister. The air crackled with that weird, otherworldly energy. It sparked off him like static electricity. She swore she saw actual sparks. He loomed over her, and hissed, "Seth is my mortal enemy."

Seeing the ferocity bloom in his eyes, she believed him. And suddenly feared this was far more complicated than she ever dreamed.

She tried to back away but couldn't move. Literally. It was as if she were frozen in place, her muscles useless.

Sick fear crawled up her spine. What was going on? How was he doing this to her? What did he want?

"I have vowed to take everything from Seth," Ray said, the syllables of his words cutting the air like shards of ice. "Everything he owns in the world. Everything he wants to own…"

He slipped the gun from her fingers and tossed it harmlessly onto the bed. He leaned down and whispered in her ear, "Including you, my dear Josslyn."

Panic grabbed her heart and squeezed tight. *Oh, God.* The man was insane!

He grasped her arms and gently eased them down to her sides. At his touch, her body clenched in unwilling reaction. A rush of hot, shivering, erotic sensation poured through her flesh, her breasts tightening involuntarily. *No!* Another wave of nausea heaved in her stomach along with the unwanted coil of physical arousal. What was *wrong* with her?

"So brave. So pretty," he murmured, brushing his lips over her cheek. "So sweetly responsive."

She shuddered in revulsion and tried desperately to pull away.

"No, don't fight me, my dear. It's no use, you see."

His strong fingers combed into her hair, bunched it and pulled back her head, exposing the bare column of her throat. She watched in horror as he drew the forefinger of his other hand slowly down the vein that throbbed there wildly. The expression on his face terrified her. He looked…hungry. As though he wanted to bite her like a—

Oh, God.

His lips parted. That's when she saw his two eye teeth begin to lengthen. And sharpen. *Like fangs.*

Oh, God. OhGod, ohGod!

She tried to scream but couldn't make a sound. She tried to struggle but still couldn't make her muscles work.

"You'll enjoy this," he murmured, touching the end of his tongue to the tip of his fang. A drop of blood blossomed and he curled it into his mouth. "I promise."

She squeezed her eyes shut and prayed to wake up from the nightmare. *This is not happening!*

Suddenly the night silence was shattered by a frantic pounding at the hall door. "Miss Haliday!" a muffled voice called. "Miss Haliday, are you there?"

Thank heaven!

Ray peered furiously at the door. Joss did, too,

summoning every ounce of strength and trying with everything she had to cry out. Still no sound emerged.

The pounding continued. "Miss Haliday!" She didn't recognize the voice. Couldn't even tell if it was a man or a woman. She didn't care. She just wanted them to come in and save her!

Ray swung his glare back to her. "Do not think this is over, Miss Haliday. I will be back," he growled. "And don't try to run. Make no mistake, I will find you, wherever you are."

He let her go, and with a rush of blood, movement returned to her limbs. She jumped away from the monster and lurched for the hall door. "I'm here!" she cried to her nameless rescuer. "I'm coming!"

Harold Ray gave her one last evil look. "And I'm warning you. *Stay away from Seth-Aziz.*"

With that he turned, and in the blink of an eye he was out on the balcony. There was a rustle of what sounded like wings, a shower of sparks, and then he was gone. Vanished.

For a second Joss was paralyzed with disbelief. And by an overwhelming incredulity that filled her whole being over what she'd just been through, what she'd just felt, and witnessed.

She quickly shook herself and rushed to the entry door, flinging it open.

"Thank you! Oh, Lord, you have no idea how—"

But no one was there.

Just a lone copper-colored cat stalking noiselessly down the middle of the Persian carpet with tail erect. Otherwise, the corridor was silent and completely empty.

Good grief. Maybe she *was* going nuts. Which might actually be preferable to...

What?

She let out a long, unsteady breath.

Merciful heaven.

What the *hell* had just happened to her?

Chapter 2

That same day
Khepesh Palace
The Western Desert, Upper Egypt

The demigod Seth-Aziz, high priest of Khepesh, needed blood. And he needed sex.

He needed to find a mortal woman and take her to his bed, sink his sharp fangs into her silken neck and his aching cock into her lush body. To relieve the hunger. And the frustration.

But that wasn't going to happen.

Not tonight. Nor anytime soon. For that would mean exposing his weakness to his followers, letting them see him as less than the powerful demigod and commanding ruler he'd been for the past five thousand years.

He'd rather die.

Which was fast becoming a distinct possibility. If

he didn't feed before his Full-Moon Slumber he would likely never awaken again, regardless of the prayers and rituals fervently murmured over his black obsidian sarcophagus by the temple priestess.

Not that there *was* a temple priestess any longer at Khepesh, the secret underground tomb-palace where he and his followers served Set-Sutekh, the ancient Egyptian God of Darkness. A week ago their last full priestess, Seth's sister Nephtys, had sacrificed her freedom to their archenemy, Haru-Re, allowing herself to be captured by the High Priest of the Sun God and agreeing to become the bastard's consort.

The thought still filled Seth-Aziz with rage.

So much so, that by sheer force of that emotion he was finally able to marshal the little strength he had left, to do what he must do.

He straightened his spine, thanked the beneficent god for his ritual costume—the dazzling silver mask that hid the pallor of his cheeks, and the shimmering black robes that covered the slight tremble in his limbs—and walked through the stately silver portal into Khepesh Palace temple.

It was midnight on the night of the new moon, the appointed time for the Renewal of Life ceremony. This was when the *shemsu,* the immortal followers of the Dark God, Set-Sutekh, went through the monthly chants, sacrifices and rituals that allowed them to continue to live forever, to serve at the altar of the Lord of the Hot Winds and Chaos, Ruler of the Night Sky and Guardian of Eternal Darkness.

Luckily, this ceremony did not require a priestess. As high priest of the temple, Seth would preside.

Assuming he didn't fall over from hunger.

That would not be good. He needed to keep up the pretense. If the council even suspected how bad off he was, they would force him to take a sacrifice, willing or not.

Which he was not ready to do.

Not yet.

Because they would want him to take *her*.

And as much as he wanted to sink his fangs into the troublesome female, even more he wanted to kill her.

The portal gates were swung open by the *shemats,* the two young temple acolytes, who bowed respectfully as he entered. He nodded to them, and paused as Sheikh Shahin Aswadi, captain of the palace guard and Khepesh's army of warriors, approached to escort Seth through the temple to the inner sanctum where he would perform the Rites of Renewal.

You look like death warmed over, my lord, Shahin whispered into his mind as he sketched a formal bow.

Since he, Shahin, and the sheikh's new woman, Gemma, had shared magic last week when Seth had been desperate for a temporary fix of mortal blood, he and Shahin seemed to have acquired the ability to communicate silently through their thoughts at will. A somewhat unexpected, but handy skill to have.

Seth allowed himself a sardonic smile. Ever since his sister Nephtys had been taken hostage, his good friend the sheikh had also assumed her role as his Official Nag.

Hardly surprising, as I am *dead,* Seth returned.

"Soon to be permanently so, if you don't stop this foolishness," Shahin muttered under his breath.

It was an ongoing battle of wills. Shahin was one of only two others at Khepesh who knew the truth about Seth's present weakness and the reason for it. But Seth didn't have the time or energy for a fight. He had duties to perform.

He glanced around at the beautiful hypostyle hall, the first of three courtyards of the elegantly luxurious temple that lay deep underground, like the rest of Khepesh, all lit up by flickering torch sconces. This was the largest courtyard, the festival chamber where his followers, the *shemsu*, came to feast and celebrate their god. Despite being filled to capacity, the mood in the hall was unusually somber for a Khepesh celebration. Normally their gatherings were loud and festive, part pomp and circumstance, part sexual bacchanalia. But on this night, the *shemsu* were feeling the weight of an unknown fate closing in upon them.

As was Seth Aziz.

"Where is your lovely captive tonight?" he asked Shahin as the crowd greeted the arrival of their demigod with a haunting, melodic chant that marked the opening of the ceremony. "Is she not with you?"

Seth could practically hear the sheikh's teeth grind under the chanting voices. "Gemma is not here," Shahin said, "because, if you recall, she is not immortal and has no need of the ceremony."

Not to mention Seth's orders to keep her well out of his path, lest he do something they'd all regret. She was, after all, the sister of the woman who'd brought his life to ruin.

"And Gemma is not my captive," Shahin added unnecessarily, no doubt simply to annoy him. "She is my chosen woman, with whom I intend to spend eternity."

Unfortunately, Seth knew that, as well. Shahin's relationship with the middle Haliday sister had gone beyond captive and master within days of her being kidnapped. Possibly hours. Seth just didn't like it. Those three accursed sisters were the bane of his existence and the source of all the current disasters befalling Khepesh.

Well, two of the sisters, at any rate. The redheaded Gemma he could tolerate, just, if she kept her distance. Shahin had done well to spirit her off to his aboveground desert oasis encampment.

The youngest sister, Gillian, the wretched betrayer and traitor, was lucky to be beyond the reach of Seth's sword and his wrath. She was presently shacked up with his former master steward and presumably ex–best friend, Rhys Kilpatrick, sharing exile with his own beloved sister Nephtys in the palace of his enemy.

But it was the oldest Haliday sister, Josslyn, of whom Seth truly wanted to obliterate all trace from his life and his universe.

It was because of Josslyn Haliday that his own sister had traded away her life to Haru-Re. It was because of Josslyn Haliday that Seth had made some of the stupidest strategic decisions in his five millennia of existence. It was because of Josslyn Haliday he'd let down his guard enough to feel, at long last, the dim, treacherous hope of having the dulcet touch of love in his life again. A hope that had proven as false as the smile of a serpent.

By the blood of Sekhmet, he wanted to wrap his hands around the woman's slim, pale neck and—

My lord! "Seth!" Shahin's urgent whisper snapped him back to the present with a jolt.

He realized he'd stopped walking and was standing in the second chamber of the temple, the Courtyard of the Sacred Pool, glaring into the lovely, water-filled basin like a mad zombie.

The surrounding crowd eyed him worriedly. Murmurs of concern rippled through the chamber.

Sweet tears of Isis.

"Sorry," he said, gathering himself. "Just saying a prayer."

Sure you were, Shahin said dryly in his mind, then he muttered aloud, "For God's sake, Seth, choose a woman after the ceremony, and take the blood you need. I don't understand why you are being so damned stubborn about it."

Neither did he. Not really. It wasn't as if he *wanted* to die or cease his existence or whatever a demigod did when he failed to awake from his immortal slumber. It was just…he was so damned tired. Tired of the weight of leadership, tired of the eternal war and strife with Haru-Re, tired of the never-ending, grinding loneliness— loneliness he'd thought was finally coming to an end. Because he'd actually let himself believe Nephtys's vision of at last finding true love and a worthy consort with that damned Haliday woman. Such a gullible fool he'd been!

He knew better. Had five thousand years of a life spent in solitary existence taught him nothing? Had the poem he'd written so many years ago, lamenting over the weariness of life on earth, not been burned in his memory like a never-ending mantra?

Nephtys's visions were so rarely wrong, he'd told himself. But by the rod of Min, *this* vision had not only proven false, but it had brought him and the *shemsu* of Khepesh Palace nothing but trouble and misery, and indeed, to the very brink of annihilation itself.

He took a deep breath, spiced with the fragrance of the thousand flowers and ten thousand sweetly scented candles that filled the hall. "I will feed," he assured his friend. "Soon. I just need to…"

"To what?" Shahin asked doubtfully when Seth's words trailed off.

He straightened. "To get this damned ceremony over with."

"Do I have your word on that?" Shahin pressed. "That you will choose someone?"

"Yes," Seth relented, just to shut the man up. "I promise. Soon."

Shahin scowled at the qualifier, but there was little he could do about it at the moment. It was time to begin the ritual.

Seth turned and raised his hands, and started to intone the opening incantation that the *shemsu* were nervously awaiting. There was a thick thread of tension underlying the love and concern of his people. It swirled and flowed through the courtyard like an invisible tide of otherworldly energy.

He closed his eyes and fed deeply off their collective magic, absorbing its awesome power into his weakening life's blood, draining every last morsel of strength from it he could.

The magic they sent him wasn't blood, and it wouldn't

keep him alive, but it bolstered and nurtured his hurting soul as nothing else could.

He continued his measured walk through the temple, coming to the dark portal of the third chamber, the inner sanctum. It was an awe-inspiring setting. The walls were clad in glittering silver and the floor made of obsidian stone so black one's feet seemed to tread upon the vast, empty void of the universe. The soaring expanse of the curved ceiling was fashioned of dark blue lapis lazuli the exact color of the night sky, spangled with diamonds that sparkled and winked in the same constellations as the trillion stars over the real desert aboveground.

It was here, in the holy of holies, that Seth's coffin rested, where he took his monthly three-day slumber at the full moon. Inlaid with precious metal and the finest gems, the elaborately carved obsidian sarcophagus lay in the middle of the small, candlelit chamber. Inside the stone nestled the fragile Egyptian mummy case into which his body had been placed upon his mortal death, so many long years ago. That he had arisen from that final sleep, and continued to do so every month since, was known only to the *shemsu*, the chosen few. That, along with an even darker secret.

That Seth was a vampire.

One of only two vampire demigods remaining in existence on earth.

He approached his sarcophagus, which also served as the central altar, lit up for display in the chamber. The altars were strewn with flowers and candles, cascades of fruit, goblets of wine and censers of smoking ambergris and myrrh—all offerings to their god Set-Sutekh, given in exchange for his blessing of another moon-span of immortality.

With a deep breath, Seth began to chant. Behind him, the *shemsu* joined in as a chorus. Together, their voices rose in a magical harmony conceived and honed over the passing of the millennia. One by one, he recited the names of each of the faithful, humbly asking for the god's continued beneficence. For only he whose name was thus spoken lived on.

By the end of the ceremony Seth was exhausted. His head was spinning and his legs on the verge of giving out.

Shahin hurried up to him and put his arm around his shoulders, lending him support under the guise of back-slapping brotherly camaraderie, now that the formal part of the ceremony was over and the feasting had begun.

"This has gone far enough," his captain declared in a low voice that carried no less heat for its lack of volume. "I'm fetching Josslyn Haliday."

"No!" Seth commanded emphatically. "I don't want—"

"I don't care what you want." Shahin cut him off sharply. "You are Khepesh's leader, and it is my sworn duty to see no harm befalls you." *You're on the brink of collapse, my lord. Clearly the lack of a blood sacrifice has affected your ability to make rational decisions.*

Seth bit down on his resentment. *I could kill you with but a single thought.*

But you won't, his friend shot back. *Because you know I'm right.*

Seth clamped his jaw, but that made his head spin even more. By the cock of Osiris, he hated this! For all eternity he would curse the malicious goddess Sekhmet for gifting him with this unholy blood weakness!

"No," he said. "I'm telling you, I will not have that woman here!" Shahin started to argue, but Seth slashed out a hand to forestall his lecture. "Fine! Bring someone else. Anyone else. But *not her!"*

His friend's assessing gaze bored into him, as though weighing his sincerity.

"By all the night gods, Shahin, I swear to you I will slay her myself if she sets her foot in Khepesh!"

With a pause and then a reluctant nod, Shahin conceded. "Very well. I'll try to find another woman willing to submit."

"It's not like *she* has consented, either," Seth ground out, taming his temper.

He shook off his friend's arm and caught himself before he fell, refusing to be half carried through the festival hall. He plastered a smile on his face, accepted a goblet of wine from a flirting woman and downed it in a single gulp. He turned a cheek to her kiss with a regretful wink. No way did he have the strength for what she was offering.

"Josslyn would do the sacrifice if Gemma but asked her to," Shahin continued to argue after the woman skipped off. "Gemma knows what it's like to be your vessel. Hell, she would do it herself if you let her."

Seth cast the other man a glance. It had been just last week that the three of them had shared the most intimate act three people could have together. It had been at once breathtakingly sensual and mouthwateringly carnal. Seth had taken blood from her then, but only a small amount. And all three were still reeling from the effects.

Mostly in a good way, but he wasn't about to take any chances.

"No," Seth said. "I don't dare touch your woman again. In the state I'm in, God knows if I could stop before she…"

He didn't complete the sentence. The circumstances they spoke of could have any number of outcomes, none of which he wanted driving an irreparable wedge between him and the sheikh. He'd already lost his best friend to this damnable situation. He would not lose another.

"Better it's a stranger," he said. "Just in case."

Shahin jetted out a breath, understanding the warning. "Very well," he repeated. "I'll do my best to find someone by morning."

But as it turned out, that was unnecessary. Shahin needed to look no further than the front gate of the palace to find a woman just begging to become Seth's sacrifice….

Chapter 3

Nephtys had plenty of warning before Haru-Re burst into her rooms in the *haram* of Petru's temple compound.

Unlike Khepesh, which was built solely under the ground, Petru Palace was gloriously placed aboveground in a magical bubble of temperate atmosphere, and flowing waters and never-ending sunlight in obeisance to the Sun God they served, Re-Horakhti. It was gorgeous, although Nephytys did miss the cool darkness of Khepesh when her thoughts turned inward...which was quite often these days.

Ray's element to call was fire, and as he approached, the sky above the lush temple garden outside her window lit up with ribbons of orange and red, showering down a rain of lightning. She could hear the scamper of hurried footsteps as the *shemsu* of Petru scattered before their furious demigod like schools of fish before a crocodile.

The door crashed open.

"You!" he roared, jabbing an accusing finger as he came at her. Streaks of fire flew from his hand, shooting onto the Persian rug. "You should stop meddling in affairs that don't concern you!"

She didn't turn to him, because she knew that would infuriate him even more. Nor did she bother to deny she was the one whose timely interruption had spoiled his assignation with the oldest Haliday sister.

"Oh, but it does concern me," she said calmly, maintaining her meditative pose while sitting on the window seat overlooking the garden, "when my intended husband goes to see another woman in her hotel room, with seduction on his mind."

Ray stalked over to her, halting with his huge body looming over her. She could feel the awesome power roll off him in hot, electric waves. The man was angry. As angry as she'd ever seen him.

Good. She was angry, too.

"I wasn't aware you were so interested in my dealings with other women," he barked.

She finally turned and glanced at him. Shimmering in a golden tempest of light and fury, the high priest was tall and broad and handsome as a demon of temptation. Which he was. Her own personal sexual demon of temptation.

Her heartbeat doubled.

"On the contrary," she said. "If I must remain pure for the year preceding our marriage, so must you, my dearest one. That is the whole point of this ritual period of cleansing. To rid ourselves of past sins." She looked at him meaningfully.

He leaned down a fraction closer. "And do you have so many sins on your conscience, *meruati,* that it will take a whole year to purify yourself of their stench?"

She returned his glare with equanimity. It was not *her* stench she was worried about. She had not had sex with another man for centuries. She had no appetite for being with any other than the one she loved.

Which, to her eternal sorrow and regret, was this man—the enemy of her brother and of her people, the architect of her misery and the ultimate betrayer of her heart.

But she'd rather he didn't know that little humiliating secret. His ego was big enough as it was. And it didn't help that despite her pain and in spite of his betrayal, she had never quite shaken the notion that under the hard, merciless exterior beat the heart of a man who was truly good.

"I am a veritable dung heap of trespass," she said evenly. At least she could have the immense pleasure of needling him.

His eyes took on a dangerous glint. "Just tell me you haven't slept with that brooding jackal of a brother of yours."

She gave a moue of distaste. *Or maybe she was wrong about him being good.* "Leave it to you to envision such a perversion."

"It was the way things were done in the days of our birth," he pointed out unappologetically. "And he is but your adopted brother, not of your blood. The way you fawn all over the man, one would think—"

"You had your chance to be the object of my fawning, Ray," she interrupted him tersely. "You threw it away when you sold me to the highest bidder."

Sparks exploded around him like a firecracker. "Lies! You were stolen from me! How many times must I say it to convince you?"

"As the number of grains of sand in the desert," she threw back.

He was the liar. She'd seen the proof.

As a captive, a lowly slave at the time, Nephtys had had no power to stem the tide of disaster that swept through her early years. But thanks to her driving need for revenge over the man who had broken her fragile young heart, she was now a powerful priestess. The most powerful in all of Egypt, and the only person remaining alive who held the secret of the spell that granted immortality.

And *that* was the only reason Ray strove to possess her again, and well she knew it. So he could use her magic to replenish Petru's dwindling numbers and gain further superiority over Khepesh and her brother.

"Nephtys—"

"We stray from the point, Haru-Re. If you want me as your willing wife, you will cease your truck with other women. I will not tolerate infidelity of any kind in my husband."

His nostrils flared and he grabbed her arms in his strong fingers, lifting her bodily from the window seat. Burning pinpricks of sparkles dusted her skin. He yanked her close to the hard wall of his chest. Her pulse beat out of control.

"Then *you* must satisfy my lust, *meruati*," he growled.

"I am a man, with a man's carnal needs. And I am vampire, with a vampire's special cravings. Are you willing to fulfill those requirements? To be my sole vessel?"

The touch of his hands, rough though it be, sent spirals of desire drilling through her flesh. Oh, how she wanted him! It wasn't fair!

"So eloquently put," she said, fighting her own traitorous flesh. Not wanting to feel this way about a man like him. A man who thought only of himself.

He combed his fingers through her riot of long, curling hair, so different from his—Ray's being thick, straight and the blackest black of midnight. Hers was the color of flame and sunset. As though she, too, were a natural part of his sun-ruled dominion, his own sexual element to call at his whim. "Just telling it like it is, my love," he said, lowering his mouth to hers.

She fought him. Didn't want his kiss. She knew what it inevitably led to. "No," she said, and pushed at his immovable body. "We mustn't. We have sworn to stay pure. It will anger the god to break our promise!"

"I have made no such vow," he said into her mouth. "And neither have you."

Her heart sped like a gazelle in flight. "My duties as priestess—"

"Do not require your chastity," he murmured, licking her lips with his warm, talented tongue. "Nor your purity. The god enjoys his pleasures through the bodies of his followers. Our bliss is his."

She swallowed, feeling her addiction to him blaze to life. A vampire's kiss was like a banquet to the starving, his dark bite the most powerful drug on earth. Surrender but once, truly surrender, and a woman could be lost forever to the ravenous cravings, desperate to feel the sting of his fangs again and again. For with his bite comes the most incredible sexual fulfillment, each climax more overwhelming than the last.

And Nephtys had surrendered to him many, many times.

One hand in her hair, the other traveled boldly over her curves, her hip, her waist, her breasts. He was watching her reaction to his touch, seeing the helpless, melting need she couldn't stop from seeping into her eyes.

He smiled. "You want me," he whispered, kissing the corner of her mouth.

"I've always wanted you, Ray," she lamented softly. "From the moment I first saw you, so proud and arrogant and beautiful, like a statue of the Sun God himself."

"Then stop tormenting us both and come to my bed."

His thumb brushed over her nipple and a starburst of agonizing desire burst through her.

She gathered her will and pushed away from him. "No. Not until you can come to me without the scent of another woman on your skin."

But his fingers were still tangled in her hair. He fisted them and drew her close again, looking angrily down into her eyes. "The reason I was with Josslyn Haliday had nothing to do with sex."

"I *know* why you were with Josslyn Haliday," she bit out, lifting her chin. "But that wasn't going to stop you from taking her anyway. Causing my brother pain just made her seduction and fall all the sweeter for you, no doubt."

"He took what was mine," he growled, yanking back on her hair. "I was merely returning the favor."

"He didn't—"

"Although, it appears he has abandoned his intended mortal plaything to her fate. Why else would she be hidden away, cowering alone in a hotel room?"

"You're hurting me!" Nephtys admonished, reaching back to pull her hair from his grasp.

She didn't want to think about Ray's assertion, for he'd hit upon a question that bothered her, too. What was Seth doing leaving Josslyn Haliday out in the world all on her own? He must know Ray would go after her with a vengeance. After the sacrifice Nephtys had made for her brother and Josslyn to be together, it pained her to think she had thrown away her freedom for nothing.

Rather than letting Nephtys go, Ray pulled her head back a fraction more, exposing the vulnerable column of her throat. She gasped as his lips grazed slowly down the length of it, leaving a trail of burning heat on her skin. His tongue flicked her fluttering pulse point. An almost painful desire stabbed through her, like a dagger of want that cut clear to the core of her center. It was the remnant of his last bite, delivered nearly a month ago, but still it carried the vampyric lust spell that could drive a woman mad for want of another taste of the fang.

"Stop," she begged.

"Why?"

"This isn't fair."

"To whom?" he murmured, sliding his instruments of torture along her collar bone. He slipped the strap of her gown over her shoulder, chasing it with his lips and tongue.

She wanted to give in. Blessed Isis, she wanted to throw herself into his arms and let him take what he wanted from her. Her sex. Her blood. Her will.

But that would be choosing the coward's path. The surrender of a weakling.

And Haru-Re would never respect a consort who wasn't as strong as he. Stronger, for Nephtys didn't have even half the power or magic that a demigod possessed. She must rely on her wits and her determination to come out on top of this most personal battle.

And at last achieve the revenge she craved.

His mouth slid down the slope of her breast and closed around her nipple. She cried out, and her breath caught as she felt the telltale scrape of fangs pressing hotly against her skin.

Sekhmet give her strength!

"No!" she cried and jerked away, this time succeeding in disentangling herself from his grasp. She dragged up the straps of her gown, covering her aching breasts and crossing her arms over them protectively.

She wanted to die of want.

He stared at her with half-lidded eyes, dark with lust. Preternatural energy roiled through the room.

She held her ragged breath. He could easily overpower her and take her. They both knew it.

His fangs slowly receded. His jaw clenched.

"You test my patience, woman," he said, his voice rough with frustration. He was clearly not accustomed to having his demands thwarted.

Well, that was about to change.

"It's for the best this way," she said, somehow keeping the words from quivering in her mouth.

He gave a humorless bark of laughter. "Tell that to my bollocks."

"Silver-tongued as always," she managed, but instantly regretted it.

His eyes cut to hers, but to his credit, he didn't give the response she clearly saw leap into them.

"You've been here only a week, and already I am at your throat," he said instead. "Do you really believe you can fight me off for an entire year?"

She swallowed, knowing the answering truth in her heart. "Must it be a fight?" she asked with an edge of desperation.

"Oh, yes." He smiled grimly. "It must. I won't give up until I have you where I want you. And that *is* a promise, my love."

And with the gauntlet unmistakably thrown down, he stalked to the door and swept from the room, leaving a churning wake of sparking energy behind him.

Chapter 4

Seth-Aziz.

That was the name of the damn bastard holding Josslyn's sisters hostage. Keeping them against their will. It must be so. If she believed nothing else of the visit from that horrible man, Harold Ray, she believed that. If they were not prisoners of this Seth-Aziz, then why did they not come back to her? Or at least contact her in person?

For Joss did not believe those bogus notes anymore. Notes could be forged.

After last night, she knew something was going on. She didn't know what, exactly. Not yet. But it was bad. Really bad.

She paced the length of her hotel room, then paced back again. She'd been pacing for four hours now, ever since that maniac Ray had appeared and then vanished from her balcony like some kind of creepy winged apparition.

Forget about sleep. No way could she even think about closing her eyes. He might come back for her. As he'd promised.

God help her.

Or…had she just imagined the whole thing?

Maybe it had all simply been one really vivid, terrifying nightmare.

But no. Because the crushed remains of his black cigarette lay out there on the verandah floor just outside the French door, motionless but oozing danger, like a scorpion in wait. Hard evidence. Proof the monster had truly been there. Hell, if she closed her eyes she could still smell a trace of that distinctive spicy smoke in the room. And that *wasn't* her imagination.

She stuck her hands under her armpits. She hadn't run up against much in this world that could make her tremble in fear, but damn, she was shaking like she was coming off a three-day bender.

Not that she'd ever actually been on a three-day bender. But this morning she was sorely tempted to give it a try.

Except that her sisters needed her. She was their only hope. Somehow she *had* to find them! Before it was too late…

Okay. Okay.

She gave herself a firm mental shake. This abject panic was getting her nowhere.

She needed a plan.

Forgetting about the big question of *why* for now, the

first thing she had to do was figure out *where* they were being held.

But how?

She took a deep, calming breath.

Plan, Josslyn! The only way to accomplish this was to go about things methodically. Scientifically. Unemotionally.

A list. That's what she needed.

Hurrying to the desk, she pulled a piece of hotel stationery from the drawer and grabbed a pen. Rapidly she wrote down the three names she'd learned last night: Harold Ray; Seth, also known as Seth-Aziz; and Lord Rhys Kilpatrick, the dead guy.

Then the pen came to a frustrating halt over the paper. That was all she'd learned. The sum total of what she knew.

Damn.

Wait. There was one more thing. She knew the approximate location of the ancient tomb where Gillian had thought Lord Rhys Kilpatrick's grave marker had been inscribed.

She wrote that down, too.

Not that the information would do her any good. Harold Ray's crazy assertions aside, there was no way that Rhys Kilpatrick could be involved in this. Not unless he was a ghost.

Although...

Against her better judgment, she wrote the word "vampire," followed by a large question mark. She added two more for good measure. Then crossed out the whole thing. No, only the facts. Not wild speculation. She still didn't quite believe what happened.

Joss blinked as a vague memory suddenly trickled through her mind. Something she'd completely forgotten. About the afternoon Gillian disappeared…

Before she and Gemma had gotten the phone call from Gillian telling them she was all right, they had gone up to Rhys Kilpatrick's alleged tomb to look for her. And something, someone…

She frowned, straining to remember. It was right on the tip of her—

With a gasp, she dropped the pen. Good God! There had been a *man* there! Dressed as some kind of Bedouin sheikh—just like those frightening men who had taken Gemma last week. And he'd been carrying Gillian in his arms! *Unconscious.* He'd spoken…. She strained to remember. That's right, he'd said Gillian had gotten too much sun and fainted.

But that's where the memory gave out. Try as Joss might, the rest was gone.

Jesus. Why hadn't she remembered this until now? And why for the life of her couldn't she remember what had happened next?

Still. It gave her somewhere to start. She underlined Rhys Kilpatrick's tomb on her list.

Jumping up determinedly from the desk, she rushed to get dressed. No time to lose. She had to get across the Nile to the west bank and search that hidden tomb. There could be vital evidence in it. Something to tell her where Gillian and Gemma had been taken.

There had to be a clue. There *had* to be.

Her sisters' lives could depend on it. And there was no way she'd let them down. They were the only family she had left.

She *would* rescue them from whatever terrible fate had befallen them. She'd find them and bring them home, where they belonged.

She would.

If it was the last thing she ever did.

The trip across the Nile River to the far west bank took two excruciating hours, and it was another hour to reach the site of the ancient tomb, which was a good distance to the north.

When Gemma's note had compelled Joss to flee from their rented villa a week ago, she'd called the car rental company and had them collect their hired Land Rover. So she had no transpo. Not that she would have dared show her face at the villa again to fetch the vehicle, even if it had still been parked there. Gemma had warned her that the kidnappers were after her, too. Harold Ray's actions in her room last night confirmed the truth of that. And if they could find her at the Winter Palace Hotel, they would surely be watching the villa in case she showed up there.

Remembering the look on Ray's face when he said he'd be back for her—God, it sent chills down her spine. She'd just as soon not make it easy for him.

So with a scarf wrapped around her head, big sunglasses covering her face, plenty of water in her backpack and a camera hanging from her neck, she threw in her lot with a group of tourists headed for the Valley of the Kings. After disembarking from the ferry, the tour bus would make a stop at Qurna, the village where the only person she could think of who could possibly help her lived—a boy called Mehmet.

Mehmet was a little con artist whom Gillian had employed as a guide while doing her research. An adolescent of indefinite age and infinite shadiness, he'd nevertheless been a reliable helper and all-around boy Friday to her sister, who had for some obscure reason trusted the creature. Right now Joss had little choice but to trust him, too. At least to the extent of renting a donkey from him. A donkey was by far the most reliable transportation on the west bank. At least for where Joss was headed.

As luck would have it, she found Mehmet hanging around the village, and after an initial hesitation and driving a very hard bargain, he was able to scrounge up a suitable animal for her. Somewhere along the line he must have decided he liked her. Just her luck.

"You are sure you don't want me to come with you, miss?" he asked. "It is long way. Difficult trail. I show you. It's better."

She shook her head. "No thanks, Mehmet. I'm just finishing up a few last details on my drawings of the Temple of Sekhmet. I'm quite familiar with the road there. But thanks anyway."

The temple was just below the *gebel* where the tomb was located, and she wasn't about to tell him where she was really going. And she definitely didn't want him tagging along so he could learn the truth. He knew all about her archaeological work, so her stated destination made perfect sense.

"I come for free," he told her earnestly, holding up his hands. "No pay. As favor to your sister, Miss Gillian," he said, a shadow of some emotion flitting through his eyes. "She very good boss lady. I am sad she went away."

"Me, too," Joss said, and politely declined his offer once again. "I'll have the donkey back by this afternoon. See you then, Mehmet."

With that, she mounted up and trotted off. She glanced back once at him as the road took a final turn going out of the village. He was still watching her. She gave him a smile and a wave. But he seemed lost in thought and didn't wave back.

It was a hard ride, and she pressed the donkey for all it was worth. Once away from civilization, she stowed her camera and pulled an old long-sleeved, full-length *gelebeya* from her backpack, which she put on over her clothes, along with a big native head scarf to hide her blond hair and fair complexion. When the few cars that appeared on the road passed her, she averted her face so no one would recognize her or suspect she was a foreigner.

Paranoid? Maybe.

She really wished she could have brought the shotgun, too, but it wouldn't fit in her backpack without sticking out like a sore thumb. Tough to explain to the tour guides and the scores of security guards posted around all the ancient monuments these days, thanks to the constant threat of terrorism.

When she reached the ruins of the Temple of Sekhmet, she dismounted to have a rest and cut the dust with a drink. Cracking open a bottle of water, she first respectfully poured a few drops onto the ground in libation, then drank thirstily.

Looking around the site of so many happy hours spent over the summer having picnic lunches with Gemma and Gillian, her heart ached. She missed them so much!

The three sisters had been apart far too much over the past several years, and it had been tough on all of them.

Gemma was a cultural anthropologist, a specialist in traditional Nubian stories and lore, and she had a new teaching position at Duke University in North Carolina. Gillian was an historian doing doctoral studies in Oxford, England. Joss herself worked for the Royal Ontario Museum in Toronto and had been living in Canada for five years. So many miles away from each other. It seemed the only time the three of them ever saw one another anymore was during the summers when they were all doing their fieldwork in Egypt.

Egypt. The country where the three sisters had practically grown up traveling with their Egyptologist father, Trevor Haliday. Their dad had become obsessed with the place, pursuing his dark demons after their mother disappeared not far from that very spot two decades ago, never to be seen again. So the four of them, father and daughters, had returned here season after season, searching for her year after year. One day Dad had simply walked into the endless sands of the country he'd loved, to be forever with the woman he'd loved too much to get over the loss of her.

It was a dual tragedy that had torn the sisters' lives apart. But it had also brought them closer, knowing that all they had left in the world was their love for each other.

People often asked how they could bear to come back to the unforgiving country that had robbed them of both parents. But the answer was simple.

All three of them loved Egypt with a passion that

flowed in their blood like the waters of the Nile. Despite the glaring cultural differences, the very real dangers and the personal heartaches it reminded them of, more than anywhere else in the world, Egypt felt like home.

Josslyn sighed and rested her back against the sandstone blocks of the temple wall, letting her gaze meander over the stark, rugged desert landscape that she, despite everything, loved more than anywhere else in the world. To the east, in the distance shimmered the graceful muddy curve of the Nile River, banked by a narrow parallel band of lush green fields. The vivid green ended abruptly in the harsh browns and blacks of the west-bank landscape. The rough dirt track that she had ridden up from Qurna cut its shallow twin ruts, hugging the edge of the fields. From there, the land began a gradual upward slope for about three-quarters of a mile, where it was blocked to the west by the rugged, towering sandstone cliffs of the *gebel*.

The *gebel* marked the western border of the Nile valley, the distinct limits of civilization—ancient and modern—the universally recognized line beyond which anyone who valued their life dared not venture.

It was there, hidden deep in the forbidding shadows of the *gebel,* that the realm of the dead, the tombs of the ancients, lay. Including the tomb Josslyn fervently hoped would contain something, anything, to help solve the riddle of her sisters' disappearance.

Why had they been taken?

Of all the tens of thousands of visitors to this vast country, why them?

Had the Haliday family not sacrificed enough to

this land of savage beauty and stark enigma for one lifetime?

Enough was enough. This was one battle Joss intended to win.

Rousing herself, she shook off her weltschmerz and remounted, urging the donkey as far up the ever-steepening *gebel* trail as it could go. She recognized at once the place where she remembered seeing the mysterious man carrying off Gillian's unconscious body. Tying the donkey securely to a small boulder, she proceeded on foot.

Just before she reached the base of the crenulated, vertical cliffs, she spotted the well-hidden tomb entrance. Nearly invisible to the untrained eye, it was a mere fingernail of black shadow sandwiched between the pink-and-beige-striped pillars of rock, looking much like the eye of a needle.

She paused to listen for a long moment before taking the last few steps up to it—for the sound of voices, the scrape of a footstep or the slide of a weapon being drawn.

But all she heard was the whistling of the wind through the sandstone formations and the far-off call of a hawk.

Nevertheless, her heartbeat kicked up.

She sensed something…a swirl of the unknown, the thick brush of some mysterious force. Her mother, a child of the sixties, had believed the earth held spirits you could hear and feel, if you only tried hard enough.

She smiled at the memory. Joss didn't believe in spirits any more than she believed in vampires. But hell, after last night…well, she was just freaked out enough that the hairs stood up on her arms at the prospect of what the ancient hills might be secreting in their hidden depths.

Suddenly, she heard a noise above her. Gravel falling.

Ohgod! Was someone there?

She froze. And nearly jumped out of her skin when a long, black shadow appeared on the ground beside her.

A scream leapt to her throat as the shadow's owner stepped out from behind a huge rock.

A scream that burst out as choked laughter.

"Omi*god!*"

It was only a cat.

Joss let out a rush of relief, half curse and half laugh. "Good grief!" she scolded it when her heartbeat had slowed to less than supersonic speed. "You scared the bejezus out of me!"

It was a pretty animal, clean and obviously well cared for, with an unusual copper-red coat and luminous green eyes. It looked kind of like the one she'd seen walking down the hall last night at the hotel. A *lot* like it, in fact. Except this cat had a round, flat, purple amulet suspended on a ribbon around its neck.

"What are you doing way up here?" Josslyn asked it, feeling a bit silly talking to a cat but feeling the need to hear a human voice, even if it was her own. "Where's your home?"

It didn't answer, of course, but it sat down in the tomb opening and stared at Joss, tail curling delicately behind it. As though it wanted to block her path.

Ri-iight.

Taking out her flashlight and the bootknife she always carried when doing fieldwork, she climbed the last few feet to the needle's eye.

"Sorry, kitty. I need to get past you."

Gently shooing the beast aside, she slid through the tall, narrow opening. After a moment's pause to let her eyes adjust to the near darkness, she flicked on the flashlight and aimed the beam around her.

Sure enough, she found herself in the typical rectangular antechamber of a tomb, a room about the size of an average home's entry foyer, carved directly into the sandstone cliff. The only decoration was a crosshatch of fake lines carefully carved into the walls, designed to make it look like fitted blocks rather than bare rock. There were no paintings and no hieroglyphic inscriptions. And no Lord Rhys Kilpatrick grave marker, either.

Damn. Could this be the wrong tomb, after all?

Murmuring a curse under her breath, she examined the walls more closely—and found something that made her gasp in astonishment.

A narrow slot had been cleverly carved between two of the faux blocks, deep in the tiny crevice was a hidden trip-latch. Unbelievable! Anyone who had not grown up trekking through tombs and temples with an Egyptologist father would never have recognized the concealed mechanism. Only during the Ptolemaic period did such devices exist, extremely rarely, and to her knowledge only in the temples. But she knew at once what it was.

Good Lord. A secret door!

The cupboard-sized passage would lead to the inside

of the tomb proper—a much larger chamber, possibly more than one. It would have originally been carved and painted with intricate murals, and, like King Tut's tomb, filled to the rafters with incredible treasures—gold, jewels, statues, amphorae and a thousand other things designed to be used by the deceased in the afterlife. Normally those treasures would be long gone, plundered in ancient times. But…

In a flash, the possibilities raced through Joss's mind.

Had Gillian found this secret opening? Had she crawled through it? If so, what had she found inside? Ancient gold? A present-day antiquity smuggler's cache? Or perhaps even a gun-filled terrorist hideout?

A chill worked its way through Joss's whole body. Any one of those reasons could be why Gillian was taken.

Grasping her knife in her fingers, she started to insert the blade in the crack, probing for the trip latch.

"I wouldn't do that," a soft, feminine voice said behind her.

With a startled exclamation, she whirled, whipping her flashlight around. A woman was standing just inside the tomb entrance. Several inches shorter than Joss, she wore a beautiful flowing gown of dragonfly green that flattered her pale complexion and her riot of rich red hair. Hair the exact same color as the cat outside, Joss noted.

The woman looked a little like Gemma. Except for her eyes. The soul that shone through them seemed as old and wise as the ages, where Gemma's were young and guileless.

"Who are you? What do you want?" Joss asked, and she noticed with a flash of unease that the woman also wore a flat purple amulet around her neck.

The woman smiled. "My name is Nephtys. And I've come to help you."

Chapter 5

Khepesh Palace had been built completely under the ground, where the taint of the Sun God never touched it. Even with the never-changing dark, most of the followers of Set-Sutekh, the Supreme Lord of Darkness, spent their waking hours during the true nighttime and took their rest during the worst heat of the day above. Some of the immortals, such as Seth's best friend, Lord Rhys, still enjoyed the daylight and kept homes aboveground in addition to their suites in the underground palace, coming and going as the whim struck, living comfortably in both worlds.

But as Khepesh's immortal leader and high priest, Seth-Aziz rarely left the palace these days, and his duties were nearly all performed in the deepest hours of the night.

But Seth liked the nighttime; he relished the peace and tranquility of the dark. It had nothing to do with the myth that a vampire is burned by the sun—Haru-Re's enthusiastic service to the Sun God, Re-Horakhti, soundly disproved that old wives' tale. Seth simply preferred the darkness to the light. It was easier to think, easier to see what was important, easier to lose oneself in one's solitude, in a cocoon devoid of the harsh light of illumination.

Occasionally during his long existence Seth had questioned his choice to serve the Dark Lord. Not because of the usual reason he'd been confronted with by others over the years—the grave misconception that Darkness equaled Evil, and that those who served its god must therefore also be evil. That was not true. He knew it to the core of his being. Good and bad did not reside in the absence or presence of light. Good and bad resided in the behavior of human beings, in the thoughts and actions of mortals and immortals, regardless of the god they served.

No, rather, Seth had questioned his choice to serve at all.

At the time of his youth, following in his father's footsteps to become a priest in the powerful *per netjer,* or temple, of Set-Sutekh the ruling deity of much of Upper Egypt under the early pharaohs, it had felt more like his destiny than choice. Especially when Seth had subsequently been anointed as High Priest of the *per netjer.* Admittedly, as a young man he'd been blinded by the awesome magic of immortality when it had been offered to him and his followers…even given the high personal price he must pay. Becoming a vampire had seemed a small sacrifice to gain such immense preternatural powers.

The early days had been rough. Learning to control the unnatural cravings, and master the power, so neither controlled nor mastered him, had not been easy. Other high priests had not fared so well in matters of conscience, the natural greed and cruelty of many of the immortal vampires coming out in ways that ended up toppling pharaohs from the throne, and plunging the entire country into many centuries of chaos and hardship.

But Set-Sutekh was the God of Chaos, so his *per netjer*, with Seth as its leader, thrived and gained more and more power and influence from one end of the Nile to the other. It wasn't until Seth truly opened his eyes and saw what the constant war and strife was doing to the mortals, the common people of Egypt, that he started to question what was happening. And his role in it.

He'd retreated to his underground palace and contemplated putting an end to it all. How could you go on living with such misery all around, and know yourself to be one of the primary causes? In his deepest depression, he'd written a long poem about a conversation between a man weary of life, and his soul, or *ba,* entreating it to just let him die.

Ultimately, his *ba* had won his personal debate, and Seth had not taken his life. He had, however, resolved to withdraw forever from the affairs of mortals, and to stop the deadly strife between his *per netjer* and all the others.

It had worked, too. In every case except one.

Petru.

Haru-Re still insisted on seizing control of all the mortal realm for his god, Re-Horakhti. Ray would not rest until Seth and Khepesh were conquered, relegated to the anonymous sands of time, as he had all the other thousands of temples of the ancient gods of Egypt.

The final battle was coming. And it was coming soon.

Lately, worry and unease had kept Seth awake for most days, as well as nights. Today he awoke even earlier than usual, and with a pounding headache.

The hunger was also growing worse every passing day, bringing with it a multitude of physical miseries along with the psychological ones.

"My lord Seth-Aziz!"

Seth gave a silent groan. Or perhaps it was just the pounding on his chamber door that echoed painfully through his skull. Did the bad news never cease?

He slid from his bed, grasping the edge of the mattress with his fingers to steady the dizziness. "Come!" he called, reaching for his robe when the lightheadedness passed. The grogginess was getting harder to shake off.

The entry door to his suite glided open. "Sorry to disturb you, my lord. But you are needed at the Great Western Gate."

Immediately, alarm shot through Seth. The Great Western Gate was the main entrance to Khepesh, placed at the end of a deep, meandering underground tunnel that led down from a hidden magical portal in the cliffs of the Western Desert. "What's happened? Is it Haru-Re?"

Had the last salvo in their endless war for supremacy finally begun, now that the enemy possessed the final weapon needed for victory? Had Nephtys given in to the bastard…?

"No, my lord," the messenger answered, shifting on his feet. "There's a, um, bit of a disturbance. The guards are…not sure what to do about it."

Seth let out a sigh and went to his armoire to pick out clothes appropriate for a public appearance. "What kind of disturbance?"

"A woman. A mortal. Demanding entrance to the palace."

Seth paused with a frown, thought, and remembered. *Ah*. The promised blood sacrifice. That was quick. "Sheikh Shahin must have sent her."

The messenger appeared acutely uncomfortable. "I don't believe so. But she insists on speaking to you, my lord. Only you."

Not totally unexpected under the circumstances. "Is there a problem?"

The man shuffled again. His face grew red. "She's, um, quite angry."

Seth was beginning to have a bad feeling about this woman. "Why on earth would she be angry? Is she not bespelled?"

"I think not, my lord."

Seth smoothed his formal black robes into place, tied a red sash around his waist, then gave the messenger a hard look. There was definitely something the man was not telling him. "Does this mortal woman have a name?"

The man avoided his gaze. "I, um…"

Suspicion suddenly curled through Seth like a serpent ready to strike.

Mithra's balls. It couldn't be. There was no way she could have found Khepesh on her own.

And besides, no, she wouldn't *dare....*

But one look at the messenger's apprehensive expression and Seth knew his suspicion was correct.

Fury flooded through him. And with it, all trace of the blood weakness fled from his bones. He could not believe the temerity of the woman to show her face here!

"By the gods!" he cursed as he flew from his rooms toward the Great Western Gate. "I will have her head on a platter! And the person who led her to our portal shall find his head on the end of my captain's sword!"

As Seth approached the monumental silver gate, he saw that a small crowd of immortals had gathered, sensing the high drama unfolding. The *shemsu* of Khepesh all knew about the Haliday sisters. And about Nephtys's vision of Seth's future consort and soul mate, a beautiful blonde whom Nephtys had joyfully identified as Gillian, the youngest sister. But Seth's embracing of the vision and admitting the young Haliday woman into the *per netjer* had led to a string of disasters... culminating in her fleeing Khepesh with Lord Rhys right after the annual Ritual of Transformation—the elaborate ceremony where Seth should have taken his annual blood sacrifice. This year Gillian had been his chosen sacrificial vessel.

Everyone knew of these events.

But what the gathering crowd didn't know was that to save Gillian, Rhys had waylaid Seth, and he had never received the sacrifice. Which was why he was now suffering the weakness that had his head reeling.

Rhys and Gillian had been summarily banished from the palace as traitors, and they had fled straight to Petru, the *per netjer* of the Sun God, ruled by Seth's enemy, Haru-Re.

When Sheikh Shahin had subsequently discovered that Gillian possessed two sisters, one of whom was also a blonde and who greatly resembled her, Nephtys had changed her story. "It must have been *Josslyn* Haliday I saw in my vision!" Nephtys had insisted.

But Seth wasn't buying it. He wanted nothing to do with either woman. Gillian Haliday had brought nothing but heartache and catastrophe to himself and to Khepesh. Because of his naïve belief in the vision, and in the possibility of love and companionship with that woman, he was in a personal hell of his own making, and his beloved *per netjer* was on the brink of annihilation by the enemy.

And he'd be *damned* if he let that woman's sister through his gates to wreak further disaster upon them all.

"Seth-Aziz!"

He could hear Josslyn Haliday's strident voice calling his name from the other side of the huge double portal even though it soared three stories high and was fashioned of pure, solid silver. He planted his feet and gathered his strength, needing all the authority he could muster. This was one battle he did not intend to lose.

"Open up! Let me in!" She pounded on the massive gate with her fists, which made a surprisingly loud echo for a mortal. "I know you're in there! Give me back my sisters! Let them go right this minute, or I'll have the U.S. Marines on your ass so fast your head will—"

"Enough!" Seth bellowed so loudly there was instant silence on both sides of the barrier. His subjects very seldom saw him angry and even less often heard him raise his voice. They knew it never boded well for anyone caught in the crossfire.

He ground his jaw and advanced on the gate, sweeping his hand at the portal guard. "Open it! Now!"

She wanted to come in? Fine. He'd let her in.

And she would never see the light of day again.

A long, deep clang resonated, and the portal wings began to move, splitting down the middle and slowly opening inward to reveal the glittering silver outer gate. Both sides were decorated in intricate hieroglyphics, the cartouches of Set-Sutekh gracing the center of each, along with the left Eye of Horus—symbol of the god who'd ripped it from his enemy. The gate was flanked by tall, lotus-shaped, fire-burning torches, flaming bright against the stygian void of the tunnel beyond.

A lone woman stood illuminated by the torchlight.

For a second Seth just stared. If he weren't so angry, and so fucking, ravenously hungry, he would have laughed.

This?

This was supposed to be his future wise and beloved consort? She looked more like a street urchin from the slums of Cairo.

Her face was sweat-streaked and dirty, and she wore an ancient striped *gelebeya* that looked like she'd stolen from an old man's clothes line. It hung about her ankles in clouds of dust. On her feet were ugly army boots. Her hair, if it was even blond, was wrapped in a scarf of the popular Palestinian variety usually worn by clueless tourists and aging hippies.

The gate reached its zenith and glided to a halt. She had no trouble picking him out of the crowd of observers, who looked back and forth between them as they stared each other down.

She was fearless. He'd give her that. Or rather, reckless. Did she really think she stood a chance here? A mere mortal pitted against a demigod?

For a long moment she regarded him, from top to bottom, her eyes betraying an emotion he couldn't quite decipher. Consternation? As though he wasn't what she'd expected? Well, that made two of them.

She took a step forward. "I've come for my sisters," she declared in a loud, clear voice.

He narrowed his eyes at her disrespect.

"On your knees, woman, and kneel before the high priest of Set-Sutekh!" the portal guard commanded her, raising his scimitar.

She faltered for a split second, then her back went up and she took another step forward, ignoring the threat. "I kneel before no man," she informed Seth archly. "Now give me my sisters!"

Seth's fists clenched at his sides, his blood simmering. *No one* disrespected him in this way!

"Come in and get them," he growled, schooling his urge to strike the woman dead where she stood. It would take so little, the merest whisper of a thought in his mind. And then he'd be safely rid of her, once and for all. "*If* you dare enter."

She started to walk, but he lifted a finger and stopped her in mid-stride. Surprise swept over her face at having her movements controlled by another, as though she were merely a puppet on a string.

She had no idea.

"Take heed," he warned, his voice gravelly with the effort to quell his boiling temper, "that if you willingly choose to enter my domain, you become mine to rule, mine to do with as I wish."

She blinked. "What's that supposed to mean?" she demanded, and he saw the first glimmer of uncertainty flit through her expression.

"Exactly what you think it means," he informed her.

He could smell her, the mortal scent of her like an insidious perfume of temptation sent to harass his senses. The salt of her sweat. A dusty hint of the fragrant desert above that clung to her clothes. The telltale tang of the dawning fear within her breast.

And under it all, the sweet, alluring scent of her mortal blood.

The vampire in him reared up in howling need, ripping with ravenous claws at his insides to come out. It wanted to gorge itself on her crimson bounty until he lay prostrate with satiety, his strength and power safely returned for another year.

Or until Haru-Re killed him.

Beneath the sleeve of her *gelebeya* her hand twitched. He sensed she held something in it. No doubt a weapon of some kind. As if that would save her.

He took a stride toward her, unable to stop himself from drawing nearer. The blood rushing through her veins was calling to him. Filling him with blood lust.

Filling him with sexual lust.

Closer now, he saw that beneath the covering of dust and the hideous scarf her face was much prettier than he'd first believed. He wondered what the rest of her looked like….

"I don't want to enter," she quickly said, stepping backward to avoid him. Her growing fear was starting to wear down her confidence.

Good.

"No?"

A lock of golden blond hair fell across her cheek from beneath its cloth prison. She pushed it aside. "No. I just want you to let my sisters go."

He yearned to rip that scarf off her head. Since he was a youth he'd always preferred blonde women. The rare, exotic color aroused him. Would the rest of her hair be as pale a yellow?

He felt his fangs begin to lengthen. And so did his cock. Along with a simmering fury that it should be this particular woman who'd awakened them both.

"And if I don't let them go?" he asked, wanting nothing more than to rid himself of her disturbing presence, to rid himself of the harrowing temptation of her blood, to rid himself of *her,* for good.

All he needed was an excuse. A means to do so that didn't violate the tenets of Khepesh that he himself had established.

"I told you," she said, but her voice caught on a quaver, betraying her. "I'll bring the law down on this place. And the American government. And the press. Whoever will listen. Trust me, they'll *all* listen."

He took another furious step toward her. There!

Right *there* was his reason! He started to summon the guards.

She lifted her chin. "And don't even think about harming me or my sisters. Because I've sent letters. Lots of them. All outlining exactly where we are and what's happened to us. To be opened in case I don't return." Her luminous blue eyes glowed with triumph. Eyes he had far too quickly dismissed as unattractive—and unwise.

He halted. He could easily sense when a mortal was lying. But she wasn't. She was telling the truth.

This was the final straw upon his patience. And thank merciful Isis, the thing that indelibly sealed her fate.

"So to be clear, Miss Haliday, you refuse to enter Khepesh of your own free will?" he asked evenly, knowing what a refusal meant. He would have no choice but to act, and no one would fault him for fulfilling his duty to protect his people. Indeed, they would blame him if he didn't take immediate and decisive action.

The letters could easily be dealt with. But she must be silenced. Forever.

The *shemsu* understood this. His palace guard had already moved into position, ready to jump to his command.

"Of course I refuse!" Josslyn Haliday declared hotly. "I want no part of your uncivilized cult. Please, I just—"

That was all he needed.

"Seize her!" he barked, and in the blink of an eye his guards had her captive. "Take her to the temple," he ordered, "where she will serve Set-Sutekh for the rest of eternity as a *shabti*. Now go!"

Josslyn let out a cry of protest, fighting the guards as they began to drag her in through the gate. Seth angrily hurled a spell of immobility at her and her screams cut off. She went limp in the grip of the guards, though her eyes still darted around wildly.

Suddenly another scream sounded, this one coming from the tunnel that led down to the palace from the desert aboveground.

"No! You mustn't!" the woman's voice cried. "Let her go! Let her *go!*"

It was Gemma, Josslyn's sister, riding a camel at full tilt toward them. A black hawk swooped in after her, circled her head once, then flew down to the foot of the gate. Before its talons hit the stone, its body stretched and grew, transforming into the shape of a man. A very angry man.

Shahin. He landed in full dudgeon, robes swirling, swearing a blue streak and yelling at his woman to stop.

I'm sorry, my lord! he called silently between curses. *The news reached her and she lit out of the oasis before I could catch her.*

Seth ground his teeth. What *was* it about these accursed Haliday women that their men were ever at a loss to control them?

"Please, my lord," Gemma cried, leaping from the camel, avoiding Shahin's grab and throwing herself to her knees on the stone floor before Seth. She looked up, her eyes pleading. "Please. Don't do this. Not a *shabti*. Spare her, at least for now! Give me a chance to talk to her. To explain. To change her mind. Seth, in the name of the magic we shared, I beg you."

It was the only thing that could have stopped Seth in his fury. But it had the desired effect. He halted.

Shahin finally reached Gemma, pulled her to her feet and clamped his hands on her arms in a firm grip.

Josslyn's horrified eyes were on the sheikh. She tore them away to fasten them on her sister, and they filled with tears.

Gemma's did, too. "It's okay, Joss. I'm okay. Everything'll be okay," she called to her. "I promise."

Not if Seth had anything to say about it.

But the sight of their anguish was an unbidden reminder of his own sister, held captive by a man she hated, and Seth's conscience felt another prick. He would do anything in his power to get Nephtys back, anything to ease the suffering he knew she must be enduring.

His temper dampened a fraction, and his conviction wavered.

Then, all at once, something dropped from Josslyn's hand. It was not a weapon. When Seth saw what it actually was, his fury returned at double force.

"By the claws of Sekhmet, *where did you get that?*" he roared.

The growing crowd of *shemsu* moved swiftly backward, away from his wrath.

In a nanosecond he was at Josslyn's side scooping up the object that had landed by her boot. There was no mistaking it. It was an amulet belonging to Nephtys—a scarab beetle made of the finest purple amethyst, with Haru-Re's distinctive cartouche carved on its belly. The bastard had given it to her, the morning after he'd taken her virginity. She'd carried it with her all these years as a reminder of the love she'd once had for the man, and of his cruel betrayal of that love.

Seth hated the sight of it, but he knew she would never have willingly parted with the scarab. Had something happened to her?

"Tell me where you got this!"

Josslyn gazed at him with silent, desperate eyes, still bespelled and in the grip of the guards. In a heartbeat he lifted the spell so she could speak and waved a hand at them to let her go. He stalked closer.

"From a woman called Nephtys," she blurted out hoarsely, steadying herself to blink up at him in terror. "She said she was your sister."

He bent over her, making her shrink down in fear. "I don't believe you. Tell me the truth!"

"I *am* telling you the truth!" she said, panic blanching her cheeks. "I just met her a few hours ago. Somehow she knew who I was and that I was searching for Gemma and Gillian. She told me they were here, in an underground compound, and she showed me the entrance to the tunnel."

If this was indeed the truth, which he reluctantly sensed it was, not only was his sister unharmed, but it seemed she was not quite the helpless prisoner of Haru-Re that he had assumed. He'd have to think about the implications of that later.

"And the amulet?" he demanded, pacing away from Josslyn, not wanting to stand so close to her. The smell of her blood was making him lose his concentration. And his will to be rid of her.

"She gave it to me to give to you. As proof she'd sent

me. She said to tell you—" Josslyn's eyes flared and her words cut off abruptly.

Seth went still inside. What schemes had his sister set in motion now?

"Tell me what?"

Josslyn's lips pressed together.

Gemma wrestled free of Shahin and rushed to her sister, throwing her arms around her. "It's all right, Joss. For God's sake, tell him what he wants to know."

"I can't," she whispered hoarsely.

"You have to. It's the only way to save yourself."

Josslyn swallowed heavily as she looked at her sister, her face going deathly pale. Her gaze flitted to Shahin, then to Seth, then back to Gemma. "I don't remember the rest. Honest."

It didn't take a demigod's powers to know that this time she was lying through her teeth. She was a horrible liar.

"Joss. Please," Gemma pleaded softly. "Trust me."

"Listen to your sister," Seth warned her quietly, the vicious need within him crouching, readying to strike. "Or suffer the consequences."

The *shemsu* eased farther back. He was even more dangerous when he went quiet.

Josslyn tried to clear her throat and failed. A tear trickled down her cheek, making a glittering track in the dust there. Gemma wiped it tenderly away.

Josslyn shuddered out a breath, hesitated one last time, and said, "She said you should remember her vision."

He could smell the fear and desperation coming off

the woman in waves. He could also feel there was more to it.

"What else?" he demanded even more softly.

She shook her head. "Nothing."

"Don't lie to me, Josslyn. I will always know when you lie to me."

Another tear broke loose and fell from her lashes. Gemma gave her a squeeze of encouragement. "It's okay. I promise."

"She said—" Josslyn closed her eyes, then opened them and met his. "She said I should offer you a bargain."

"What kind of bargain?"

"A bargain for my sisters' freedom."

Inwardly he cursed Nephtys. She knew damn well he had no power to grant either Gemma's or Gillian's freedom. They had both willingly joined the *per netjer,* and only death or banishment freed them from that obligation.

So it wasn't difficult to discern what Nephtys had in mind with this little scheme of hers. She'd sent the Haliday woman straight into his arms, into his bed, as a gift, all done up in a dirty striped ribbon, in hopes that she would somehow make up for her sister Gillian's colossal failings in that regard.

"Joss, you don't have to—" Gemma began.

With a swift thought, he strangled her words.

"In exchange for…?" he prodded Josslyn. He wanted to hear it spoken aloud. He wanted to roll it around in his mind and savor it before he spit it out. And he didn't want the sister's infernal interference.

"In exchange for…" Josslyn reluctantly said, "allowing you to use me…to ease your need."

For a long moment there again was absolute silence around the gate.

Gemma glared daggers at him. The *shemsu* held their collective breath. Josslyn was no doubt praying he would refuse her. And he, well, he was carefully weighing his options.

If she was offering herself to him of her own free will, to use her as he saw fit…well, that put a different spin on things than him having to pursue her, to talk her into submitting to the blood sacrifice…or anything else he might desire of her.

Not that he wanted anything more to do with the woman after slaking his voracious need for sustenance. At least not in the way Nephtys had envisioned.

However…

Spurred on by the prospect of feeding, the blood lust pounded through his flesh like a thousand marching feet. Adrenaline had brought him this far in their battle of wills, but it was now taking all his powers to keep from giving away the state of his ebbing strength to his people. The smell of her blood was driving him mad with hunger, driving his temper to the breaking point. And his ungovernable cock was not helping matters. It had grown instantly hard at the thought of having Josslyn Haliday at its complete mercy, offered up to him at her own suggestion.

The fact was, he could make any bargain he wished, because he held all the power. Because she believed he possessed what she wanted, and she had no idea that it was indeed she who possessed what he so desperately needed.

He made the logical decision.

He leveled a gaze at Shahin. "Get your woman and hold her," he ordered. His captain of the guard obeyed, pulling Gemma from Josslyn's embrace and banding his arm around her. Although, to be sure, it looked more like an embrace than any kind of compulsion, and she didn't put up too much of a fight. It helped that Gemma had actually come to trust Seth over the past weeks since their intimate encounter.

Though that was probably about to change radically.

"Are you willing to do that?" Seth asked Josslyn. "To submit yourself to me? To become the vessel of my sacrifice?"

The color drained from her face. Her eyes grew wide as saucers. "Wait. *Sacrifice?* What kind of sacrifice?"

And didn't *that* just figure? "Nephtys didn't tell you?"

"Tell me what?"

Seth's lips curved in a humorless smile, showing her the tips of his long, lethal fangs.

"My dear, I am vampire. And my need? It can only be slaked with your blood."

Chapter 6

Vampire!

The word screeched through Joss's entire body, striking a cacophony of fear within her. It couldn't be true. It *couldn't* be.

"Are you kidding me?" she managed to croak.

Twenty-four hours ago she would have rolled her eyes in incredulity at Seth-Aziz's outrageous assertion. But at the moment, she was acutely aware that no one else around her was laughing. Not even Gemma. Not that Gemma *would* laugh. In her work as an ethnographer, Gemma was forever being spooked by the tales of ancient gods, vampires, and shape-shifters told to her by the local village women. Like their flower-child mother, Gemma believed in such things.

Joss didn't.

At least she hadn't until last night, when she'd almost been bitten in the neck by that horrible man Ray, who'd suddenly seemed to grow fangs. And then, just now, when the man embracing Gemma had shifted from a hawk into a human being right before her eyes. All while Joss's body was being held mutely in place by some horrific power that she couldn't begin to understand.

It was tough not to believe even the impossible when presented with compelling evidence like that.

My God, she'd landed smack in the middle of the twilight zone!

"I assure you," Seth-Aziz said, his dark, sexy eyes watching her like he wanted to devour her whole, "I do not kid."

Great. So he was actually asking her if she'd let him drink her blood. And heaven help her, those fangs did not look like the fake kind attached by some expensive cosmetic dentist.

A spill of something tangible in the air brushed over her like soft, warm fur, raising the fine hairs all over her body. Ever since she'd first approached the huge silver gate, she'd felt the thick, powerful aura of some indefinable, otherworldly energy enveloping her, like last night, only a thousand times stronger.

His aura?

Deep down, she was suddenly, terrifyingly convinced he was the real thing. An honest-to-God vampire.

Lord, was she losing her mind?

Had she and her sisters stumbled into something very, very evil and scary that would mean the end of them all?

She thought suddenly of her vanished mother, and wondered in horror if *she* had stumbled onto the same cult of unnatural beings? Was that why she'd disappeared all those years ago, so close to this very spot?

Oh. Mygod.

In growing desperation, Joss licked her lips and glanced to Gemma for help. Oddly, her sister didn't look terrified in the least. She seemed more angry at Seth-Aziz, that he wouldn't let her speak, and kept giving him furious looks. When Joss finally caught her attention, she just shook her head and mouthed the words, "I'm sorry."

No help at all.

Joss glanced back at Seth-Aziz, who continued to regard her with those disconcertingly dark and mysterious bedroom eyes.

They were irresistibly hypnotic, seeming to draw her down, down, down, into their black depths, luring her in with an erotic promise of God knew what. Tempting her to give in to his dark blood bargain.

Tempting was the word, all right. Though not classically *GQ* handsome, Seth-Aziz was far more attractive and alluring than any man had a right to be— tall of build, dark of hair, broad of shoulder. There were surely worse things she could imagine than to be bitten on the neck—or anywhere else for that matter—by this man.

Wait.

No.

What was she *thinking?*

And yet, what choice did she have?

"If I agree to this…exchange," she said, shaking off the unwanted sexual stirrings and banding her arms across her midriff, doing her best to ignore that weird energy swirling about her, "do you swear you'll let my sisters go at once?"

Seth-Aziz tipped his head in an off-kilter nod. Another brush of dark, brooding power tingled over her skin. "If they wish to leave Khepesh, I promise I will not stop them."

"Or your guards, or anyone else? They'll be free to go at any time?"

He lifted his hands, palms up. "Agreed."

She suddenly realized her fingers had strayed to her neck, touching the place she imagined he'd put his lips when he bit her. His gaze had followed the movement, watching her like a predator watches his prey.

Her face heated and she forced her hand down again. She tried to recall the many Egyptian vampire stories Gemma had repeated to her and Gillian over drinks on the verandah, tales of wicked shape-shifters going from village to village in the dead of night, stealing away young women to service a powerful vampire demigod with their blood and their bodies.

She glanced nervously at the shape-shifter Shahin. *Jesus.* To think those stories could be true, that it may even have happened to her own sisters! And was about to happen to her...

Seth was watching her expectantly through lowered lids.

"Will it hurt?" she blurted out, a shudder going down her spine like a washboard.

He smiled knowingly, showing off those glistening white fangs again. "On the contrary," he said, his voice a velvet rumble. "It will be quite pleasurable for you. For both of us."

She shivered as a lick of heat curled through her center and touched the pearl of her need. And recalled that according to the stories, a vampire's bite induced a sexual gratification unlike any other a woman could ever experience.

"And after…after you finish, you'll let me go?" she asked, fighting off an avalanche of apprehension. *This was a really, really bad idea.* Lord, what if she *liked* it?

His smile grew sultry. As if he could read her thoughts, he said, "After being with me, I assure you, you will not want to leave Khepesh."

Oh, God.

She was pretty sure her face was beet-red by now, though why she should be affected by his false flattery, she had no clue. She looked like a filthy beggar dressed in this old rag, and it was crystal clear that until her mention of a bargain, he'd had absolutely no interest in or attraction to her as a woman. He was too powerful, too good-looking, not to get this reaction from females all the time. He was just humoring her to get to her blood.

"Let's say I *do* want to leave," she pressed, swallowing down the insanity running through her head.

Instead of answering, he reached out and tugged off her scarf. Her hair fell in clumps around her shoulders. It had been hot under the cloth and she reached up convulsively to run an embarrassed hand through the sweaty mess. Which was stupid, because she didn't *care* how she looked to him.

His gaze moved over her like a Realtor assessing the

potential value of an overgrown, run-down, fixer-upper. Which made her cheeks flame even more.

He said, "You will be free to join your sisters, if that is your wish."

Behind her, she heard a commotion, and she turned to see Gemma wrestling to get free of Shahin, who still held her in his grasp. Towering and muscular in his human form, Shahin wasn't about to let her go. But Gemma didn't appear frightened of him. She still looked mad as a hornet, glancing between Joss and Seth-Aziz. Still unable to make a sound.

Joss turned back to him, suddenly even more nervous. "I don't know what you've done to my sister's voice, but I want to speak with her before I agree to any of this."

Seth-Aziz didn't even consider her request. He shook his head immediately. "No."

An avalanche of foreboding tumbled through her. "Why not? What are you afraid she'll tell me? Are you lying about something?"

His eyebrows drew together. "What possible motivation would I have to lie?" he returned. "Indeed, why would I bother to bargain with you at all if I didn't mean to keep my word?"

He glanced pointedly at the armed guards standing at the ready, scimitars in hand. They'd taken her prisoner once, barely lifting a finger. They could grab her again, was the implication, and he could easily force himself on her if that was what he wanted to do.

Still. He hadn't denied her accusation.

Something wasn't right. She could feel it in the electric brush of tension arcing between them. In the increased roil of the weird, supernatural energy that permeated every molecule of this place.

She glanced covertly around, searching for the camel that Gemma had ridden in on, praying Seth wouldn't sic those guards on her before she and Gemma could reach it. But it must have wandered off, around the first bend in the tunnel. They'd just have to make a run for it.

"Okay," she said, "In that case, you can forget the whole thing."

She did an about-face and started to stride away, back toward Gemma, the tunnel and the camel. She'd just grab her sister and they'd—

"*Stop,*" Seth-Aziz ground out. "Do *not*—"

But just then Gemma broke free of Shahin and ran up to her. Joss grabbed her hand and started to sprint for the tunnel and freedom. To her confusion, instead of going along, Gemma pulled her firmly to a skidding stop. She shook her head and grasped Joss's upper arms in firm fingers. "No," she clearly mouthed.

"What the hell, Gem?" Josslyn cried in dismay. "We've got to get out of here!"

Again Gemma shook her head and glanced in appeal at Seth-Aziz. Glowering fiercely, he crossed his arms in front of his chest. Gemma looked back at her and sighed. She pulled Joss into a tight hug and kissed her cheek. Joss could feel the conviction in her gestures, the intense desire of her sister to reassure her. Then she mouthed "Go back" and turned her around so she was again facing Seth-Aziz, and gave her a little shove.

Joss balked. She couldn't believe this was happening! Did her sister *want* her to become the…the next human sacrifice of a vampire?

Apparently she did. From behind, Gemma once again put her arms around Joss and gave her another hug. Then she let go and gave her an even firmer push toward Seth-Aziz.

Her meaning couldn't be clearer. *Go to him. Submit to him. Do whatever he asks of you.*

Seth-Aziz's expression betrayed nothing. It had gone from glowering to carefully blank as he stood splay-legged with his arms crossed imperiously over his chest, as though he owned the entire universe and they were just visitors.

Joss swallowed heavily. She trusted her sisters more than she trusted anyone else on earth. She did. And if Gemma said she must do this, to free her and Gillian, then she must. Joss was the oldest, the responsible one. The one the other two looked up to. Depended on. It was up to her alone to keep the family together. And she would do it. So they could once again be just that—a family.

She thought of their mother and father and how much it had hurt to lose them. She couldn't lose her sisters, too.

She just couldn't.

No matter the sacrifice.

So she straightened her shoulders and took a deep, shaking breath and began to walk back toward the gate.

To the vampire lord, Seth-Aziz.

And toward a terrifying, unknown fate.

Chapter 7

The sun cast a warm, pink glow over the temple garden as Nephtys sat by the sacred Pool of Re-Horakhti, gazing into its still waters hoping to catch a glimpse of something, anything, that brought a sign from Seth-Aziz or Khepesh or even Josslyn Haliday.

She hadn't had a vision all week. Not since arriving in Petru. She dearly missed the Eye of Horus, her favorite scrying bowl. It had been left behind in her rooms when Haru-Re had sprung his sinister trap and spirited her away from Khepesh.

She ground her jaw as, instead of a glimpse of the future, a scene appeared from the recent past—the worst day of her life.

"Bring the Haliday woman to Petru!" Haru-Re had ordered his minions as Nephtys looked on in despair.

"No!" she'd protested. *"What do you want?"*

"You know my price," he'd told her, his eyes glittering with imminent conquest.

She'd known only too well what his price would be. *Nephtys herself.* Her freedom in exchange for Josslyn Haliday.

But she had paid it willingly. The mortal woman's union with Seth may be the last hope for the survival of Khepesh. She didn't know how, but she knew their fates were somehow linked. But more important, Nephtys had wanted to safeguard her brother's happiness. She would rather die a slow death herself than deprive him of the future he deserved.

So she had given herself over to Haru-Re. To become the consort of the enemy, bound to him forever.

There had been a short time after her capitulation that Ray had changed and seemed to turn almost... kind. And happy, of all things. She had thought against all odds that the goodness deep within him had shown itself at last. That she'd been right about him. But then he'd become angry again when she'd insisted they wait to wed. And the result had been his visit to Josslyn last night. It infuriated her!

She thrust her hand agitatedly into the pool, churning the still waters into a whirlpool, shattering the unwanted vision and the vexing memory. Jerking away, she glowered up at the disc of the sun, traveling along its golden path across the sky, just as it had yesterday and the day before and a trillion days before that. Doomed to repeat the same journey forever.

Just as she seemed to be.

She couldn't believe after all this time she was right back where she'd started.

The bastard had won, after all.

She took a deep, calming breath.

No. Not necessarily. There may yet be a way to achieve her desired revenge and come out on top. But only if she executed her plan very, very carefully…

And to do that, she needed to know if her first move had succeeded.

Once again, she endeavored to empty her mind and gazed down into the waters of the pool, seeking a different vision. One that would be more productive. But it was impossible to focus. Irritating thoughts of Haru-Re kept invading her mind, ruining her hard-won serenity.

She should just give up and wait until her agitation waned. But she didn't know how much time she had. Ray probably wouldn't be gone much longer, and she'd already incurred his wrath this morning by slipping out to find Josslyn. She'd made the excuse of going for a ride, which in the end he may or may not have believed. She didn't want to push her luck.

He was currently out chasing down some unfortunate *shabti* who'd had the questionable judgment to run away from Petru during the night.

Poor thing. Nephtys didn't like the creature's chances once Ray caught up with her. He didn't tolerate deserters. The woman would feel his anger, for certain. Nephtys just hoped she herself didn't bear the brunt of his displeasure when he returned. After their run-in last night, and again this morning, his patience with her was on a very short fuse.

"Well?" a breathless voice asked, hurrying up to her.

It was Gillian Haliday, a hopeful expression on her

face. Nephtys put aside her frustrations and smiled in greeting. She'd grown quite fond of the young woman in the short time they'd spent together, here and before they'd both been forced to leave Khepesh.

"You were right," Nephtys told her. It had been Gillian who'd unknowingly presented her with exactly the information she'd needed to set her plan in motion. "Josslyn was at the Winter Palace Hotel, just as you guessed."

She thought it best not to mention the fact that Ray had also been there. Thank the goddess Nephtys had shown up when she did, or Josslyn Haliday would now be living a nightmare, and Nephtys would be faced with the untenable choice between her growing friendship with Gillian and her fury at the bastard for having it off with another woman when he'd promised himself to her.

Nephtys didn't give a damn about his accursed carnal needs. She only hoped that after sending Josslyn to her brother, Seth had more control over himself when it came to such things than Nephtys's own betrothed.

"So you found Joss?" Gillian asked, elated. She looked excitedly around the garden, as if expecting her sister to be sitting here, too. "Where is she? You brought her here to Petru, right?"

"Not exactly." Nephtys patted the granite edge of the pool beside her. "Sit."

"What?" Gillian sank down on the stone rim, looking crushed. "Why not? Surely, she didn't refuse to come? Not when—"

She glanced over at an older couple sitting on a bench on the other side of the garden.

Oh, dear. This was not going to be easy. "Gillian…"

The young woman turned back to her and comprehension suddenly dawned. Her mouth dropped open. "Oh, no. Nephtys, please, God, don't tell me you sent her to Khepesh!" Gillian jumped up, a stark portrait of accusation.

Nephtys grabbed her hand and pulled her down again. "*Kitet,* little sister, you know better than anyone about the vision I was sent of the future. Seth needs—"

Gillian put her hands over her eyes. "Seth!" She lifted them to reveal a pained expression. "Seth-Aziz is a freaking *demigod!* He can have any woman he wants! *I'm* the one who needs her. Josslyn should be *here,* in Petru, with me and our parents!"

This time they both looked across the garden's splash of brightly flowering plants to the older couple. The man was holding the woman's hand, patting it, speaking softly to her. The woman was staring vacantly at the horizon, seemingly unaware of the man beside her.

"*We're* her family. Not Seth!"

Nephtys's heart went out to Isobelle Haliday, and especially to Trevor Haliday, for what they were going through. But she also knew her brother needed Josslyn far more than they did, regardless of what Gillian thought. What was the happiness of one small family against the fates of so many? If Nephtys's vision was correct, Josslyn could be the key to saving Khepesh. How could she take the chance of not allowing it every opportunity to be fulfilled?

In addition to serving Nephtys's purposes.

"I understand how you feel," Nephtys said. "But you know what she will suffer if she comes here." She folded her hands in her lap to keep them from balling into fists. "Haru-Re also knows about my vision. There's little doubt he would take out his antipathy for Seth by ruining Josslyn."

Despite a vain attempt to deflect it, pain razored through her at the thought. Selfishly, not for Josslyn's sake, but for her own. Because she would then be forced to watch Ray's dalliance with another woman. Until he tired of toying with her, and Josslyn ended up in the same pathetic state as Nephtys herself. Vamp-addicted, alone, and abandoned.

Men were such cruel brutes.

At least this one.

Gillian bit her lip, frowning. "He wouldn't do that. Not after he's chosen you to be his consort. That would be—"

"Despicable?" Nephtys's attempt to keep the cynicism out of her voice failed. "Obviously you don't know him as I do."

"Then why the hell do you love him?" Gillian asked in exasperation.

The woman was so incredibly naïve. "Who says I do?"

Gillian made a wry face. "Don't even try. I can see it in your eyes, whenever you look at him." She glanced over at Trevor and Isobelle Haliday, where the love on her father's face shone like the sun that was rising behind him.

Nephtys sighed. *Sweet Isis.* Was she equally transparent?

"You're wrong. I don't love him," she said firmly, "I hate him." But her statement lacked conviction even to her own ears. "I do, however, love my brother, and I know you love your sister. Therefore, I don't want anything bad to happen to either of them. That's why I sent her to Khepesh. I hope you'll forgive me one day." She took Gillian's hand. "And at least she'll be close to Gemma."

Gillian jetted out a breath. "This is so stupid. We should all be together. My sisters and I and my parents. You and Seth. Hell, you and Haru-Re. Jeez, someone should knock some sense into those two idiots. Why keep fighting each other in a war that no one wins?"

Nephtys smiled wanly. "For the same reason the sun shines in the daytime and the moon lights up the darkness."

Gillian simply didn't comprehend the forces at work. How could she? She'd only known the immortals for a few short weeks. This war had been going on for millennia, ever since the dawn of Egyptian civilization. Between the Sun God and the God of the Night; between order and chaos, between enlightenment and darkness.

There were those who believed it boiled down to the essential fight between good and evil.

But that was wrong, Nephtys knew. Both Seth and Ray were good men, each in their own way. Neither condoned real evil, as many of the ancient rulers had done. They were both beloved of their immortal followers, and had long ago left mortals out of this war between demigods.

No, she knew it was a much more personal battle going on between her brother and her captor. Of which, unfortunately, Nephtys herself was at the heart.

She just prayed Josslyn Haliday had not now been tossed into the volatile mix like an accelerant in gunpowder.

"It's just the way of things," she said. "There has always been strife between them, and there always will be, until one *per netjer* is irrevocably defeated."

Gillian shook her head. "That's what Rhys says. But I still don't get it."

"Listen to your man. There is much intelligence under that rakish exterior." Nephtys squeezed her hand and let it go. "I'm sure it must be hard on Lord Rhys, being here," she said sympathetically. True, the pair had betrayed her brother, but only because they were in love. And Seth had been working with faulty information, thanks to Nephtys's incorrect interpretation of her vision, or he would surely have blessed their union. Seth only wanted his people to be happy and content.

Sitting on the rim of the pool, Gillian raised her knees and wrapped her arms around them, resting her chin on a fist. "He misses his home and his friends terribly."

"I know he does. He and Seth were very close."

They sat in contemplative silence for a few moments. Nephtys dipped her fingers into the warm water of the sacred pool and stirred it. "If you and Lord Rhys could go back to Khepesh, would you?"

Gillian glanced again at Isobelle and Trevor Haliday. She shook her head, though Nephtys could see that thinking about it hurt her—the prospect of having to choose between her parents and the man she loved. "No," Gillian said. "I couldn't leave them. My father needs me."

"Rhys loves you. And your father made his choice

when he left you and your sisters behind," Nephtys reminded her gently.

"That was different," Gillian said, forgiveness softening her voice. "He knew we'd be okay. We had each other." Her gaze settled on Isobelle. "Mom had no one to take care of her here. She would have spent eternity alone. Like *that*." Her lips thinned. "Damn, I wish there were some way to…" Her words trailed off.

But Nephtys knew exactly what Gillian was thinking, because she was thinking it, too. "To reverse the magic that turned her into a *shabti?* I've never heard of a spell like that. But I promise, I'll make it my business to find out."

Gillian smiled in gratitude. "If anyone can do it, you can. You're amazing at magic."

Nephtys smiled back and touched her fingertips to the young woman's cheek. "And you, *kitet*, are getting quite handy with the spells, yourself. I'm very proud of your progress. What does Lord Rhys think of his lady becoming a temple acolyte and learning the ways of mystery?"

Gillian rolled her eyes. "He says he wishes Petru were the *per netjer* of Isis instead of Re-Horakhti."

Nephtys let out a laugh. The temple maidens of Isis were notorious odalisques, their skills honed in a magic of the…more earthy variety. "Typical male. Thinking only of his pleasure."

"And is that so very wrong?" Ray's deep voice cut across the garden from a shadowed doorway leading to the palace. How long had he been standing there listening? He ground out an aromatic cigarette and stepped out into the pastel glow of the spell-filtered sunlight. Nephtys's heart skipped a beat. "After all," he said, "doesn't a man's greatest pleasure lie in giving pleasure to his woman?"

Nephtys barely resisted an unladylike snort. "*Lie* being the operative word," she returned sharply.

Ray's eyes narrowed. "You insult me already, and the day has barely begun."

Gillian sprang to her feet and cleared her throat. "I, uh, just remembered there's something I need to be doing." With that, she hurried off.

"A wise woman," Ray murmured, watching her timely retreat.

"As opposed to me, I suppose," Nephtys said pleasantly.

He leveled his gaze on her. "Did I say that?" he snapped.

"Difficult morning?" she asked conversationally, determined not to rise to his bait. She refused to give him an excuse to impose his will on her.

"I've had better," he said with a scowl. "I could use a good fuck."

She lifted a brow, unoffended by his crudity. He liked to shock. She was used to it. "So much for your ritual purity."

He flung himself down on the granite rim of the pool and lifted his soft brown boot onto it, leaning back on one elbow. His hair was mussed from the morning breeze, and his golden robes fell about him carelessly, making him look achingly sensual. Every inch the seductive demigod he was.

He regarded her. "What are you up to, *meruati?*"

Her pulse fluttered. "I don't know what you mean."

"Josslyn Haliday has vanished."

"Has she?"

"Do not pretend ignorance," he said evenly. "Your so-called ride this morning, it didn't happen to have anything to do with her sudden disappearance, did it?"

"You think I've done away with the woman? So you can't have her? Really, Ray. I'm not that desperate."

"Hardly. You've sent her to your donkey's ass of a brother, haven't you." It wasn't a question.

She pressed her fingertips together. "Even if I have, and I'm not saying it's true, I don't see that it's any of your business. We have a deal. You have me. You leave her alone."

"Ah, but I *don't* have you, do I?"

Her mouth dropped open as a tingle of alarm rushed through her. "You wouldn't *dare* go back on your oath to me, Haru-Re. Even a demigod must honor his word to a priestess."

"Only if she has honored hers to him," he said silkily.

She snapped her mouth shut. "Do not even go there, Ray."

The corners of his lips curled up. "Actually, our deal was Seth's consort for mine. If he now has his bedmate in hand, and between his sheets, I want mine, too."

"I've told you, the purification ritual—"

"Is bollocks and you know it. You're stalling and I want to know why." He slid his boot from the pool's edge and lithely rose to stand in front of her, hands on hips. The air around him started to glow dimly. "It's not as though you've ever refused to fuck me before. Therefore, there must be another reason. Tell me what it is."

His huge body nearly blocked the sun completely. And yet it emitted a light all of its own. Her heart beat faster. Her traitorous nipples beaded. His power never failed to excite her. "You assume she'll just go along with what is asked of her. That she will simply say yes and fall into bed with him. She may not. She may despise my brother and refuse him."

Ray waved a dismissive hand. "He is vampire. It will take him five minutes to have her begging to feel the thrust of his cock inside her."

She regarded him coolly as an involuntary slam of hurt went through her chest. "Like all the women *you've* had begging for you?" she retorted.

His brows slowly knitted. A shadow of insight passed across his features. "Is that what this is about? You resenting the women I've fucked in the past? What, did you expect me to live like an aesthetic, chaste and pure until you deigned to come back to me?"

She'd had enough of this conversation. She stood. "I would never have come back to you," she clipped out, and attempted to walk past him.

He blocked her path and seized her arms. The air crackled. He pulled her close, but she turned her head, refusing to look at him. She didn't want him to see the lie in her eyes.

He bent his head and skimmed his lips along the edge of her cheekbone. She could feel the sparks bounce off her skin. "If you wish to continue your infernal purity ritual, you had better pray to the gods that Josslyn Haliday *does* refuse your brother. Because if she goes to him, if she binds with him as his consort, if she spreads her legs for him even once, I will know. And I will claim my rights with you, as well, my love."

His fingers closed around her jaw and he forced her face around to look at him. The sky lit up. And then he kissed her.

His mouth covered hers, touching his tongue to the seam of her lips. Against her will they parted. She didn't know if he was bespelling her or if it was her own infernal weakness, her accursed inability to resist him. But the damage was swiftly done. The taste of him overwhelmed her senses. And her wits.

She moaned, and let herself be kissed. Allowed him to run his hands over her body and press his hardened cock against the inward curve of her belly.

"Nephtys," he murmured, "it's torture having you so close but not in my bed."

Her addiction for him roared through her in a firestorm of need, kindled by their erotic encounters over the past month. He knew *nothing* of torture. *She* was the one whose body craved him like a vicious drug.

"Come with me," he urged her, starting to walk her backward toward the door to the palace. "Come to my rooms. Let me—"

"No!"

She wrenched her burning body away from him, shaking with the stinging need that coursed through her veins. A need she knew only he could satisfy.

"Nephtys—"

A need she must deny herself at all cost.

"No, Ray," she repeated, her body trembling.

"When will you put an end to this foolishness?" he growled, his anger flaring to life with ribbons of flame around his head like a Medusa. Sparks rained down on them both. "You want me! You've already admitted it. Look at you! You're as needy as I!"

He was right, but she had to be strong.

"It doesn't matter." Her heart beat out of control at her dared defiance. "My life and my body are my own to bestow as I see fit. You must respect my wishes."

He glared down at her, his eyes the windows to a roiling cauldron of emotion. But he didn't shout. He didn't curse. Instead, he said darkly, "That works both ways, *meruati*. You would do well to remember that."

She gazed up at him, struck by a brief shock of uncertainty. Was that…a glint of *hurt* in his eyes?

No, surely not. How could she possibly have the power to hurt a man with no heart? She couldn't. He was just feeling the pain of sexual frustration.

Wasn't he?

Whatever it was, he whirled and walked away.

Leaving her with the uneasy feeling that he had just let slip a shield that he hadn't meant to. And she'd glimpsed a hidden part of him that he'd never intended to reveal. A part that was vulnerable.

The question was, would she use her newfound knowledge against him?

Or would it only make her love him more…?

Chapter 8

Josslyn blew out a breath and smoothed her trembling hands down the front of the costume she'd been given to wear for her presentation to Seth-Aziz. As his human sacrifice.

Oh, sweet Jesus.

She tried not to think about it, but her heart was pounding like a bass drum.

After she'd given in to his notorious bargain, the vampire lord had taken one look at her and ordered two servants to "Clean her up, and bring her to me." Then he'd turned on a heel and stalked off. After going a few dozen yards, he'd halted, turned again and swirled his hand at her, and suddenly two delicate silver cuffs were circling her wrists, attached by a length of fragile-looking silver chain. There were no clasps.

"Don't bother trying to escape," he'd told her, "the chain is stronger than it looks." He'd turned again and continued down the soaring marble hallway, finally disappearing into the bowels of the palace.

Then Joss had been led away by two of the mysterious female attendants she'd heard someone call *shabtis*.

As an archaeologist, Joss was very familiar with the term *shabti,* or *ushepti*. It was the word for those ubiquitous, pretty blue doll-like statuettes found by the dozen, hundreds or even thousands, in every ancient Egyptian tomb from Alexandria to Aswan. Their purpose was to serve the dead in every capacity imaginable in the afterlife.

The two *shabtis* helping her bathe were most definitely real, live women, but they seemed as oblivious to the world around them as their ceramic sisters. As though they'd been drugged. Or hypnotized. Robbed of all personality. It was downright spooky. And heartbreaking.

Joss had been thoroughly washed, dried, oiled and perfumed and her face carefully made up with kohl, sparkling eye shadows and pounds of mascara that made her look like something straight out of *The Arabian Nights*. Then she was silently handed an outfit to wear.

By this point she'd been half expecting one of those typical bikini-top-and-see-through-skirt getups that belly dancers wear. But she'd been surprised—and completely mortified—when it turned out to be one of those long, skin-tight and totally see-through pleated-linen gowns seen gracing the women depicted in most ancient Egyptian art.

Good lord.

It was, admittedly, gorgeous; a beautiful shade of

shell-pink shot through with silver threads, shimmering with a sheen like the wings of a hummingbird.

It felt as fragile as a dress made of tissue paper and lay against her body like a gossamer glove. How would it ever hold up to the strong hands of a feeding vampire? She had the sinking feeling it wasn't meant to.

Like everything else she'd experienced today, the thin silver cuffs and delicate, ornate chain that still bound her wrists defied logic. Though solid to the touch, and unbreakable when she tried to snap the chain apart, other objects would melt right through it—the towel the *shabtis* dried her with, the fabric of her gown, even the *shabtis* themselves when they brushed her cleansed hair until it shone like spun gold.

What was the true purpose of the restraints, then? She was afraid to ask.

Finally she could drag her preparations out no longer. She was ready to be brought to Seth-Aziz.

It was time to be sacrificed.

Her heart thundered as she was led to the high priest's rooms. Her feet were bare, and the smooth, seamless marble floor felt cool and hard underfoot as she followed the two *shabtis* down a long, long corridor. Silver torch-sconces lit their path, illuminating soaring silver columns, elaborate carved reliefs, exquisite painted murals and luxurious tapestries on every wall. The collection of glass, precious-metal objects and statuary that decorated the niches along the way would have robbed her of breath at any other time.

The people she passed in the halls greeted her with formal bows and curtsies, as if she were some kind of royalty. She felt strange, and very exposed in the insubstantial gown. But if they paid her outfit any mind, it was only to openly admire it, and her. Normally she would have been dying of embarrassment. But at the moment all she could think of was the coming ordeal.

And Seth-Aziz.

He was, she reluctantly acknowledged, the most dazzlingly sexy man she'd ever seen. His soaring, muscular body was worthy of a well-trained athlete, his coal-black hair the perfect length to be infinitely touchable. Even his stern, aristocratic features appealed to her, far more than any vapidly perfect movie idol had ever done.

But it was his black eyes that really got to her. Sharp and furious one moment, they could be sultry and provocative the next, drawing her in, making her want to drown in their enigmatic depths and unveil the mysteries behind those fathomless orbs.

They were on her now, those intense, watchful black eyes, as the *shabtis* ushered her through his nearly dark suite of rooms. Only a few scattered candles burned, casting eerie shadows on the walls and furniture as they lit a path through the darkness.

A few more glowed in the chamber where he awaited her. It was like a luxurious cave inside, a chiaroscuro of dark and darker, with just enough light for her to see where they'd taken her.

His bedroom.

Her heart stalled, then took off like a racehorse. The bed was huge and heavy, taking up the whole center of the room. Its intricate headboard was wrought of star-glittering silver, as so much of Khepesh seemed to be. The bed linens were of crimson-colored satin, and a mound of pillows was scattered carelessly about, as if he'd just risen from a nap.

But Seth-Aziz was not in the bed.

Thank God.

He was reclining on a soft white, upholstered chaise, a silver goblet in his hand, his long legs stretched out before him, crossed at the ankles. His outfit was the same as he'd had on earlier. Well. Parts of it. He still wore the black breeches in the style of the desert nomad, along with a black, floor-length robe, or *bisht,* of the finest silk, that flowed off the white chaise like a black silk waterfall. But he'd taken off his tall black boots, and the black tunic he'd been wearing was gone, too, leaving his bare, olive-skinned chest framed like an exquisite work of art by the black edges of the *bisht.*

As she drank in the sight of his body, he watched her expression with a gleam of satisfaction in his eyes.

He was magnificent, and he knew it.

Nevertheless, she felt her nipples ruche and a warmth invade her belly. It had been a long time since she'd been with a man. And never, ever had she been with a man like Seth-Aziz.

Not that sex had been part of their bargain. *That* had never been mentioned.

Even so, there was an unmistakable, simmering charge of sexual expectation that permeated the air between them.

But for some reason Seth didn't seem happy about that. Or her. Or something. He looked positively fierce as his gaze glided down the length of her, taking in the gown and her body. Missing nothing in its slow descent.

She glanced nervously down at herself, her cheeks burning, wondering if he found fault with her. Suddenly it mattered. She wanted him to think her attractive. Though for the life of her she couldn't imagine why. The man was a *vampire*.

Her hands started to tremble at the reminder. The links of the chain that bound her jingled softly. She couldn't make them stop.

Slowly he placed the goblet on a low table beside the chaise and rose to his feet.

God, he was tall. He towered over her.

He reached out and touched her hair, letting his fingers sift through the long, golden strands. "So beautiful," he murmured, his voice low.

His strange, otherworldly energy enveloped her, brushing over her skin, invading the hidden places of her body. She shivered in unbidden relief. She wanted to please him...

He came closer, taking her face in his hands, tipping it up to his. A ripple of power shivered through her where he touched. Desire reared up, hot and potent.

She put her hands to his chest. More electricity. Hotter desire. *And a frisson of terror.* She started to shake harder.

"Are you afraid?" he asked.

"Yes," she admitted. "Terrified."

"Good," he said, and she gasped softly. "You would do well to fear me," he said, his eyes drilling into hers. "Do not ever think to betray me, Josslyn Haliday, for it will go badly for you if you do."

"I wouldn't," she said unsteadily. "I won't."

She couldn't look away. She was having a hard time

forming a coherent thought. The feel of his hands on her, and of hers on his chest, the accidental brushing of their lower bodies, the intensity in his gaze, were all scrambling her brain.

He compelled her head to one side, and his fingers scraped her hair back, exposing the side of her throat.

Her heart beat out of control. Was he going to bite her now? So soon?

She saw his nostrils flare, and he leaned in to put his lips to the side of her temple. Not in a kiss. Just a touch. Her skin sizzled with pleasure where his mouth grazed it. Her nipples hardened to tight pebbles. Wanting his mouth to touch her there, instead.

She stepped in closer, pillowing her body into his, sliding her hands around to his sides, feeling the hard, solid wall of him against her palms. The chain binding her wrists remained a cool, solid line between them. But that was the only thing about them that was cool. The rest of her was hot. And so was he. Scorching hot.

The long, thick length of his cock pressed into her belly. A breathy moan escaped her. God, she wanted him.

His lips moved down to the sensitive spot just below her ear. A sharp fang scraped erotically along her skin. She shivered violently as a jolt of sexual need rocked her clear to her toes.

His hands moved inward over her shoulders, his thumbs hooking in the neckline of her fragile gown. He slid them back again, pulling the neck of the gown farther and farther apart, until she heard a rip, and the delicate fabric tore down the center.

It ripped. And ripped. And ripped. Until the gown fell away and she was naked before him.

Her body throbbed with want.

"Seth-Aziz," she whispered, pressing herself tighter against him.

She felt his desire in the quickness of his breath, the intensity of his touch, the lengthening and thickening of his cock. And the razor's edge of his fangs at her throat.

He murmured, "Josslyn, you must give me permission."

She couldn't stop now if she wanted to. It was like a compulsion within her, this raging desire she felt for him. She wanted to know what it was like to be taken by him. She wanted to know what it was like to be bitten by him.

"Yes," she said. "I give it to you. I give myself to you, Seth-Aziz, in every way."

She felt a low, rumbling growl from deep in his chest. His fingers dug painfully into her flesh. Sweeping her up into his arms, he strode the three steps to the bed. He lay her down, threw off his *bisht* and lowered himself on top of her. She spread her thighs to accept him, the smooth fabric of his trousers still coming frustratingly between them.

The silver chain jingled, then melted through his body as she put her arms around him. But suddenly it jerked, and pulled her arms up over her head, as though the links were attached to some invisible pulley on the headboard.

She gasped, struggling against its unrelenting pull.

"What are you doing?" she cried. A buzz of fear washed over her.

Followed closely by his hands. They blazed an electric path over her hips and along her ribs, sliding up and over her breasts. He touched her there, running his thumbs over the aching tips until they stood at painful attention. He pinched them, and she gasped again as her body bowed up in a deluge of pleasure.

"The hunger is strong," he said, his voice rough with need. "And I want you helpless."

A candle sputtered out.

"I don't like—"

"I don't care," he cut her off gruffly. "This is my end of our bargain. And I want it like this."

His mouth came down on her then, and all objections flew from her mind.

He tasted like sin. Dark, rich and velvety. Like her favorite sweet and her favorite memory all rolled together. She opened for him, and his tongue invaded her, seeking, laving, dueling with hers. An orgasm built and exploded in a shimmer of sensation before she knew what was happening.

Her cry of pleasure spurred him on. His kiss was as deep as the darkness he lived in. She tugged in frustration at her bonds, wanting to put her arms around him and pull him closer still.

He deepened the kiss even more. She felt a sudden prick on her tongue and sucked in a breath. A tinge of copper blossomed in her mouth. He growled low in his throat, and his body ground into hers.

A renewed craving swept through her. It was like she hadn't just come. Like she hadn't come in years. Her thighs shook. Her lungs were breathless. She jerked at her chains, wanting to get to him.

More urgent now, he moved down her body, his tongue licking a trail of sizzling, shivering embers along her skin. He found her breast and his tongue circled the nipple, driving her mad with need. She arched up, thrusting the aching tip into his mouth. He bit down. His fangs sank into her flesh.

She screamed, detonating into another climax, this one bringing her up off the bed in a conflagration of pleasure.

She didn't think— She didn't know he'd—

Oh, *God!* Her body shook as he sucked her breast, the climax going on and on, bringing the chains taut as she strained against their hold. She could feel the slick smear of blood on his lips, but she didn't care.

She gave a groan as she came down from the peak. She wanted more. *More.*

She felt him lift his head, but she didn't have the energy to open her eyes. She was exhausted, exhilarated.

He shifted to the other breast. She barely had time to take a breath. The sharp sting of his bite pierced her again. Her body convulsed, and an even more intense pleasure swept over her. She screamed with it, reveling in the pure carnality of it. Of him. She was barely hanging on to consciousness. She fought to stay with him. She wanted to feel everything, every sensation, every amazing second of his touch.

She was panting uncontrollably now, gasping, crying out, floundering in a viscous sea of his power and of endless pleasure. Lost to all sense of time, of self, of her own will.

She dragged her eyelids up and saw him looking down at her. There was blood on his lips, more on his chin. A smear of scarlet slashed across his cheekbone, and he had a harsh, savage, unreadable expression on his face. His long, sharp, blindingly white fangs gleamed as they dripped with her blood. Her heart quailed. She fought to keep her eyes open as he slowly, oh so maddeningly slowly, lowered them toward the throbbing vein on the side of her neck.

Oh, God.

His mouth closed over her throat.

Her eyelids fluttered closed and she stilled her heaving breath.

A burst of harrowing pain razored through her flesh and then blossomed into the most excruciating pleasure she'd ever experienced. It seized her. And shook her. And turned her instantly inside out.

A scream froze in her throat, choked off by the tingling feel of her life's blood gushing into his mouth. Blackness began to descend over her mind.

And as she lost consciousness, she wondered…

Would she ever awaken again?

Chapter 9

He drank.

Sinking into the dizzy delirium of a feeding that was far too long overdue, Seth let the precious liquid slide down his gullet, swallowing convulsively. It hit the pit of his stomach like a dozen shots of the strongest liquor all at once.

His body bucked under the impact, nerve endings buzzing like a hive of hornets attacking an intruder in their nest. His whole body burned like acid.

And then the buzzing ebbed, and the succor flowed into his veins, renewing his strength, expanding his power, banishing the weakness as it absorbed into his starving body.

As he slowly recovered, his cock stretched and thickened, desperately seeking the potent release of blood sex. He craved the intensity of being inside a woman when he fed. He ached to be inside this one.

Her blood was like a rare aphrodisiac. He wanted to ram himself into her and take her like she'd never been taken before. Until she screamed his name and begged for mercy.

Except she already had. And then she'd fainted. He wasn't going to take her like that. Unconscious. Unaware.

He wasn't going to take her at all.

This was Josslyn Haliday, the woman who had brought him nothing but trouble, and the only thing he wanted from her was this. To fulfill Sekhmet's curse and nourish his blood for another year.

Having sex with her would complicate matters. It was possible to bind a woman for life if she allowed herself to surrender completely to his powers. His seed did not carry the possibility of new life. It carried the germ of addiction, as did his bite. It took a strong woman to resist their combined force.

He wanted no part of a possible bond with her.

He only wanted her blood.

So he took it. Greedily. Plenty of it. Filling his belly and his veins with the power of her mortality and the essence of her life.

Even unconscious she writhed and moaned in pleasure, her darkened mind drowning in the dreamworld of his irresistible magic, her legs splaying in invitation for more. It was difficult to turn away from the pleasures she offered.

But he did.

And when he'd drunk his fill, he rolled off her body, his chest heaving with gratification, his body thoroughly sated—in that way at least—and his strength finally, finally restored to full.

He lay there for a long while, listening to her steady, rhythmic breathing, making sure she was recovering from her ordeal. He'd taken much, but not enough to harm.

Physically, anyway.

It couldn't have been easy on her. Submitting herself like this to him, for her body to be used by a stranger in ways she'd probably only imagined in nightmares before today. All for the sake of her sisters.

A prickle of shame sifted through him at that. He hadn't lied to her, exactly. But he had misled her badly. Her sisters were already free, because, although not yet immortal, they had both joined the *per netjer* and sworn with their lives to keep the secrets of the immortal world safe. Josslyn would never be allowed back into the mortal realm unless she did, too. Gemma knew that. It's why she was so angry with him, for his half-truths. Well he was angry, too. He'd lost *his* sister, and it would be a miracle if Khepesh survived another year. All because of the woman lying next to him.

It didn't matter if Nephtys had sent her to him, believing this woman was destined to be his soul mate. *He* didn't believe it. And he didn't want her. Every time he'd look at her she would only remind him of the part she'd played, however unwittingly, in the eclipse of everything he loved.

She stirred, and her hand reached for him in her sleep. He moved away, not wishing her touch. But he turned to look at her for the first time since the fever had cooled.

A bolt of shock went through him. *Sekhmet's teeth.* Her fair skin was smeared with scarlet streaks of blood; the linens beneath her were soaked with dark pools of it. He wiped a hand over his face. It came away stained with crimson.

Had he been such a savage with her?

Normally he took his sacrifices with barely a spilled drop. Never like this. Okay, last week, sharing magic with Gemma and Shahin, it had gotten a bit messy— but only because he'd been unaccustomed to stopping after only a few sips and the blood had poured from her wounds before he could heal them. But this…

He made a moue of disgust with himself. He'd obviously lost control. It was unforgivable.

Sliding out of bed, he gently gathered her in his arms and carried her to the bath chamber, sending a spell ahead of them. By the time he'd bespelled his trousers off, the deep Roman tub was filled with steaming, spice-scented water. He stepped in and sank down with her still in his arms into the warm, fragrant bath.

"Mmm," she murmured, curling into his body as he settled and reclined against the slanted back of the tub. He waved a hand over her eyes so she wouldn't awaken yet. He didn't want her getting the wrong impression.

With a wet Red Sea sponge, he gently cleansed the blood from her face and throat, taking extra care around the puncture marks. Even so, she gasped in pleasure as he passed the sponge over them. The bite of a vampire was infected with a spell of erotic sensation that lasted several weeks. Every time the wounds were touched, she would experience a jolt of orgasmic pleasure.

He dropped his gaze to her breasts. He'd also bitten

her there, as he'd suckled on her nipples. Two tiny red punctures sat above each pretty, rosy tip, further proof of his loss of control. Merciful Osiris. When had he last done *that?*

And yet, an unwilling spill of desire rippled over him at the sight of his marks upon her flesh. Without thinking, he rolled out from under her and canted over her. Lifting her upper body from the water, he put his mouth to one lush breast. He tongued the nipple and it reacted instantly, coming to pert attention. Pleased, he did the same for the other.

She moaned and unconsciously lifted up, offering them to him. He shouldn't, but he couldn't resist the temptation. He covered one and sucked, licking and teasing it until her moans turned throaty. He switched again, this time sending the sensations of his tongue down between her legs along with her breasts. It was a magic spell every *shemsu* woman he knew enjoyed tremendously.

Josslyn did, too. Her thighs fell open, and her hands reached for him, her fingers grasping his hair for purchase. Her cries became more urgent.

He brought her to the brink and then swept the tip of his tongue over the bite marks. She shattered. Her body convulsed, making at least the dozenth climax of the night. He could make them go on till dawn if he wished, so much mastery did he have over a woman's body.

The discomfort of his own unfulfilled need was small enough payment. This was the only reward he could give her for her sacrifice. He would take no relief for himself, but he was, after all, a gentleman.

At length her body quieted, and he felt her swallow.

He lifted his head just in time to see her awaken and gasp, and start to scramble backward in the tub, water sloshing. Then suddenly she seemed to remember everything and halted in mid-scramble.

"Oh!" she cried out breathily.

"How are you feeling?" he asked. He sat up, giving her space, running his hands through his wet hair to get it out of his eyes.

She watched him, her own eyes like full moons, and licked her lips. "I think you probably know," she said.

"Better than you've ever felt in your life?"

She nibbled her bottom lip as she thought about that. "I'm not sure," she finally said, reaching up to touch her neck.

He grabbed her hand. "I wouldn't." More water sloshed.

She looked spooked. "Why not?"

He chose his words. "Let's just say...there are ramifications of a vampire bite."

She blinked. "Such as?"

He figured a demonstration would illustrate his point best. He lowered his hand to her breast, and before she could scoot away, he brushed his thumb slowly and deliberately across the two tiny wounds.

She gasped and instantly dissolved into another orgasm.

He teased it out, and made it good for her, solely using his touch on the bites.

When her body calmed and she opened her eyes again, she looked stricken. "My God," she whispered. "That's—"

He leaned back. "Yes. I know."

"Is this… Is it permanent?"

"Regretfully—" he paused "—or possibly mercifully, no. A few weeks normally."

She sat up and glanced down to scan her body. "Did you…are there more?"

"No," he answered. "Just those, and your neck. A bandage usually protects them fairly well against the reaction, if you are bothered by it."

"Who wouldn't be?" she murmured hoarsely.

He just smiled. He rarely indulged in blood-play of the variety Haru-Re enjoyed so much—biting a woman just for the sensual pleasure of it. He was only compelled to feed once a year, and that's what he did. He wasn't interested in the unpredictable complications of hedonistic excesses. Such as those his own sister suffered because of Ray's indiscriminate lust.

Seth had, however, often enjoyed a woman's company beyond her sacrifice, and he hadn't found one yet who wasn't enthralled by the after-effects of his bite.

"Indeed," he said, and noticed Josslyn had caught sight of his rampant arousal, rising from the water like a stubborn column from a temple ruin. Her cheeks blossomed like opium poppies.

Her gaze shot to his, the obvious question burning in them.

"No," he said. "We didn't have sex." He lifted a shoulder with a wry smile. "At least I didn't."

She bit her lip again.

"And no," he anticipated her next question. "I don't want to." His cock might want to, but it would survive the deprivation.

He rose from the water, not bothering with modesty.

He was proud of his close-to-perfect body, so why hide it? And if she grew a little covetous, well, so much the better. A man was allowed his vanity, wasn't he? If nothing else.

He shook the water from his hair and flicked his fingers at his robe, which flew to him and slid onto his body. "Stay as long as you wish," he told her. "I'll have clothes laid out for you."

He was on his way out of the bath chamber when she called after him, "Wait. What about my sisters?"

Ah. So very single-minded. He turned back to her. "Your sisters are free to move about the country as they please. You'll find Gemma with Sheikh Shahin at his oasis encampment, where they live. Gillian, I'm afraid, is not here. She's in Petru, situated about fifty kilometers to the north, on the east bank of the Nile, living with her lover, Rhys Kilpatrick, and your parents."

She surged up so fast a deluge of water splashed from the tub. "My *parents?*" she exclaimed, her expression stunned.

He frowned, instantly regretful. "I'm sorry. How thoughtless of me. Of course you didn't know. You must ask Gemma when you see her. It's best she tell you."

"They're *alive?*" Josslyn asked in shock. "*Both* of them?"

"I believe so. As I said, better speak to Gemma about it. I really only know the sketchiest details."

"My God," she breathed. "So it's really true?" She looked overwhelmed. Tears filled her eyes, and a reluctant tenderness for her tugged at his heart. Sitting there in the middle of the huge bathtub she looked small and fragile, like a beautiful abandoned waif in the body of a woman.

The ends of her flaxen-colored hair hung in wet strands on her back, but the tangled curls around her head were dry, surrounding her face like an intricate golden halo.

He wanted to go to her and hold her in his arms, give her comfort in her emotional chaos.

"Can I see them?" she whispered hopefully.

Which soundly crushed the ill-advised impulse. "If that is what you wish," he said. Haru-Re would no doubt be thrilled to have her at Petru. Despite his earlier resolve of indifference, the thought sent a stab of anger through him. "In either case, I am finished with you," he stated, briefly wondering with no little irritation if it was more to convince himself than her.

He turned and walked out, but not before he saw her lips part in surprise. "So I'm free to go?" she called hesitantly after him. He heard the water swish.

"Whenever you like," he said over his shoulder.

As far as Shahin's oasis, at any rate. If she and Gemma decided to flee to Petru, good riddance to them. In the meantime, he could count on Shahin to see that Josslyn didn't go anywhere in the outside world where she might reveal their secrets. Yes, and to retrieve those incriminating letters she'd sent.

Eventually Seth would have to decide on her final disposition—*shemsu* or *shabti*. But at the moment he had more important things to see to, now that his strength had returned.

"I'll have one of the guards take you to your sister at the oasis," he called back to her.

She appeared at the bath chamber door, rivulets of water running down her lovely body, her brilliant blue eyes uncertain. She lifted her wrists. "What about these?"

He stared at them for a moment, irrationally unwilling to remove the silver cuffs and chain, the indisputable claim of his ownership over her.

He did not want her in his bed. But against all reason, he didn't want her in any other man's bed, either. As long as she stayed inside Khepesh, that was a distinct possibility. Every immortal was allowed to bed anyone in the *per netjer*, given mutual consent. Josslyn Haliday was a beautiful, sensual woman. He had no doubt there would be many of the *shemsu* men, and probably some women, who would be delighted to invite her to linger awhile in the palace.

Not a good idea. He wanted her out of his sight. Out of the reach of temptation.

"The cuffs will disappear when you leave Khepesh," he told her, casting a spell to make it so.

Then he walked away, doing his best to ignore the lost expression on her face as he left her standing there alone.

Chapter 10

Josslyn recognized a dismissal when she heard one.

It vaguely surprised her, but to be honest, she was so overwhelmed by everything that had happened to her today, along with the incredible news of her parents' still being alive, that Seth-Aziz leaving her was a blessing.

She needed time to absorb it all.

Her head was spinning with questions and confusion, strange physical feelings and a landslide of unfamiliar emotions.

Or maybe it was just loss of blood. She was tired. So damn tired.

She found a towel and dried herself and managed to make it to the bed before she collapsed. Seth, or more likely a servant, had somehow found time to change the sheets before he left. They were now midnight-blue, neatly tucked in, covered by a satiny duvet in a subtle pattern of stars. She crawled under it and rolled herself in a ball, feeling small and insignificant in the massive bed and the huge, high-ceilinged room.

She slept. And she dreamed of him. Naturally.

Broad-shouldered and handsome as ever, Seth-Aziz was twice as tall as she, and cold as ice as he stared angrily down at her. Malevolence poured off him as he told her over and over in an endless loop that he didn't want to have sex with her.

"All right already!" she cried, slapping her hands over her ears to keep from hearing the disdain in his voice. "You don't want me. I get it, okay?"

She awoke with a lurch and found herself sitting up in bed, her chest heaving with a desperate mix of anguish and mortification, her hands still covering her ears.

There were more candles lit, and a few sconces burned on the walls, making the room much lighter than before. She jerked her hands from her ears and heard her sister's anxious voice.

"What the *hell* went on here between you two?" Gemma asked. "I thought you'd never wake up!"

Joss snapped around. Her sister was sitting on the edge of a chair, watching her with worried eyes.

"Gemma!" she cried and reached out for her. With a look of relief, her sister leapt up and onto the bed, and they hugged fiercely. "Oh, Gem! Am I glad to see you!"

"You have no earthly idea. I've been so worried about you, sis! You've slept for hours and hours. Are you okay?" Gemma pulled back, holding her arms, examining her for— "Omigod. He really did it." Her sister's gaze had fastened on her neck. "Does it hurt? Is it…" Her question broke off, and her eyes darted for a nanosecond to her own wrist. "Never mind. You don't have to talk about it if you don't want to." She pulled her into another hug. "Shahin wanted to take me back to the oasis, but I wouldn't go until I saw for myself that you're all right. And I wanted to say I'm sorry for not being able to talk to you earlier. It really was horrible of Seth to put that spell of silence on me, and he's going to hear about it, believe me. But thank God you're finally here with us and out of danger."

It was always tough to get a word in edgewise when Gemma got on a roll, but that last bit grabbed Joss's attention. "Danger?" she cut in, pulling back. "So you know what happened to me? At the hotel? You *know* that guy?"

Gemma froze in alarm. "Something happened to you? What guy?"

Joss rubbed her hands up and down her bare arms in a sudden chill. Gemma saw it, noted her nakedness and slid off the bed to fetch a dress that was hanging on an armoire across the room while Joss told her about the encounter in the hotel room with Harold Ray. And about his final warning.

"I *knew* the bastard would find you. But don't worry about him," Gemma assured her, handing her the long, flowing dress. "Seth will protect you from Haru-Re now that you're here."

Joss wasn't so sure about that. "Haru-Re?" she asked.

"He's a demigod, a vampire like Seth," Gemma explained. "High priest of the Sun God, Re-Horakhti. His real name is Haru-Re, but he likes being called

Ray." She rolled her eyes at the double meaning. "How on earth did you get away from him?"

Joss pulled on the dress and told her about the knock at the hotel room door that came in the nick of time, and the copper-colored cat she'd seen in the corridor afterward. It made no sense then, but after today…

"Nephtys," Gemma declared, blowing out a breath of recognition. "Thank God she found you at the hotel."

Joss blinked, sitting back on the bed, recalling— "Good grief," she said. "There was a cat at the tomb, too. It was wearing an amulet around its neck. When Nephtys appeared moments later wearing the same one, I thought I'd started hallucinating."

Gemma smiled. "It was her, all right. Her Set-animal is a temple cat."

"Set-animal?" More shape-shifting? The memory of seeing the man, Shahin, change from a hawk to a human sent a shiver down Joss's arms.

"Shape-shifting is part of the deal when you become one of the *shemsu,* an immortal," Gemma said. "You get to choose the animal you'd like to share your *ba* with."

Joss knew about the ancient Egyptian belief that each person possessed three different souls: the *ba,* the *ka,* and the *akh.* The *ka* carried one's earthly spirit, or creative spark, while the *ba* was more bound up in the physical, existing in its own body and able to take on any shape it wished as it traveled between the mortal realm and the underworld. As a guide to the living, a person's *ba* directed his words and actions toward *"maât,"* or truth and goodness, keeping him on the path to heaven.

Upon death, the two souls joined to become the *akh*, the person's essence that lived on in the afterlife.

Joss stared at her sister in stark disbelief. So she was saying this stuff was really true? That these people had somehow found a way to harness the powers of their *ba* and… No. It was too incredible. If she didn't know better, she'd think Gemma had gone stark, raving mad.

And yet…she'd seen it with her own eyes. Shahin *had* shifted. How else to explain that?

Gemma waved a hand as if the whole shape-shifting thing were inconsequential. "You'll learn about all that stuff later." She frowned. "Although I'm not sure how, now that Khepesh no longer has a priestess. That was Nephtys's job. Before she…" For a second, Gemma looked troubled.

"Khepesh?" Joss asked, not about to let her get off-track.

"Here," Gemma said, indicating their surroundings with an all-encompassing gesture. "Khepesh is the name of our palace. Our *per netjer*."

Joss didn't miss Gemma's use of the word *our*. Twice.

Joss was also fluent in hieroglyphics, so she knew what *per netjer* meant without asking. *Home of the god*. And the word *Khepesh* bore a complicated circular meaning involving the foreleg of an ox, a type of scimitar, the connotation "strong of arm" and the Great Bear star constellation—known to ancient Egyptians as "the foreleg of Set-Sutekh." An appropriate name for the abode of the god himself.

If he existed.

Josslyn was more than skeptical when it came to pagan gods, despite the undeniably strange goings on here at Khepesh. She was strictly a one-God kind of person. So were Gemma and Gillian, which was why she couldn't understand what either one of them was doing here. And yet, Joss had definitely seen signs of supernatural goings-on. Heard things that made her believe. Hell, definitely *felt* the power here. How could she deny what her own senses were telling her?

Still, accepting the existence of vampires and shape-shifters in the world was a far cry from attributing that presence to the manifestation of some ancient pagan god. Or even a demigod.

Gemma had obviously accepted it all. But then, she always was a bit woo-woo, like their mother had been.

Joss gazed at her sister, a thousand new questions assaulting her like a hoard of insects—on top of the million questions she already had pinging around in her brain like pinballs.

"Gem," she said carefully. "What the hell *is* this place? And how did *we* end up here? Seth-Aziz told me Mom and Dad are alive, and Gillian is living with them in some place called Petru. For God's sake, I've just been bitten by a freaking *vampire!* Yet here you sit, looking happier than I've ever seen you. Please, Gem, tell me what's going on here, before my head explodes!"

Seth had spent the entire afternoon arguing with the six other members of the Great Council of Khepesh. About how to get Nephtys back. About whether to take the offensive in the war with Haru-Re instead of sitting back and waiting to be attacked. About the council sticking their noses in where they damn well didn't belong.

The council had actually ordered him to bring Josslyn Haliday to the council chambers so they could speak with her! When he'd told them he'd sent her away to Shahin's oasis, they'd even intimated that he had made a grave error, rebuking him for going against Nephtys's vision of the future and not immediately taking Josslyn as his consort.

The bunch of superstitious old goats.

It was an outrage!

He would decide with whom he would or would not spend the rest of eternity, with no help from his meddling sister *or* the Great Council!

Furthermore, he was *not* being irrational.

He was *not* losing control of his element to call—which happened to be the element of chaos. It was not his fault that everything around them was falling apart at the seams! It was all that damn woman's fault!

And another thing was for *damn* certain. When he decided to take a new consort, his choice of soul mate would *not* be a woman who was a goddamn living magnet for trouble and catastrophe.

By the balls of Mithra!

He ground his jaw. For a man used to maintaining cool, reasonable authority and an even temper at all times, this entire day had been one long nightmare of emotional uproar.

He needed to calm down.

To gather himself.

To figure out a strategy to deal with this newest mess the blasted woman had sent hurling into his life.

Hell. He needed to run.

He stormed into his private rooms, heading straight to his bedroom to change into clothes that wouldn't be—

"By the *gods!*" he gritted out.

There were two women curled on his bed, head to head, one with a mass of auburn curls, the other a tangle of golden tresses. When he burst in like a whirlwind, they shot up with startled faces.

"Seth!" Gemma exclaimed in surprise, reaching for her sister's hand. Josslyn said nothing, but her face flooded with something that looked a lot like mortification.

"What are you two doing here?" he demanded, further irritated by the cheeky woman's use of his name instead of the proper form of address. He lasered in on the blonde. "Why isn't she gone?"

"We were talking," Gemma said, irritatingly unafraid of him. "Must have lost track of time. Sorry."

Sorry?

Unperturbed by the thunderous expression he summoned, she lifted Josslyn's wrist. "And what is this all about?" she pointedly asked, referring to the silver bindings that still hung from it. "My sister is not a prisoner, and I was led to believe that you abolished slavery in Khepesh a thousand years ago. Why is she in chains?"

It was a flaming wonder that Shahin put up with the blasted woman.

Seth schooled his knee-jerk impulse to show her exactly *which* of them in the room was the demigod. "I do as I please," he told her with chilly precision. "And it pleases me to see her bound."

Gemma's lips pressed together. Josslyn's gaze flipped back and forth between them, unsure whether to be afraid of him or not.

Which gave him just the idea he was seeking.

He stabbed a finger at Gemma. "You. Out."

Josslyn's uncertainty increased visibly.

"What are you going to do to her?" Gemma asked, suspicion rife in her tone.

In reply he ground out, "I have also abolished public flogging, but I am dangerously close to reinstating it."

She—wisely—silently lifted her chin and rose with exaggerated dignity from the bed, shook her gown into place and regarded him. "Be nice to her," she admonished. "My lord," she added in a belated and not entirely successful show of respect.

"I shall take it under advisement," he said, glaring at her until she turned to Josslyn and kissed her on the cheek.

"Remember what I told you," she said quietly. "And don't worry about Seth. He's all bark and no bite." She realized her mistake and did her best to suppress a smile. "Well. Mostly."

And then she swept out of the room, head held high.

"Has she always been this trying?" he asked Josslyn when the dust had settled.

"No." She crossed her arms tightly over her middle, the silver chain jingling musically. "Usually she's a lot worse."

Seth couldn't decide whether she was joking or not.

He looked at her and hated that he was teetering

dangerously on the edge of being amused by the pair. The only people allowed to make him laugh were Nephtys and Rhys. And on rare occasions Shahin, but not often. The sheikh was even more somber than he.

Seth shook off the unwanted appeal and hardened himself. Then he started to remove his clothes.

She watched him nervously.

"Take off your dress," he ordered her.

She didn't move. "I—I thought you were finished with me," she said, her color rising.

He could feel the warmth of her blush all the way across the room. Because her blood flowed in his veins, his own body felt a whisper of whatever hers did. If she cut herself, he would sense her pain. If she felt hunger, or panic, he would know it.

"I've changed my mind," he said. "There's something I want to show you."

Something that would frighten her away from him for good. If they both objected, even the Great Council could not force a union.

He felt her heart flutter. "What is it?" she asked.

He stripped off his boots and silk Bedouin trousers. He was naked and she still hadn't moved. "The dress," he repeated impatiently.

Hesitatingly, she pulled the long, flowing garment over her head and clutched it in front of her body. Covering herself as she waited uneasily on the bed.

"Come here," he said.

"Seth-Aziz," she began.

"I don't like to be kept waiting."

She obviously didn't like to be ordered about. She

obeyed, but with tangible reluctance. He felt her heart beating a tattoo in her chest.

When she reached him, he lifted a hand and made a slight movement with his fingers, and with a quick spell, he dressed them both in soft, loose trousers, tunics and knee-length boots. Hers were all in black; his top was black and his pants and boots tawny-brown. He took the opportunity to rid her of the handcuffs. They'd be disappearing shortly anyway.

She gaped in astonishment at the instant transformation, taking an unsteady step backward, her hands flying up. "How did you—" But she didn't complete the question. She was learning.

He turned and strode toward the door. "Follow me," he commanded, and he didn't wait to see if she would obey this time.

After a moment, he heard a quick exhale, and her footsteps approached behind him. Inwardly he smiled and led her through the maze of corridors toward the Great Western Gate.

It was well after dusk, the sun having been consumed by the darkness several hours ago, and most of the *shemsu* were up and about the palace. They smiled and greeted him as he strode past.

"Taking your lady out for a run, my lord?"

"May Set-Sutekh, God of the Night Sky, watch over you both, my lord."

He didn't bother to correct their assumptions about him and Josslyn. They'd understand soon enough that they were wrong.

He reached the gate, and without breaking his stride on the marble floor, he whirled once and spoke the magic words with which the god had gifted him on the night of his transformation long, long ago. The powerful spell that would change his human flesh into his immortal form. Mihos Rukem. The Black Lion of Egypt.

His body grew massive and muscular, his head enormous under a thick black mane. His huge paws could crush a man with a single swipe.

At his shift, Josslyn lurched backward, stifling a scream. He felt it build in her lungs, but she refused to let it out.

He rose on his powerful hind legs and gave a mighty roar, his rampant form towering over the people who had gathered to admire him. He was their demigod, their sovereign leader, their protector, a lion in his own right even as a human. He was the most powerful lord on earth, and he could shift into any creature he wished. He shared his *ba* with all living things. But Mihos Rukem was his favorite.

As the great lion, he could run like the wind, vanquish any enemy and strike fear into the hearts of every mortal who gazed upon him.

But tonight, there was only one mortal he was interested in frightening.

He came down on all fours and prowled over to her, circling around her with a low growl. He could feel the surge of fear that stabbed through her, the painful beating of her heart, the strangled breath.

Even in his lion form, he was much bigger than she, his size more equine than feline. His shoulders reached almost the height of hers, but the top of his head was far above that. The length of his back was nearly eight feet, his tail another three. Except for him, this ancient species was extinct, from deep in the African past, a primal, untamed and savage beast.

She did not scream. Or run. She turned in a slow spin, keeping his black eyes in her sight even as he padded around her, growling, brushing against her with his shoulder, shaking his massive mane at her.

And still she would not scream.

They would see about that.

He hunched his body down low, pushed at her with his blunt nose and shoved her onto his back.

She gave a small cry and grabbed his mane with her fingers, her legs sliding down around his ribs and her knees gripping him as if he were a horse. At the last second he spun a spell around her, so she wouldn't fall off. He wanted to scare her, not hurt her.

The guard had already opened the gate for them.

Seth took off at a lope through the midnight-dark tunnels that led to the desert above, digging his deadly claws into the cool earth underfoot. He picked up speed, inwardly chanting the spell that opened the hidden portal high up on the *gebel,* where no human dared climb.

He burst up into the warm desert night like a shooting star returning to the sky.

And he ran.

With the woman clinging to his back, he streaked across the desert sand, heading away from the Nile Valley, away from the *gebel* and Khepesh, away from all humanity, mortal and *shemsu.*

He carried her far into the night, deep into his realm, the domain of Set-Sutekh, Lord of the Night Sky, Guardian of the Moon, God of the Hot Winds, Chaos and Darkness.

He ran until his breath was ragged and his paws left tracks of blood with each footfall from meeting the rough ground. He ran until his mind was free of the turmoil of the day and his heart was filled with the peace of the desert night.

Then he slowed to an easy lope, and eventually he came to a halt. He stood, his lungs sucking down gulps of air, at the top of a rocky plateau that overlooked the vastness of the continent of Africa, the moonlit sands undulating in a glittering sea for two thousand miles to the west.

He felt Josslyn slide from his back and collapse on the sand at his feet. She lay there for a brief moment, suspended in movement, staring up at the star-strewn sky, her eyes wide.

"Oh. My God," she said in a strangled voice.

And then…and then she started to laugh.

Chapter 11

Nephtys paced back and forth at the garden window. Something was going on. She could feel it in her bones, in the way Haru-Re was avoiding her and in the buzz of tension that permeated the palace. Petru was mobilizing for an attack on Khepesh. She was certain of it.

She must warn Seth!

But how? After her "ride" yesterday, Ray had placed her under constant guard. There was no way for her to escape to warn her brother. And no one else was being let in or out of the palace, either, not without specific permission from the high priest. So her spies were useless.

The only possibility was the ancient spell that Ray had discovered and she'd subsequently stolen. The spell by which he had invaded first her dreams, then her meditations. The one by which he had come to her inside the formerly protective walls of Khepesh, to spring the trap that had forced her capture.

He'd found it on a scroll buried in the library of Petru. It was an immensely powerful but difficult spell to invoke, a rare type of love spell that only worked between two people with a strong emotional connection—love.

The magic enabled the spellbinder to be there, physically, with the object of the spell, even though by all appearances the receiver—or in Nephtys's case the unwitting victim—was just having a dream. Except it wasn't a dream. Ray had actually been there, as solid and real as she was. He'd fucked her, bitten her, threatened her, all the while being there with her in the all-too-real flesh.

The more often he'd used the spell against her, the stronger his hold over her had grown. She was terrified that his growled prediction would come true, and one day soon he'd be able to invade her world while she was wide awake.

Not a pretty thought.

Suddenly Gillian burst into her room like a whirlwind. She glared at the guard who'd followed her in until he went out again and closed the door.

"Nephtys!" The other woman rushed up to her and whispered urgently, "Rhys says they're readying the guard to invade Khepesh! *In the morning!*"

"I knew it!" Nephtys slapped her hands over her mouth to muffle the sound of her cry. "All evening I've had a terrible feeling something bad was about to happen."

"Haru-Re and his captain called Rhys in front of the council, to ask him about the interior layout of Khepesh," Gillian went on. "They all tried to act casual, but Rhys thought their questions were a little too specific. He bribed a servant who later overheard some of the plans." Gillian wrung her hands. "What do we do? Gemma and Josslyn are both there!"

"There's no other way. We must use the dream spell to warn Seth."

Nephtys went swiftly to the small meditation chamber off her bedroom to fetch the carefully hidden scroll where she'd copied down the magical words. It had actually been Gillian who had managed to get hold of a copy first, a few weeks ago.

"But how?" Gillian asked nervously. "It's only just gotten dark. Neither Seth nor my sisters will be asleep now. Probably not for hours!"

Nephtys had never used the dream spell herself to contact her brother. She was too afraid Haru-Re would sense it and somehow inveigle himself into Seth's mind and turn her love into a weapon against him. Gillian was still a fledgling at magic and did not yet have the skills to work the spell by herself. But with Lord Rhys's help last week, she'd managed to invoke the spell and had successfully reached out to her sister Gemma.

"We must try," Nephtys said, desperation clawing through her body. "And keep trying until one of them falls asleep. This is too important."

She didn't know what she'd do if anything happened to her brother…if Ray killed him. The very thought brought stinging tears to her eyes. "We can't let Haru-Re win this war!"

Seth was the only family she had, Khepesh the only true home she'd ever known. If she lost them…

Gillian looked disheartened. "Rhys says Khepesh

is badly outnumbered. He says it'll be tough going for Shahin and his warriors to defeat Haru-Re's armies."

"If they have proper warning..." Nephtys said hopefully. But they both knew how difficult the coming battle would be, even with forewarning. Barring a miracle, many immortals would die come morning, and victory was by no means assured.

They sat tailor-style on the floor cushions and emptied their minds for several minutes in preparation. Then they joined hands, and Nephtys poured her power into the younger woman. Gillian recited the magical words of the spell.

First she tried Gemma, with no success. Though she could feel her sister's presence, she couldn't get through to her mind.

"It's no use. She probably just woke up," Gillian lamented. "Shahin prefers the nighttime to do his patrols, and no doubt she's adopted his sleep schedule."

"Try Josslyn," Nephtys urged. There was no time to lose.

Gillian glanced over at her, a worried look on her face. "I've never contacted Joss like this before. She might think it's just a dream and not tell Seth about it."

"You'll just have to convince her."

Gillian looked doubtful. "She's kind of a skeptic."

Nephtys glanced around and picked up a small alabaster statuette of Re-Horakhti. "Here. Give her this. It'll still be there when she wakes up, so she'll have proof you weren't a dream. Have her speak to Gemma if she's still unconvinced."

Gillian took the statuette. "That should help. Hopefully I can get through to her."

But Josslyn wasn't asleep, either.

"You've got to try Seth," Gillian said, giving up.

Nephtys's heart began to pound painfully. "I'm so afraid. What if Ray somehow senses what I'm doing? What if he hijacks the spell? He's a demigod, Gillian. Far more powerful than I am."

"What choice do we have? Somehow Seth has to be warned about the attack, and my emotional connection with him isn't exactly love. You have to do it."

Nephtys knew Gillian was right, but she didn't like it. Not one little bit. Haru-Re was not just powerful, he was ruthless when it came to Seth. He wouldn't hesitate to use her to get to her brother. Not to mention what he'd do to her…

She took a deep, calming breath. She nodded, closed her eyes and began to speak the magical words, calling to Seth, praying he was asleep to hear her plea.

Naturally he wasn't. No matter how she called to him, hammering on the walls of his mind, he didn't hear her.

But Haru-Re did hear her. Just as she'd feared.

It seemed like mere seconds later that the hall door thundered open and Ray appeared in the arched doorway surrounded by a strobing halo of golden light. His dark eyes glittered with a maelstrom of fire, like fine black opals. They latched on to her like rivets and held her pinned, helpless, as he growled to Gillian, "Get out."

Gillian got out.

"Who gave you the spell?" he asked. His voice was deep and now completely void of emotion. Which was even scarier than when he yelled at her. Sparks spangled the air around him.

"No one," she answered, forcing equanimity into her

tone when she felt none. "It's amazing what you can find in the library when you know what you're looking for."

"Clever girl," he said, his tone betraying a reluctant hint of admiration along with his sharp annoyance. But the sparks did not diminish.

"How did you know I was using the spell?" she asked, though there was little doubt of the answer.

He regarded her. "The question is, how did *you* know of our plans?"

"What plans?"

She didn't fool him for a second.

"How much have you learned? Enough to foil our attack? Have you warned him, that hyena of a brother of yours?"

Like she would tell Ray the truth. "Of course I warned him! The spell worked perfectly," she said smugly. "Seth knows everything, so you can call off your dogs. It won't work."

A muscle worked in his jaw. Pinpoints of flame shot from his shoulders. "I am very disappointed in you, *meruati*. See how easily you lie to me. And how readily you betray me, your future husband."

She was not about to feel guilty. "I learned both skills from the master," she retorted.

He sighed, and to her surprise, the flames died down. She could have sworn she heard a hint of weariness in the low rush of his breath as he approached her. "Such bitterness. Where did it come from?"

"You know very well what caused it, Ray. *You* did."

He reached out and stroked along her cheek with his warm fingertips. "Nephtys, I can sense your hurt. It is like a living thing, eating you alive. But it's old news.

Let it go. I was young and foolish and didn't know what I had in you, didn't understand how precious your love and devotion were. Nor how rare. Not until you were taken did I even begin to understand. But then it was too late. Does it count for nothing that I have been trying to get you back from the bastard who took you from me for five millennia?"

She refused to be placated by the false sincerity of his words.

"Took me?" she spat back, the pain and outrage flaring up within her like a backflash of flame from the embers she'd carried for so long, burning her from the inside out. "*Took* me? You *sold* me, Ray."

"No, Nephtys. You were *stolen* from me. By Seth-Aziz's father."

Lies!

"Why would he steal me? Did he not offer you enough gold to satisfy your avarice, so you refused him a sale? Perhaps he would not pay your asking price because I was spoiled goods, tainted by your insatiable lust and infected by your vampyric poison?"

"There was no asking price!" Haru-Re snapped, grasping her arms. She thought he would shake her, but he just held her with a grip like the talons of a falcon, his favored Ra-animal. "He knew you were from the far north, a princess of royal blood. He wanted to open trade with your people. He thought your 'rescue' and a match with his son would pave the way. He made me several offers, yes. But I turned them down. Every last one. And not because they were too miserly. Trust me, they weren't. But nothing would tempt me. So he took you from me. *I did not sell you!*"

Momentary shock sliced through her. This was the

first she'd heard of such a scheme by the man she'd come to think of as a second father. The plan to marry her to Seth was perfectly plausible and not terribly surprising. But the other—the betrayal—had that really been her adopted father's lie all along, and not a heartless cruelty by the man standing before her?

That betrayal had been the reason she'd hated Ray with a vengeance. Had cried and mourned and plotted revenge and been a wretched mess for five millennia over his callous rejection of her true and faithful love.

"I saw the scroll!" she cried. "Your written agreement. The bill of sale for me, signed by you."

His fingers gentled on her arms. "Forged by Seth's father, no doubt, to turn you against me, *meruati*. He knew you had feelings for me. That even though you were a slave, you were my lover. My favorite. My refusal to sell you told him as much. He lied to you. He must have known you'd never agree to wed Seth if you still loved me."

She stared at him, her heart squeezing as if caught in a vise. *All these years...*

"You're lying," she whispered hoarsely. "You're *lying*."

She wrenched herself free of him and started to run.

It couldn't be true.

It couldn't.

Because if it were, it meant she'd wasted her entire life in heartache and misery.

And all for nothing.

Chapter 12

"**My** *God!*" Joss exclaimed for the dozenth time. She felt exhilarated, awestruck, captivated and more alive than she'd ever felt in her life. "Seth-Aziz! That was *amazing!*"

The huge lion regarded her with half-lidded, unreadable feline eyes. His head was lowered and his mouth slightly open as he fed his winded lungs with air. His upper lip curled in a snarl, showing vicious teeth as long as her fingers.

But she was no longer afraid. Lions were supposed to be scary. But this was Seth-Aziz. He hadn't hurt her before. He wouldn't now, even in his majestic *ba* form.

He padded closer to her on paws the size of her whole head, his unruly black mane falling about his leonine face as he looked down at her from high above. She could smell him, the strong, musky scent of a wild animal.

"*This* was what you wanted to show me?" she said, flinging her arms out in a sand angel, unable, unwilling, to quell the joy in her voice. "Thank you," she said. "Oh, thank you! I shall never forget that ride as long as I live!"

She reached upward and touched the riotous fur of his shaggy mane. It was thick and coarse, yet the strands were light as air between her fingertips. She lifted her other hand and combed her fingers through the formidable black halo. He stared down at her. She touched his rough cheeks, and drew her palms over the warm, bristly fur that covered his face. His nose was broad and flat, reminding her of a mysterious sphinx.

His nostrils flared, and he came closer, within inches, bringing those enigmatic eyes close enough to see the striations of his irises. They were on her like lasers, watching every move she made, drilling into her with a predator's intensity.

She wasn't worried. Gemma had told her story after story of his enlightened leadership and his immense love for his people—everything he did, he did for the good of Khepesh and his followers.

A man like that would never hurt her.

She stroked the backs of her fingers along his massive jaw. Okay, so he wasn't exactly a man at the moment. She knew she should be scared witless of this giant beast with its deadly strength and its saber-like teeth, but she was unable to summon any emotion save awe.

"You're magnificent," she murmured. "Truly."

She lifted up to place a kiss on one surprisingly

smooth-haired jowl. A low, rumbling growl sounded deep in his chest.

She smiled and lay back on the ground and closed her eyes, just savoring the moment.

He let out a roar.

Startled, she opened her eyes again. He was now standing right above her. His large body blocked out the spangle of stars above, his paws on either side of her, not touching her but effectively pinning her down.

She felt a brief pang of apprehension. Not fear, really. But… God, what was he doing?

"Seth-Aziz?"

His head lowered toward her, coming closer and closer, until his large, cool nose touched her cheek. She could feel his hot breath on her skin, and smell the distinctive scent of his lion's pelt. Under it, she caught a drift of the man himself, the unique sage and spice his skin carried, that she remembered so well from this afternoon.

"Seth…" she whispered, lifting her hand to the edge of his face, sliding her fingers into the fringe of mane that rimmed it.

With another growl, his mouth opened, and opened more, and then the angle of his head turned, and he placed his jaws around her throat, spanning it from ear to ear.

She could feel the pointed tips of his huge teeth scrape against her tender skin, the hot lion saliva soaking her in its languorous warmth.

Like blood.

Oh, Lord. Her heart thundered.

His body crouched down, lowering itself until she

could feel the hair of his belly poke into the soft fabric of her tunic, and the muscles of his massive haunches press into the sides of her thighs.

He was aroused.

Oh, dear *God.* Okay, now she was getting scared. She grabbed handfuls of his mane, tried to drag him away, but it was no use.

With another low growl, the sandpaper touch of his tongue scraped under her ear, a solid, living, vibrating force against her fluttering throat. The spell of the vampire bite under her opposite ear came instantly to life, sending a dark, agonizing ribbon of want through her center, just as he'd warned her it would.

Jesus. What was he *doing?*

The points of his teeth clamped a smidgen tighter around her throat, just enough so she didn't dare try to move away. The twin bite marks throbbed erotically, sending pangs of need shooting through her veins, the spell working its undeniable magic on her flesh. Her body awakened with a sensual jolt, quickening with a burst of desire. His supple lion's tongue moved slowly along its path with powerfully restrained intensity, toward the center hollow of her throat. When he reached the shallow dip, she wanted to swallow but didn't dare. His teeth were like an iron maiden around her vulnerable flesh. One slight move could slide his tongue onto the vampire bite and send her body into a mortifying paroxysm of pleasure.

The speed of his breath had gotten faster, the sensual crush of his body over hers a fraction heavier. His thick arousal pushed more insistently against her belly.

Ohgod ohgod ohgod.

She knew what would happen if his tongue went any closer. She could feel it already, the explosion that tingled and teased at the fringes of her physical craving.

His tongue moved. Blinding need tore through her. Her nipples zinged painfully. The pulsing pearl of want between her thighs begged for more, more, *more*. His tongue kept moving.

"No," she whispered desperately. "Not like this!"

But it was too late. The tip of his tongue glided hotly over her vampire marks. They flared to life.

She started to come apart. With a cry, she threw her arms around his head...and suddenly realized he'd shifted. It was Seth's lips and tongue bringing her to climax.

She plunged into the blissful agony of orgasm. She bucked and quaked and finally just let herself go, abandoning all vestige of control. She rode the storm and soaked in the pleasure, dizzy with its preternatural intoxication.

Suddenly her clothes were gone, and his were, too, and their naked bodies slid together, causing a cry of excruciating need from the core of her being. She opened her legs and rejoiced when his body surged between them. He thrust, and his cock plunged into her. He was long and thick, and filled her to the hilt. She moaned in exquisite pleasure.

His mouth moved up and covered hers, latching on with toe-curling erotic suction. The wet thrust of his tongue imitated the movements of his cock between her legs. In and out. In and out. Hot. Hard. *So good.*

Too good.

She cried out as another orgasm swept through her body.

This time he came with her.

He roared his release with a shiveringly familiar, growling timbre to his primal mating call.

After the quivers subsided, a moan of pleasure and fulfillment soughed through her. Every nerve in her body felt wonderfully sated. "Ohhh…Seth…"

She clung to him, her arms surrounding his muscular back, the weight of him substantial and solid between her legs. Even in human form he was impressive…and impressively large. "That was…" She swallowed. *The most incredible sex she'd ever had in her entire life.* "Unexpected."

He grunted, rolling her so she lay on top of him. He folded his arms loosely around her.

She opened her eyes and with a shock realized there was a bed under them. "How on earth—" she began. "Right," she corrected herself. She didn't think she'd ever get used to his world of magic and spells and shape-shifting. "Is there anything you can't do?" she asked, gazing down at him.

He took a final deep breath and let it out. "Unfortunately, yes."

Once again he didn't look like a happy camper.

She felt a crush of disappointment. Apparently she was alone in thinking their lovemaking had been amazing.

What. Ever. She was a big girl. She'd live.

With an effort, she summoned the proper sangfroid appropriate to a moment of passion that had caught them both by surprise. "You needn't worry," she reassured him. "Just because we made love, believe me, I'm not going to demand you take me as your consort or anything. I know you didn't really want this, or me."

He gazed up at her for a moment with those black, black eyes that made her shiver. "Gemma's been talking to you, I see." His voice was cool and neutral.

She nodded and slid off him. He didn't try to stop her. She landed on the mattress and sank into it. It felt good under her body. Like a soft, cradling embrace. Unlike him. So much for the vastly exaggerated "romantic vampire" myth. "Yeah. She told me about Nephtys's vision and the rest of it. Something you probably should have done."

"Why?"

"Why?" She rolled her head to give him an incredulous look. "You don't think that might be something I'd want to know, and, oh, maybe have a say in?"

"Why?" he repeated.

"Are you serious?" Wow. "So it never occurred to you that I might not *want* to marry you, or whatever being a consort entails?"

"No," he said.

Incredible. No ego there, or anything.

"Anyway," she said. "You've obviously changed your mind, so it doesn't matter anymore. And I'm fine with that."

More than fine. Honestly.

She gazed up between the four tall corner posts of the bed he'd conjured for them, artfully tied with sheer silk curtains wafting in the breeze from the finials. The square of indigo night sky above was spangled with a million stars, glittering and winking like diamonds.

It was so beautiful. Like everything about Khepesh and this man. And for a single, crazy moment she thought, jeez, too bad he *didn't* want to marry her. Because where would she ever find another man who was quite so handsome, sexy and…thoroughly magical? But…

"Sex isn't everything, Seth-Aziz," she said, figuring that was the reason he couldn't understand why she wouldn't want to become his consort. He'd only see how much she enjoyed their bed play.

"Call me Seth," he said, ignoring the real substance of her statement. Apparently vampire demigods were no different from other men when it came to being obtuse. "I appreciate the show of respect," he told her, "but we're lovers now. You can drop the formality."

How casually he made the mental switch from adversary to intimacy. For her the transition wasn't so easy. Nor was the assumption of their relationship quite so simple.

"What I mean is," she said, "lovers or no, we just met. We might not even like each other. Hell, fifty percent of mortal unions end in divorce. And, well, forever is a really long time." A *hell* of a long time to be tied to someone who openly resented you. Even if he was a god in bed.

"None of that matters," he said, not looking at her.

Was he even *listening*?

"In any case, it's all moot. I'm glad you changed your mind. About both things," she added. "I'm not usually one for jumping into bed with a man five minutes after

I meet him, but...I'm glad I made an exception with you."

"You didn't have a choice," he said impassively.

She hiked a brow. His aloof tone was really starting to bug her. "Are you saying you wouldn't have respected my wishes if I'd told you to stop?" A strange thing to tell her now. Kinda spoiled the mood.

"You *wouldn't* have told me to stop. Your mortal blood in my body has bound us physically. If I want you, and bid you come to me, it's impossible for you to refuse. You'll never want to refuse me."

She blinked. She could have sworn it had been her own idea to sleep with him. But this unnatural world was so insane, she supposed it could be his influence making her think so.

"Oh," she said, even more deflated. "That sucks."

"Why? You just said you enjoyed our coupling."

"I did. At least I think I did. But if that's true, how much of my desire was real? How do I know if I really enjoyed it, or if your vampyric powers just made me think I did?"

He finally looked over at her, his eyes questioning. "What difference does it make?"

Double wow. He really had to be kidding. "A big difference," she said. "Like, oh, the difference between mutual consent and rape."

"Rape?" he echoed. "Surely not, if you enjoyed it? If you wanted me?"

"But if you *caused* that want, if it's impossible for me to refuse..." She turned away and gazed back up at the stars, extremely unsettled. She sighed. "I guess we'll never know the truth."

Fabulous. He'd managed to totally ruin the moment. Now all she wanted to do was forget all about it.

"Josslyn—"

She sat up. "I think you'd better take me back to my sister now."

He sat up behind her. His hand touched her shoulder, and she tried not to shudder. His other hand extended a goblet of wine around to her. "There's no hurry. Let's just relax for a while before—"

"No, thanks. I'm really not in the mood any more." She looked about for her discarded tunic and pants. Not that she remembered taking them off... "My clothes?"

Again he ignored her question. "Josslyn, there's something I need to—"

"I'd also like to see my parents," she went on, taking a page from his own playbook. "Hopefully I can arrange passage back to the States for all of us. They'll need new passports and—"

His hands grasped her arms from behind. "Josslyn, stop. You know that's not going to happen."

She frowned at him over her shoulder. "The passports? I think it'll be possible. Somehow I don't believe the State Department is so organized that they know my parents are supposed to be dead."

He lifted her from the mattress as though she weighed no more than a feather pillow and turned her to face him. "I'm not talking about the passports, Josslyn. I'm talking about you leaving Egypt."

"What's the problem?" She summoned forth her most indifferent mien. "As I recall, this afternoon you couldn't wait to for me to leave."

He didn't even have the grace to deny it. "Things are different now."

"Seth, I told you. This was just sex. I have no interest in making it anything else." Especially now that she knew the truth.

"Neither do I," he said, driving the invisible knife further into her heart. "But unfortunately, these things are not solely my decision. The Great Council also has a say when it concerns the welfare of Khepesh. And they've ordered me to bring you to appear before them."

"Me? I have nothing to do with the welfare of Khepesh."

"Some would disagree. They wish to meet you."

"Why?"

"To see if you're suitable."

She stared at him. She was getting a really bad feeling about this. She might think his priestess sister's woo-woo vision of their supposed future together was just so much hooey, but these people apparently believed in such things. "Suitable for what?" she asked warily.

"You know very well for what." He leveled his dark gaze upon her. "To become my consort."

Chapter 13

Seth felt Josslyn's consternation and rejection of the idea as swiftly and strongly as he'd felt his own when presented with the order.

Unfortunately, things really *had* changed, now that he'd slept with her.

By the gods! How had he let this debacle happen? One second he was roaring at her, doing his best to scare her so badly she'd never want him in a million years, and the next he was plunging into her, unable to think of anything but making her his—all his, completely his, in every way.

Utter disaster. Now that he'd taken her body as well as her blood, the Great Council would see it as a foregone conclusion that he'd agree to take her as his consort. After all, why would he refuse? He'd never before refused to take a woman to wife whom they'd recommended. Especially after tasting her blood and being with her carnally. The choice of consort had never mattered one way or another to him. Women didn't understand him. They weren't interested in understanding him. They were only interested in having mind-blowing sex with a vampire and in the wealth and prestige that being the consort of the high priest of Khepesh and demigod of Set-Sutekh could bring them. There had been a few exceptions over the years, but not many. And those few, Haru-Re had taken a special delight in seeing captured for his perverted amusements.

Part of Seth didn't want another consort. Ever. But another part of him longed for a soul mate with a dull, aching pain in his heart that only the love of a wife who truly understood him could banish. But that was just a dream.

And his wishes were secondary. The only thing that mattered was what was best for Khepesh.

He'd always trusted the neutral objectivity of the council to help him decide which woman to choose, unless he felt strongly enough about one to simply do it without consulting them. In every one of those cases, they'd invariably agreed with his choice.

This time he'd felt strongly enough about Josslyn Haliday to reject her without consulting them. But this afternoon they'd gone against his express wishes and summoned her to the council chambers. They weren't convinced by his arguments. Still, he was pretty sure he could have swung them over to his opinion in the end.

But that was before they'd shared their bodies.

That had changed everything.

He feared he'd sealed both their fates when he'd given in to his fleeting lust.

Except it wasn't so fleeting; already he wanted her again with a need that ate at his insides like a phantom crocodile.

He reached out for her at exactly the same instant she turned away from him.

"Where *are* my clothes?" she asked, still searching for them on the disheveled bed. She got on all fours and peered over the side at the ground.

He groaned silently. Her sexy bottom was to him, lifted as though she were displaying it for his pleasure. Tempting him to further seal their fates.

He moved quickly, quietly, and was behind her before he could think about what he was doing. But again she foiled him.

"I don't understand what could—" She straightened and turned. "Oh! What are you doing?"

"Take a wild guess." His rampant erection made it easy.

She went red as a ripe pomegranate. "Jesus, Seth. Seriously? After what we just talked about?"

"I did not rape you. Don't even try. You wanted me as much as I wanted you."

It had been obvious in the way she'd touched him as Mihos Rukem. In the way she'd eagerly spread her legs for him as he'd thrust into her. Fuck the magic of the bites. It had been all *her* begging him to take her.

"That's a matter of debate," she ground out. "But either way, having sex again would be pointless, because I won't be your consort. I'm leaving."

He grasped for patience. "Josslyn, you have to know I can't let you go."

"So Gemma was right. She said you'd threaten me."

"Threaten?" he said. His lip curled. How naïve she was.

"She said if I didn't join your cult willingly you'd force me to stay. Or turn me into one of those awful *shabtis* as you were about to do before she saved me."

Oh, that. "Seems to me," he reminded her, "it was *you* who knocked on *our* gate."

"Seems to me," she shot back, "you just said you don't want me."

He gave her a sardonic look and lay back on the bed. "As a consort. Obviously I do want you as a bedmate." His still-engorged cock was hard to miss. He looked like a reclining statue of Min, the outrageously endowed God of Fertility.

"You said I could leave anytime after I let you take my blood," she reminded him tersely.

He stacked his hands under his head to keep from reaching for her. She had a wonderful body, and he was so ready. "Technically, what I said was, you may join your sisters. You are free to do that. After you speak with the Great Council."

She studied him with a shrewd glare. "Really? You *lied* to me? Why am I not surprised?"

"No. You simply heard what you wanted to hear."

"You really are a bastard, you know that?"

He shrugged. "I do what I must, for the good of the *per netjer*. And frankly, if you are unhappy with your fate, blame your sisters. If it weren't for them, or at least Gillian, you wouldn't be in this position."

She glowered. "Is it so easy for you to shift the blame for your own heartlessness?"

He pressed his lips together. "You know nothing of me or my heart, Josslyn Haliday."

"Oh, I think I do," she retorted.

"Is that so?" Irritation spread through him lightning fast. And he'd been feeling so good.

Time to change the direction of this conversation before he lost his temper completely.

"Come here," he beckoned with outstretched hand.

Immediately, suspicion swept over her. "Why?"

Mithra's *balls,* but the woman was annoying!

"Can you not, just once, do as I ask without an inquisition?"

Her eyes darted to his arousal. Her tongue peeked out and swiped over her lower lip. "Probably not."

"I can make you," he warned.

Her brows beetled. "You wouldn't." But he could feel her rising uncertainty.

"I would." And he did, bringing her over to him with merely a thought.

Her mouth made an "O" of surprise as he compelled her to crawl to him on all fours.

"Hey!" she squeaked.

"I told you, I have something to show you," he said.

"I can see it just fine from here," she retorted, but he could feel the jumble of feelings that rushed through her, putting the lie to her dismissive tone. There was resentment and anger, sure, but under those, he also sensed a surge of excitement. *And desire.* Unwilling? Perhaps. But definitely there.

He stretched his arms out to her and waited. He had all night. Eventually she would come to him, and they both knew it.

Several heartbeats later she gave up and lowered herself into his waiting embrace. He put his arms around her, pulling her against his body, side to side, in a nestle, so they were both gazing up at the night sky. He felt her surprise. He knew what she'd been expecting.

"Do you ever look at the stars?" he asked. "Like this, in the darkness of the desert, so you can see every one of the trillion different worlds hovering out there in the universe?"

She glanced at him for a moment, absorbing the change of topic, then looked back at the sky. "Yes," she said at length. "I like looking at the stars. Though it can make you feel a bit small and insignificant at times."

"Mmm. I know what you mean." He adjusted and pulled her a shade closer. He enjoyed the warmth of her body and the softness of her skin against his. He lifted a hand and pointed at a constellation. "Do you know that one?"

She nodded. "The Big Dipper."

"We call it the Foreleg of Set-Sutekh."

"Khepesh," she said, startling him with her ready knowledge of his language. "I learned to read hieroglyphics before I could read English," she explained with a wry smile when she saw his surprise. "One of the hazards of having an Egyptologist dad."

He made a face. "And me, I struggled to learn those incomprehensive symbols as a teenager under the merciless tutelage of my father's scribe. I can't tell you the number of beatings I endured before mastering them to his satisfaction."

"Tell me about the ancient times," she said, settling in. "What you've done with yourself for all these years.

What was it like to live under the pharaohs and see the rise and fall of a civilization?"

He hesitated. He'd never talked about his past to anyone before. Not in any detail. But for some reason, perhaps her sincere curiosity, he wanted to share it with her. "You understand you cannot reveal any of what I tell you outside of Khepesh? No scholarly papers. No reinterpretation of the frescoes at Amarna. No helping your former colleagues fill in the gaps of Egyptian history."

She blew out a breath. "I don't see how I could, if you really aren't planning to let me go anywhere."

"After you've joined the *per netjer* and spent a certain amount of time as one of the *shemsu*, you are free to travel as you wish. The only requirement is you must return to Khepesh once a month at the new moon for the renewal ceremony. Assuming you have no other duties to keep you at the palace full-time, that is."

She ignored his not-so-veiled hint. "So I could theoretically go back to my job in the States?"

"It could be years. And it's not recommended. The logistics alone would be formidable… Not to mention keeping any knowledge gained here strictly to yourself. Remember, the punishment for breaking one's oath of secrecy to the god is death."

She shivered. "A long and painful one, I presume."

"Depends on how you feel about beheading. It's the traditional way to kill an immortal. One of the few that brings permanent death. That and a few rare kinds of poison." His smile turned lopsided. "Sheikh Shahin is very skilled with his blade, if that's any consolation."

With a muttered curse, she shivered again, and he

surprised them both by giving her a squeeze and kissing her forehead. "Don't worry. It won't happen. You'll like your new life with us. Remind me to show you our library. That alone will keep you busy for a millennium or two."

"Library?" she said, looking up at him with renewed interest. "With papyrus scrolls and ancient texts? Like the one they burned in Alexandria?"

He nodded. "Only better, and more complete. Lord Rhys practically lived there his entire first century. Your sister seemed equally enraptured by it."

"Gemma?"

He frowned at the reminder. "No, Gillian."

"Figures. Gemma was always more into the present than the past. Gillian is much more like me."

Only in looks, he thought, shaking off his residual resentment of the other woman. "Anyway. There are a multitude of pastimes to occupy yourself with at Khepesh. No reason at all to be unhappy."

She sighed. "I'm not unhappy, Seth. I'm just…"

He touched her chin and gently cradled her face in his palm. "Just what, *heret-ibi?*"

She stilled for a second at his endearment. She obviously knew what the words meant. "She who belongs to me." But they could also mean "my heart's desire." He decided not to think too carefully about which he'd intended.

"I'm just a bit overwhelmed," she finally said. "A lot's been thrown at me today."

"You've handled it well. Better than most," he told her.

"Thanks," she said. "I think."

He felt her relax a little in his arms. He gathered her closer, resisting the temptation to roll his body over hers and have his way with her. He was still hard as a marble column, wanting her with undiminished lust. But he wanted her trust more. Though Set-Sutekh alone knew why, his admiration for her was growing as strong and compelling as his unrelenting hunger for her body. She was as smart and brave and sexy as Isis herself.

"So," he said with a mental self-admonishment to patience, "you wanted to know about the ancient times." He dug in to tell her the long saga of his seemingly endless life, and his all too few adventures. "Well, I was born in the twelfth year of Neferkare, in what you know as the sixth dynasty…"

Joss listened with avid fascination as Seth spun out his story of passion, violence and mystery. Mostly he told her about the Egyptian pharaohs and queens about whom she'd studied most of her life: the ruthless palace intrigues, the rapacious bids for power by the temples and their *per netjers,* the bloody wars fought over the most absurd and petty things. The cruelty, the hardships, the lost friends and lovers. The devotion to his god and his duty. And through it all, the loneliness of a man who ruled with stern authority and infallible wisdom, who saw to everyone's happiness but his own.

He even told her about a poem he'd written during the troubled times of his early immortality. A poem she recognized with shock and amazement was the "anonymous" one known as "The Man Who Was Tired of Life," which they taught in university classes all over the world today. Not just classes in Egyptology or hieroglypics, but in philosophy and literature classes, as well. She'd taught it herself, in the graduate seminars she'd conducted.

Stunned, she gazed at him with new eyes and an exploding awe and admiration, as he recited it for her in his own language, filling in the blanks that the tattered papyrus had created for modern scholars, and giving her his meanings for the many disputed passages.

Afterward, she fell into an awestruck, almost worshipful silence, listening to the recollections of the man whose great loneliness and heaviness of heart she had glimpsed years before knocking at the gate of Khepesh.

Occasionally she'd make a comment or ask a question or exclaim with shock or even laugh with delight at some incident he related. But mostly he talked, and she soaked everything in with an absorption she'd never experienced. He was endlessly fascinating, and sensitive, and filled with a goodness she couldn't fail to recognize.

When the sky grew light and his words began to slow to a trickle, she found herself captivated by the man who by virtue of his character, wisdom and sense of duty had been granted the status of demigod by the ancient god he served.

"Wow," she said when his long narrative came to a halt. "Just. Wow." She was lying on her stomach on the bed with her feet in the air and her chin resting on her palm, watching him with a whole new appreciation and respect. "I am…pretty speechless."

He glanced over at her and for a second seemed taken aback to see her there. As though he'd forgotten he was telling his life's story to someone else, so deeply had he immersed himself in his personal ramblings.

He cleared his throat, a wince of embarrassment sweeping over his handsome features. "By Thot's feather. I didn't mean to drone on and on like that. Forgive me."

"Are you kidding? It was absolutely spellbinding. I learned more tonight than I could have in a lifetime of digging in the dirt or floundering in the intricacies of hieroglyphics."

He gave her a dry smile. "I'll assume that's a compliment."

She laughed. "Absolutely. My God, Seth. You are— Damn, she really was speechless. "Completely incredible."

She leaned up and kissed his jaw. She couldn't reach any farther without scooting up. But before she'd raised her lips, he had lifted her and brought her body over his.

"I need to get back," he said, but he made no move to do so. Nor to shift her body off him. He tunneled his fingers in her hair and searched her face, his own inscrutable as always.

Well. Okay, maybe not so much. His black eyes had gone all bedroomy again, half-lidded and sultry, and the hard planes of his stern face were shadowed with desire.

She smiled.

And then he kissed her.

She didn't mind.

The kiss was a slow, sensual exploration of each other's mouths, drawn out and enjoyed as though they had all the time in the world. Which, she supposed, they did.

He didn't seem the least bit tired of life now. Which made her happy.

"Mmm," she whispered on a sigh. "Good."

He kissed her with the full surfeit of his sensuality, but gently, persuasively. He didn't push, didn't bespell. He just let the kiss take its course. As did she.

His hands began to travel lightly over her body. Tentatively at first, and when she didn't object, bolder.

She touched him back. His broad chest, his muscle-corded arms. His well-toned backside. She enjoyed touching him. His body was a living sculpture, powerfully male and infinitely beautiful. It was a body a woman could get lost in for days, years. The body of a protector and a lover.

Her lover.

She shivered with a spill of desire that purled through her whole being from head to toe and every space in between. Not the desperate sexual need of her blood sacrifice, and not the frenzied carnal fever of the first time they'd come together as one. But more of a quiet desire, a drowning ache in her whole body, a yearning to belong to this unique, utterly amazing man. Completely.

Heret-ibi.

Or perhaps she already did.

He glanced at the rising glow of the coming sunrise and then pushed out a breath between kisses.

"We must go. The council will be waiting. Best not to anger them with further delay."

Her pulse leapt. She'd forgotten all about the summons. She worried her lower lip with her teeth, at once terrified. No way was she ready for this. "I don't want to. Can't you make some excuse?"

"It'll do no good. They'll know the truth. It's all right, love. They only want to ask you questions."

"To find out if I'm suitable," she said, recalling what he'd told her earlier. "To be your consort."

With his tongue he touched her kiss-swollen lip on the spot where she'd worried it, soothing the hurt. "Yes."

"But you don't want me as your consort. And I don't want to be forced into marriage."

"They can't force you," he said after an infinitesimal pause. "You must enter the *per netjer* willingly, and you must give your consent to become my wife. Just as you had to agree to the blood sacrifice. We aren't barbarians, Josslyn. There are laws."

She swallowed. "You really think that's what they want with me?"

"Quite sure."

"So all I have to do is say no?" She watched his eyes, but he gave nothing away. The man could make a fortune at the poker tables.

"Theoretically," he said. "In truth, I have no idea how they'll react. No one has ever said no to them."

Great.

"But I should definitely tell them no, right?"

He gazed at her with that sphinx-like mien. "I may have been hasty in my judgment of you…measuring you by the yardstick of your sister."

Okay. What was *that* supposed to mean?

Surely not… Her pulse suddenly leapt in consternation.

She wriggled out of his arms and sat up. "What are you saying, Seth?"

"I'm saying Nephtys may be much wiser than I gave her credit for."

She blinked down at him. "You can't possibly believe in that…that *vision?* You can't want to base your whole future on a crazy dream your sister had!"

"My sister's crazy dreams are almost never wrong."

"*Almost* never," she emphasized, but she had the sinking feeling he really did believe it.

This was in*sane*!

"So what do you want me to do?" she asked, a shade desperately. Desperate, because suddenly she wasn't nearly as certain of her own resolve, either. She liked him. She really, really did. And she'd never been so attracted to a man in her life. But was that enough to build forever on? Forever was a freaking long time.

"That's your decision, *heret-ibi*," he said, sitting up. He took her hands. "Just tell them what's truly in your heart."

"What if I don't know? How can I possibly say, after knowing you less than a day?" She squeezed her eyes shut. "How can *you* know?" She opened them again and saw a rare smile grace his lips. Her heart gave a little flutter. It was amazing what that smile did to his face.

"I don't have to know," he said. "I simply accept."

Her pulse thundered at the implication. "But what about love?"

"Love?" he echoed. "Love has nothing to do with it."

At that, her chest squeezed painfully. "Oh," she whispered.

"I must do what is right for my followers. What is best for Khepesh." He lifted her fingers to his lips. "They'll ask you to be my consort, Josslyn. I'd like you to say yes."

She swallowed heavily and felt her stomach sink like a stone. Because she knew what she must do. For *her* sake.

For the sake of her heart.

"I'm sorry," she said, and pulled back her hands from him. "I can't."

Then into the painful silence a sardonic laugh cut through the shimmering dawn like the blade of a guillotine.

"She's right, you know," Harold Ray's hated voice said triumphantly. "She'll never be your consort, Seth-Aziz. Because you'll be dead by sunrise!"

Chapter 14

Seth launched himself up from the bed, sending Josslyn tumbling. In a swift spell he dressed them both in their Bedouin clothes, at the same time spinning to attack his enemy.

At once he saw it was no use.

They were surrounded.

He had been so caught up in the moment, in Josslyn's reaction to him, that he had let his guard down. For how long had he left them vulnerable? Too long, obviously. Three dozen men on ghost camels had formed a double ring around the dune where Seth had conjured their love nest.

Mentally, he berated himself. But it would do little good now.

He was a dead man.

Haru-Re smiled down on him scornfully, incandescent with victory, and Seth wanted to retch. What had he done? By the gods, what had he done? He was dead and Khepesh would be no more.

He snapped his fingers and the bed disappeared from under them, leaving him and Josslyn standing on the warm desert sand. He suddenly wished he'd gone barefoot in it more often, and absurdly, his feet itched to be rid of his boots.

"Better kill me now, Haru-Re," Seth ground out, wresting back his focus. "For I will never surrender to you. And you can burn Khepesh to the ground, but the *shemsu* of Set-Sutekh will never bow to your god."

Anger swept over Haru-Re's features. He spurred his camel forward and raised his golden scimitar. Its razor-sharp edge gleamed in the pale rays of the coming dawn. "I believe I'll oblige you, you whoreson of a scorpion."

"No!" Suddenly Josslyn jumped in front of him, shielding him from the deadly blade with her body.

Both he and Haru-Re were so shocked they each froze where they stood, Ray's sword in a slant above his head, poised for the coup de grace.

"You don't want to do this," Josslyn said into the stunned silence, her voice loud and strong. "Think about it, Ray. What will Nephtys do when she learns you've murdered her brother? Her only living family? Do you think she'll ever forgive you?"

Fear stabbed through Seth at her reckless boldness. She was going to get herself killed, too!

Ray's eyes narrowed dangerously. He didn't lower the sword. Instead, he bored into her with his furious glare.

But Josslyn didn't back down. "You've given her an

oath of marriage, but what will it be like to go through eternity bound to a woman who loathes the very air you breathe?" She returned Ray's glower, feet spread in challenge and her fists planted on her hips.

By the staff of Osiris, *she* was the incredible one!

To Seth's shock, Ray's stony glare melted into guarded amusement. Slowly, the scimitar dropped to his side. His eyes cut to Seth with a flash of derision. "Letting females fight our battles for us now, are we?" he mocked.

"Only when she is evenly matched," he returned.

A shower of sparks glanced off the golden blade.

Seth smiled. If he was going to die anyway, he'd rather go down in flames than cowering in fear.

"For once we are in agreement," Haru-Re said, returning his attention to Josslyn with a slow, evil smile. "I think I shall enjoy taming this one." His voice lowered. "Especially breaking her to the fang."

White-hot rage erupted in Seth so swiftly he didn't think—*couldn't* think—he just reacted. In a blur he shifted. With a mighty roar he was on Haru-Re, Mihos Rukem's powerful lion's body knocking the enemy off his camel and sending the deadly scimitar flying through the air. Bedlam erupted all around them, men shouting and being tossed from camels that suddenly went berserk, butting and braying, biting and spitting. Sand flew in whirlwind dust devils. The light of the coming dawn dimmed.

It was chaos—Seth's element to call.

And through it all, the only one who didn't move a muscle was Josslyn. She watched in confusion, rooted to the spot.

Seth leapt toward her, tossing her onto his back with a single jerk of his massive head. He bounded forward through the pandemonium and started to run.

But a sudden burning pain seared into the flesh of his rear haunch, and he stumbled. Josslyn screamed. Another agonizing stab of pain, and he went down, hearing the snap of an arrow shaft as he hit the ground. The muscles of his leg were already numb. *The arrow had been poisoned.* The edges of his vision blurred. His consciousness slipped precariously. With his last vestige of strength, he shifted back to human form. When he was laid to rest in his sarcophagus, it would be as Seth-Aziz, the human.

"No!" Josslyn screamed. *"No!"*

Vaguely, he felt his lover fling her body over his, protecting him from any more arrows.

"Cease fire!" he heard Haru-Re's shouted order. "I want her alive!"

And that's when he knew her fate would be far worse than his.

In one last futile effort to help her, his element to call surged to life. But this time instead of lending help, the chaos turned inward on him, spreading confusion in his own head instead of among the enemy.

Questions rippled through the fabric of his mind like stones skipping on water.

Why had she done it? Risked her own life to save his?

What did it mean that he wanted to tear Haru-Re limb from limb, if he could but raise himself from the dirt where he'd fallen?

How had it happened that he'd lived five thousand

long years, only to meet the woman he was destined to love forever, on the very day he died?

To whom could he speak today? Where was the god he had faithfully served and sacrificed every happiness for? Where was his god, now when he most needed his help and intercession?

Behold, his name was surely detested. More than a monarch, whose subjects mutter sedition when his back is turned.

Death was in his sight today.

Yea, death was in his sight today.

Like the smell of myrrh.

Like the perfume of lotuses.

Death was in his sight today.

Like the clearing of the sky on a starry, starry night.

Like a man who yearns for something he does not know...

But in his heart Seth knew just what he longed for.

And her name was Josslyn.

Chapter 15

Nephtys's heart stopped dead in her chest when she saw them bring her brother in on a stretcher.

"Seth!" she screamed, running to him like a child to its calling mother. Undignified for a priestess of her rank, but she didn't care.

He was lying on his side, two arrows protruding from his thigh, one feather-tipped and the other broken off next to his body. Blood matted his fawn-colored Bedouin trousers, a red pool of it staining the cloth of the stretcher under him. His eyes were closed, his features slack. There were no signs of life.

Before Nephtys could get to him, Ray intercepted her. He grasped her arms and held her as she struggled. "Stop."

"Let me go! What have you done to him?" she cried.

All at once she noticed that the guards walking behind

the stretcher were holding another woman fighting to get free, much as Ray was holding her. She was tall, blond and irate enough to spit nails. She looked like a slightly older version of Gillian.

Josslyn Haliday?

Oh, no! Their eyes met and she saw Josslyn's were red-rimmed and swimming with tears.

Nephtys's heart sank and she stopped pulling against Ray's grip. She gave a sob of despair.

Sweet Isis. All was lost.

"By the orb woman! You will *not* weep for that bastard!" Ray exploded, his voice rising with each word until the palace walls shook like thunder. "*I* am to be your husband, not Seth-Aziz! You should be celebrating my glorious victory, the capture of my enemy, not wailing over a brother who doesn't give a hyena's fart about you!"

She gasped. "How dare you!"

"He doesn't love you, Nephtys. He hasn't even *asked* to buy you back. And he is too damn busy mounting his new concubine to bother mounting a rescue!"

She let out a cry, cut to the quick. Not by Seth's supposed lack of caring—she knew it wasn't true, he'd just been waiting for the right time to strike—but by the cruelty of Ray's deliberate attempt to wound her with his accusations.

Flame seemed to shoot from his eyes, singeing her very eyelashes with the heat of his fury.

She shrank away from him, stinging with hurt. And terror. He could crush her like a beetle under his boot with a single thought. And he looked angry enough to do it if she crossed him now.

Apparently Josslyn Haliday was not so easily intimidated. Or maybe she was just unaware of the danger contained in that temper of his.

"Please, Haru-Re. I beg you," Josslyn pleaded. "Let me see to Seth's wounds. Why let him die? What good will it serve? You have him in your power now, a prisoner. Surely that is a worse punishment than death?"

Nephtys held her breath, astounded by the bravery of the woman to attempt reasoning with a demigod in a blind rage.

Ray whirled to Josslyn. Nephtys could see the calculation in his face, weighing her fate for daring to speak.

"You, too?" he seethed, more disgusted than incensed. "Am I surrounded by women who are in thrall to my enemy?"

He pointed a finger at Josslyn, his arm straight as a spear, but he turned to Nephtys. "You show her the way to Khepesh, and less than twenty-four hours later I find them fornicating like two dogs in heat!"

Josslyn flinched and opened her mouth to protest, but she wisely shut it again.

"What *is* it about the son of a jackal you females find so fucking irresistible?" he roared.

Astonishment jolted through Nephtys. Of all the bizzare things for Ray to be infuriated over... Her brother was *dying!*

"Ray! What is *wrong* with you?" she demanded.

"Exactly! What *is* wrong with me?" he blasted back. "Why does no one love *me* with such passion and loyalty?"

"By the goddess, Ray, this is not time to be—"

But suddenly... It was like his words hit a switch and a light went on in her mind.

He made me several offers, yes. But I turned them down. Every last one.

It works both ways, meruati. *You would do well to remember that.*

Why does no one love me...

But the agonized look on his face said one thing loud and clear.

He meant *her.* Why did *she* not love him?

Her gaze sought her brother, nearly lifeless, then returned to Haru-Re. And looked at him from a whole new perspective, seeing his behavior in a completely different light than she had for nearly her entire life.

Her heart stalled, and her world shifted, turning completely upside down.

Sweet blessed goddess.

He loved her. He did!

And just as she had, everything he'd done ever since, good and bad, he'd done because of that love.

He'd loved her back when they were together, and she'd been ripped from his arms against her will. And against his.

But she'd turned against him.

Instead of trusting him, trusting his love, and acknowledging the good she had always known was in his heart, she had believed the lies of others and thrown his feelings in his face, letting her own love and goodness turn to hatred and a burning need for revenge.

All for a betrayal he had never, ever been guilty of.

No wonder he'd turned vengeful and cruel, and

struck out at her, wanting to hurt her as badly as she'd hurt him!

Could he really still be in love with her, even now, and could his long-festering jealousy be driving his actions to this day? Was it truly possible?

She knew in her heart it could. Because her own jealousy had driven her actions in exactly the same way.

She was the reason he'd become what he was.

Merciful Isis.

Could he ever forgive her?

"Sometimes," she answered, her heart breaking for all they'd lost, "it happens that two people take one look at each other and know in their hearts that they are two halves of a single soul." She gazed into the eyes of the man who was her own other half and always would be, her heart pounding and her limbs trembling. "It would be a shame if something, or someone, came between them and they had to wait a thousand lifetimes to join those souls together and live as one. Don't you think?"

He stared at her hard. "What are you trying to say, *meruati?*" His voice was like the tear of raw silk.

Her brother groaned in his unconsciousness, and she glanced at him again. His life may depend on what she said next. But that was not the only reason she needed to say it. At long last, it was time to tell the truth. To lay her heart in her hands and offer it up in all sincerity.

Swallowing, she pulled her gaze from her dying brother and met Ray's angry, penetrating stare.

"I'm saying," she said, gathering every ounce of courage to say what was long overdue, "that I love you,

Haru-Re. I've always loved you. Let Josslyn have Seth. Don't put her through the misery I've had to endure, an endless, empty life without the man I love."

For a moment he looked stricken, then disbelief swept over his features. Finally, when she didn't move, didn't laugh at his gullibility or try to hide the tears that welled hotly in her eyes, his lips parted and for a split second he looked so vulnerable that her heart melted into a soft, warm puddle.

Seth moaned again. Josslyn tried to shake off her captors and go to him. "Please, Haru-Re," she pleaded.

Without taking his gaze from Nephtys, Ray raised a hand and flicked it at Josslyn's guards. "Put them in the garden suite and bring her whatever she requests."

They released Josslyn, who rushed to the stretcher as they carried it off toward their assigned quarters.

"Thank you," Nephtys whispered. She wanted to go to Ray and put her arms around him. To sink into his embrace and show him how grateful she was to him for sparing her brother's life, and how sorry she was she'd ever doubted him. But she didn't dare move.

"If this is a ruse, you'll bitterly regret it," he growled.

"It's not," she assured him.

"So you'll come to my bed." It was a statement, rife with skepticism, but the question that rang within it was unmistakable. "No spurious protests?"

"If you still want me," she said.

"You'll become my consort? Right away?"

"Yes."

"Tonight?"

Her head felt light. "If you wish it."

"Why?" he asked. "Why the sudden about-face? Is this you maneuvering because Khepesh is defeated? Do you think you can play me?"

"No, Ray. That's not it at all. It's because…" She shook her head sadly. "Because you are so wrong about not being loved. Look around you." A crowd of *shemsu* had gathered, each face looking more concerned than the next. They respected, and yes, sometimes feared their leader, but they had always loved him. "Your people love you, Ray. And so do I." His eyes narrowed, still suspecting a trick.

She could see it wasn't going to be easy to convince him of her change of heart. And she didn't really blame him for his cynicism. "I believe what you told me last night," she said. "About not wanting to sell me. And Seth's father stealing me away and lying about it. I should have trusted you, Ray. Trusted us, what we had." She hung her head. "I'm sorry. So sorry."

It was a long time before he spoke. By the time he did, they were alone in the great hall of Petru, the *shemsu* having recognized a moment of import for their leader and giving Ray the privacy he needed to deal with it. With her.

"And if Seth-Aziz dies?" he asked.

Her heart stuttered at the terrible thought. She loved her brother dearly, and it would devastate her to lose him. "A big part of my heart would die along with him," she admitted. "But I know that much of the blame for this…vicious animosity between you two can be laid at my door. If Seth dies, his death will be upon my hands as much as yours. I understand that now."

She felt the full weight of his regard drill into her, making her dizzy from the wash of power that pulsed from him, swirling about her, wrapping her in its electric web.

"What if I no longer want you?" he drawled. "What if I was merely using you as a means to get to Seth-Aziz? What if, now that I have poisoned him and taken him captive, I plan to throw you away like a bad penny?"

She flinched, her skin almost scorched from the heat accompanying his words. "Then I suppose my purity ritual will last much longer than I anticipated," she said shakily, praying it wasn't true. She licked her dry lips. "But I'll wait as long as it takes."

Ray let out a long, measured breath, apparently finally convinced. "Seth-Aziz won't die," he said at length. "The poisoned arrows were not deadly. Just toxic enough to knock him out and make him sick as a bloated vulture when he wakes up."

Relief swept through her, and her tears threatened to spill over. "Thank you. Oh, thank you!" She wanted to go to Ray and fling herself into his arms for joy, but she had to know one last thing. "I don't understand. You've wanted him dead for eons. Why not kill him now when you have the chance?"

A grim, humorless smile flashed over his lips. A muscle ticked under his eye. "Because Josslyn Haliday convinced me that you'd never forgive me if I did."

She felt a tickle of warmth track down her cheek and tasted salt. "Oh, Ray," she said in a strangled whisper. And this time nothing in the world could keep her from going to him.

She slid into his waiting arms and her whole body

gave a sigh of happiness and relief when he wrapped them around her and laid his cheek against the top of her head. She half expected him to sweep her up and carry her to his rooms, to his bed, and demand she prove the sincerity of her confession of love and her promise to give herself to him.

But he didn't. He just stood there, breathing into her hair and holding her so tight that she couldn't tell where her body left off and his began. *At last.*

It felt good. So very good.

And it filled her with hope for her future, a future she could finally share with the only man she'd ever truly loved.

But at the same time, she felt a gnawing pain in her heart. For she knew her own happiness had come at the price of her brother's.

For him, and Josslyn Haliday, and their beloved Khepesh, there would be no future happiness.

And possibly, there would be no future, at all.

Chapter 16

"Oh, thank God. Joss!"

Josslyn looked up from where she was sitting on the bed next to Seth, desperately cutting away the fabric of his trousers from the vicious arrows protruding from his thigh.

"Gillian!" When she saw her baby sister, Joss dropped the knife and leapt to her feet, colliding with her in a huge hug, overjoyed to see her after so many weeks of worry. "Oh, Gillian, is it really you? Are you all right, Jelly Bean?"

"I'm good. And you? You're not hurt?" Gillian searched her face and body and immediately spotted the vampire bite on her neck. "Oh, Jesus, Joss! You let him do it."

Joss glanced anxiously at Seth, who was lying as still as a corpse on the luxurious bed. "Who would have thought, eh? I still can't quite believe it myself," she said, "but yes. Oh, Gillian, he's…he's so…"

How could she put into words how she felt about Seth already, after knowing the man just one short day? It would sound crazy. Especially for practical, logical Josslyn Haliday. Love at first sight? Her sister would think she'd gone off the deep end, or was bespelled…. Which, well, maybe she was. But Seth was right—that didn't make her feelings any less strong or true.

"I'm so scared for him. Gillian, he's been poisoned. He once told me that poison was one of the few ways an immortal can be killed."

"I'm afraid it's true," Gillian said. "Rhys has told me that, too."

Seth looked so pale, his skin so translucent it was almost blue. There wasn't even a hint of the powerful, magical energy that usually swirled like an invisible maelstrom around his body.

Joss let her sister go and hurried to sit back down next to him, forcing herself to continue to hack away the trouser leg. Her hands were shaking so badly that she was making a complete hash of it.

"I have no idea how to stop the poison from the arrows from killing him," she said. "And I'm terrified to pull them out for fear he'll bleed to death. I've asked for a doctor, but they say there isn't one here at Petru—there's no need because they're immortal. I have to help him! But how?"

Her sister's arm came around her and she sat down on the bed, too. "Don't worry. Rhys will be here in a minute. He's interrogating the guards about the poison and has sent for the temple priestess, who specializes in herbs and potions." Her sister frowned. "Probably the priestess who prepared the arrows in the first place."

Alarm sizzled through Joss. "Are you kidding me? She's not touching him! Over my dead body!"

Gillian's eyes widened and she held up a hand. "It's okay, sis. Rhys will be here. He's Seth's best friend. If anything happens to him, trust me, heads *will* roll. Rhys is beside himself with worry." She puffed out a breath. "Obviously, Haru-Re is going to know now that Rhys's loyalty still lies with Seth and Khepesh. Things could get ugly."

Joss shook her head. "Not if I can help it. I'm getting you all out of here as soon as possible. You and Mom and Dad. And Gemma, too. We're going back to the States where we belong. Away from this madness." Now that Seth had been captured and Khepesh was most likely to be destroyed, there was nothing to stop them. Though the thought was surprisingly painful... What would happen to him? Just yesterday she wouldn't have cared; but now...

No. She couldn't think about her own feelings. She had to protect her family.

She could feel Gillian's gaze on her as she reached for a cloth and a basin of hot water from the nightstand and started gently to wash the blood from Seth's exposed thigh.

"Joss," Gillian said carefully. "I'm not going back. I love Rhys. Wherever he ends up living, I want to stay with him."

Josslyn paused in her task and looked at her sister. She saw a mirror of her own growing feelings for Seth, but much, much stronger because of the time they'd had together. "You're really serious about this guy."

Gillian smiled. "Yeah. I am." Then her expression grew somber. "And about Mom… I don't really think Dad will want to take her away from Petru. It wouldn't be…good for her. You haven't seen how she is, Joss. She's…" Gillian closed her eyes and got such a pained look on her face that Joss's heart actually hurt.

She nodded and continued to wash Seth to keep from dissolving into tears. She was old enough to remember how brilliant and vibrant their mother had been when she was with them and still…herself. "I've seen *shabtis* in Khepesh. I was horrified. It breaks my heart to imagine Mom like that. God, how it must be killing Dad. How is he? I want to see them both so badly!"

"He wants to see you, too, sis. But he says he can wait, that you should take care of Seth first. As for how he's doing…" She gave a sad smile. "He's dealing pretty well, all things considered. Nephtys has promised to try and find a reversal spell in the library to bring all the *shabtis* back to themselves."

Hope soared within Joss as she stroked the wet cloth over Seth's leg. Imagine having both her parents back, alive and well! Having all of them together again, as a family! And if Seth lived, everything would be perfect again…even if they couldn't be together. "Oh, Gillian, that would be awesome! Do you really think it's possible to reverse the spell?"

"I'm praying it is."

Seth moaned when her ministrations got too close to the arrows, and Joss sent up a prayer for him, too. He just *had* to survive this! She swallowed down a thick lump of fear for him...and a spurt of guilt.

"I'm so sorry, sweetheart," she whispered. "Oh, Seth, this is all my fault."

Gillian raised her eyebrows. "Joss. You know better. Khepesh and Petru have been at war since the dawn of Egyptian civilization. How could this possibly be your fault?"

From her work, Joss was well acquainted with the eternal strife between the gods Set-Sutekh and Re-Horakhti, whom modern scholars call Horus and Seth. Khepesh and Petru were the ancient homes of their followers. But that wasn't what Joss had meant. If it hadn't been for her, Seth-Aziz would never have been out tonight in that desert in the first place, naked in bed with his guard down, vulnerable to capture by his enemy.

Joss felt herself blush, and kept her head ducked so Gillian wouldn't see her red face.

But Gillian was a smart cookie. She let out a choked sound. "Seriously? I'd heard that Seth was caught with a woman...ahem, in flagrante. So that was *you?* Damn, girl!"

"Sort of," Joss confessed, chagrined. "We weren't actually— I mean—" She made a face. "He'd conjured a beautiful bed for us out in the desert, and we were watching the stars and talking when Haru-Re and his men surrounded us."

Gillian's brows hiked up further. "Watching the stars and talking, eh?"

"It's true!"

Their eyes met and they shared a moment of amused

sisterly understanding before their gazes both went to Seth's wound.

"He has to be okay, Jelly Bean. He just has to be. I don't know what I'll do if he…" She couldn't even say it.

"Seth-Aziz is not going to die," a refined British voice said from the doorway.

"Rhys!" Gillian cried, hurrying to meet a tall, roguishly handsome man as he strode into the suite. It was the same man Joss had seen carrying her unconscious body down from the old tomb on that day last month.

"Did you find out about the poison?" Gillian asked him in a rush. "Is there an antidote?"

He gave her an affectionate peck on the lips. "Slow down, darling. The poison's not deadly," he said, including Joss in his glance.

A huge avalanche of relief coursed through her. "So he'll be all right?" she asked. "Truly?"

Rhys nodded. "Just sick as a dog."

He strode over to the bed, gave Seth's wound a quick, efficient study, felt his pulse and blew out a breath. "He'll do. We just need to get those arrows out of that leg before he wakes up."

Finally Rhys looked up at Joss. He gave her a disarming smile. "Hello again." He peered about her, feigning concern. "Should I be worried you have a shotgun hidden somewhere?"

She couldn't help smiling back. The man was definitely a charmer…when he wasn't carrying off innocent maidens to preternatural fates.

"Not that my shotgun would do me any good," she

pointed out dryly. "It has an alarming tendency to misfire when I'm around you immortals."

A grin lightened his face. "Yes. Well. Sorry about that. Couldn't have you accidentally shooting your sister, now could I?" He gave Gillian an adoring wink. Then his grin faded and he turned back to Seth, examining the entrance wounds of the arrows. "Don't worry, old man. We'll have you fixed up right as rain in no time."

"You're sure? How long will he be knocked out like this?" Joss asked Rhys, worry rushing back over her.

"Hopefully long enough to extract these nasty things. Seth is an extraordinarily powerful demigod. The good news is he'll heal quickly. The bad news is he may wake up while I'm working on him. That could be painful." He winced. "For both of us."

"You?" Joss and Gillian said in unison. They traded looks. "You're a doctor?" Joss asked. "Or...have medical training?"

"I was in the British army in Africa in 1885. I did my share of sewing up saber wounds and digging lead from the bodies of my men." A black shadow passed through his eyes, accompanied by a chill of dark energy that sent goose bumps hurtling over Joss's arms. "Some of them even lived."

Oh, God.

He jetted out a breath. "Of course, I wasn't an immortal back then, and I wielded no magical powers. I'm hoping I won't actually have to resort to using a knife for this procedure." His brow beetled. "Damn it all! Nephtys should be here. She'd be able to do this with her eyes closed. Where the hell is she?"

"With Haru-Re," Joss said. "They were, um, discussing their relationship when I left them."

Rhys grimaced. "Of all the bloody times to pick."

"Ray went all postal when Nephtys was more concerned about Seth's welfare than in Ray's victory in capturing him," Joss said.

Gillian rolled her eyes. "Now there's a shock."

"She *was* shocked," Joss said. "When Haru-Re just now as good as admitted he's in love with her."

"Like anybody couldn't tell *that* after being in the same room with them for five seconds."

"About bloody time she opened her eyes," Rhys muttered. He returned his attention to Seth, who had started to stir. "Right. I'd better do this before he regains consciousness."

"What about the priestess you sent for?" Joss asked anxiously. "Shouldn't you wait for her?"

He shook his head. "She's bringing an elixir that will dull the effects of the poison, but he should be awake to drink it, so he can heal his wounds."

Joss bit her lip and reached for Seth's hand again. "You're sure about this?"

Her sister and Rhys exchanged a look. They both smiled.

"What?" Joss asked, straightening and glancing between them.

"You like him," Gillian said warmly. "Seth-Aziz."

"Of course I like him," Joss returned. "He's a very interesting man."

"And handsome," Gillian pointed out.

"Powerful," Rhys added.

"Sexy," Gillian said.

"Intelligent," Rhys said.

Joss watched the rapid exchange like a ping-pong match.

"Oh, yeah," Gillian chided. "And you *slept* with him."

"*And* let him bite you, so it must have been good," Rhys concluded, brows crooking wickedly.

Joss pressed her lips together. "Not that it's *any* of your damned business."

"Oh, it's very much our business," Rhys stated. "But that's a discussion for another time, when Seth is out of the woods."

"What do you need us to do?" Gillian asked as he sat down on the bed and placed his hands gingerly on the other man's leg, circling the protruding arrows with a triangle formed by his fingers and thumbs.

"Take both his hands and hold them tight. I'd just as soon not be hit by a bolt of chaos."

Joss blinked. "A what?"

"Chaos is Seth's element to call." When she gave him a blank look, he explained, "When you become immortal, there is always an element that finds you and binds with you, giving you its power, manifesting itself through you. It becomes your element, and you can call on it at will. Shahin's is earthquakes. Haru-Re has fire. Seth's element is chaos, and it is an immensely difficult one to master. He is the only immortal ever known to possess it."

"What is yours?" Joss asked Rhys as he closed his eyes to begin…whatever he planned to do to get the arrows out of Seth.

"Not sure yet." His lips curved. "I'm still young. I've

only been immortal for a hundred and twenty years or so. I should begin to get a feel for what my element is in the next few decades."

Good lord. A hundred and twenty was *young?*

"Focus your energies," Rhys instructed, his voice going deep and intense. "Send all your strength and positive thoughts into Seth's body."

Great. More woo-woo stuff. Nevertheless, Joss faithfully obeyed. After the past few days, she'd stopped being able to tell what was real and what was mere superstition. Everything seemed to blend as one in this supernatural world. And she would do anything, anything at all, to help bring Seth back to her.

To *life*, she mentally corrected.

He didn't belong to her, she reminded herself. He didn't *want* to belong to her. Except for short intervals, while they were in bed. He'd said so several times. That last proposal—if you could even call it that—was just because of the sex. And the council's orders.

Which was fine. Because she didn't want to belong to him, either.

Honestly she didn't.

As she and Gillian took hold of Seth's hands, Josslyn felt a rush of energy surge through the room. Rhys was the source, it was his power she felt. It swirled and twirled in a tingling whirlpool; it went through her body like electricity, gathering in an invisible vortex that focused and centered over her lover's body. Seth's hand jerked in hers, and she had to grab it with all her might to hang on to it. She could see Gillian do the same.

To her amazement, the longest arrow shaft slowly began to move, easing itself agonizingly slowly from the depths of Seth's muscular thigh, causing wet runnels of blood to spill over his flesh and stain his skin crimson.

She tried not to think about how she had kissed and touched that very spot just a few short hours ago. How the inside of her own thigh had slid intimately against it as he'd filled her with his long, thick manhood and moved within her so erotically she hadn't been able to think straight.

With a painful groan, his fingers now clamped on to hers, and she bit her lip, tasting her own blood. Somehow Rhys was keeping the leg still as he concentrated. And the magic was working. Joss was impressed, and so thankful she nearly wept.

It seemed like hours before both arrows were out, though in reality it must have been minutes. To Joss's horror, Seth woke up halfway through the second procedure. He didn't open his eyes at first; he just clenched his teeth and asked through them, "Sekhmet's blood, Englishman! Am I dead, then? Is this your Christian hell I've landed in, to be endlessly tortured?"

How he knew Rhys was the person working on his leg, Joss had no clue. But her heart leapt with joy at his bad temper—a sure sign of life and vitality. He had seemed so far gone, she'd been terrified he'd never wake up again.

For a brief moment Rhys's eyelids fluttered up. He, too, appeared immensely relieved. "Actually, my lord, I think it may be the Muslim version of heaven. Although there are only two beautiful virgins attending you, stroking your hair and holding your hands…and come to think of it, I rather suspect they are not virgins, either. But they are beautiful, my lord."

Still without opening his eyes, Seth squeezed Joss's hand. "That they are, Englishman."

Her heart melted and soared, and she squeezed back.

He was going to be all right.

At least for now…

Chapter 17

The second arrow parted from Seth's leg with a sickening sound of bloody flesh, and he let out a long string of vivid curses. After it was over and the pain subsided, he looked up at Josslyn. He felt a tired smile curve his lips. It was good to see her.

"Drink this, my lord," the soft voice of a priestess said from behind Joss. He reluctantly pulled his gaze from her.

"What is it?"

"The elixir will chase the poison from your blood and lessen the pain in your limbs and stomach." The priestess respectfully offered a golden chalice to him. He wondered why she was being so deferential.

"And yet, is not this evil potion that's turning my insides to fire of your doing?" he asked her with narrowed eyes.

She responded with her gaze cast to the floor. "I

simply do what my high priest commands," she said quietly.

He had the oddest feeling that she didn't approve of her ruler using her skills to hurt others. Interesting that someone with scruples had made it to such a high position at Petru.

He grunted and labored to sit up, waving off Rhys's help. He needed to do this himself. He held out his hand for the chalice and drank the brew down with a grimace.

"In that case, I'm surprised I'm still alive." He handed her back the goblet. "Or perhaps that has just been remedied…" Haru-Re had tried to kill him with those arrows. Why would his enemy now try to lessen his discomfort?

He was gratified when Josslyn gasped and shot a horrified look at the other woman. She looked ready to pounce on her.

His fierce, beautiful protectress.

"The elixir is as I said," the priestess assured him. "As for the other…I prepared two quivers of arrows for my lord Haru-Re: one with lethal poison, one not." Her eyes slid to Josslyn, whose expression was still a scowl. "I understand it was at your lady's urging that my lord made the choice he did."

As the priestess bowed her head and took her leave with the empty chalice, Seth turned to Josslyn, the memory of her impassioned plea for his life out in the desert when they were surrounded filling him with pride and no small wonder. "Yes, I remember."

Her cheeks blushed. "Well, I wasn't about to let him kill you without putting up a fight."

Her bravery put him to shame. How different she was from his preconceived notions of her! "You never cease to surprise me, Josslyn," he murmured. He was nearly as sorry to lose his budding relationship with her as he was to lose Khepesh. "I owe you my life."

She squirmed under his praise. "Don't be ridiculous. Anyone would have done the same."

"I doubt that," he said.

Nephtys's prediction about Josslyn had been uncannily accurate. At least the part about her wisdom and perfection as a candidate for consort of the leader of Khepesh. It ripped his heart out that he had lost his *per netjer,* and along with it the chance to fulfill that prophecy.

Shame swept through him. He still couldn't believe the war was lost! He had been conquered. And without even setting foot on the battlefield, without shedding a drop of enemy blood. He was the prisoner of his nemesis and had lost everything. He alone was the cause of Khepesh's downfall.

His disgrace was deep.

He didn't deserve to be the high priest of Set-Sutekh. He didn't deserve to be the leader of Khepesh. And he certainly didn't deserve to have a woman as worthy and courageous as Josslyn Haliday to sit at his side for eternity.

His heart grew bleak as the emptiness of his future hit him hard. Even more so than when he'd written that poem four thousand years ago.

"You should have left me to my fate," he ground out in despair. "I would be better off dead. And you would be better off without me."

"Don't say that," she protested. "It's not true, and you can't mean it."

He let out a long, unsteady breath. "I've never been more serious in my life."

"I know this is difficult for you, my lord," Rhys stepped in. "More so than anything you've ever had to endure. But the *shemsu* of Khepesh need you to be strong, for their sakes, even if you refuse to do it for your own. You can't give up. Haru-Re may have you in his possession for now, but he has yet to seize the palace or engage our warriors in battle. There is still hope for victory."

Seth let out a humorless laugh. "Perhaps in a parallel universe, as your woman is so fond of saying." It was one of Gillian's favorite expressions, and he'd always found it ironic. Until today.

With a raised hand, he beckoned Josslyn to return to his side. She looked so worried. He felt guilty for his uncharacteristic bout of self-pity, but he felt even more guilty for dragging her into the dangerous mess that had become his life. That, at least, he could remedy.

He summoned his most autocratic mask. "Either way, Lady Josslyn, you will be generously rewarded for your intervention, if it's in my power to do so."

She shook her head. "Seeing you regain your strength is reward enough," she assured him, but she appeared the slightest bit wounded at his cool formality, though she tried to hide it.

It was best this way. She wasn't a follower of Set-Sutekh. She wasn't immortal, hadn't even known about the existence of the *shemsu* three days ago. She wouldn't see the impossibility of his situation. Nor the precariousness of her own, because of the prophecy. If Haru-Re believed she was special to him, she would pay a steep price. Thoth alone knew what would become of her here at Petru. He couldn't bear to be the reason for her unhappiness.

He must distance himself from her, convince Haru-Re she meant nothing to him.

For her own good.

But she made it very difficult. She helped him to lie back on the bed again. Adjusting his pillow, she tenderly pushed a fallen lock of hair off his forehead. "Rest now," she told him softly.

Gillian and Rhys stood watching him with their arms around each other and exchanged quiet smiles.

"Nephtys was right," Gillian said with a clueless sigh. "You two are so right for each other. You belong together."

His heart ached as never before. He pressed a final kiss to Josslyn's palm and reluctantly let it drop.

She stepped away from him. Because of the blood connection, he could feel her discomfort at her sister's observation. But he sensed it wasn't because the idea was so distasteful to her. Far from it—the thought seemed to fill her body with a strange kind of…rightness.

Which was even worse.

Because he felt it, too, in his own.

He arranged his face in a frown, searching for a diplomatic way of crushing those sweet feelings for him that he could feel blossoming within her. "No. Nephtys was wrong," he said. "And so was the prophecy."

After an infinitesimal hesitation, she plastered a false smile upon her full, lovely lips and covered the hurt in her eyes. "Yes, the idea is absurd," she told Gillian with shoulders squared. "I don't believe in psychic visions, you know that. And Nephtys definitely got her wires crossed on this one. I'm going back to the States as soon as I can. Seth and I have already discussed it."

Her sister's mouth dropped open and Rhys's brows shot up.

"Is this true?" Gillian asked Seth incredulously. "You're just letting her go?"

Josslyn was certainly stretching the truth, and she was also referring to a conversation they'd had when he'd been of a vastly different mind about her. Nonetheless, he went along with her. As much as the whole idea of her leaving Egypt made him see red, he would far rather she was safely away from Haru-Re.

"Is that a problem?" he asked Gillian, reinforcing Josslyn's statement with a wisp of a spell of acceptance. "Will she be a danger to the *shemsu* who remain here? Will she expose us—you—to the outside world?"

"No! Of course not," Gillian said, affronted. "Joss would never betray Khepesh, or even Petru. Not in a million years. I just thought…" She shook her head, acquiescence already seeping in to let her sister go. She frowned.

Seth kept his face stoically impassive to prevent himself from betraying how difficult this rejection was for him.

"Unfortunately, my permission doesn't matter," he said. "Whether Josslyn stays or leaves is no longer my decision to make." His voice felt brittle and the taste of the words was as bitter as bile. "I am Haru-Re's prisoner. And knowing him, Khepesh will soon be razed to dust.

Would she be better off here, a captive of Haru-Re, living the life of his defeated enemy and possibly robbed of her mind and her will, as your mother? Or would she be safer and happier back in her home, living the life she had planned and forgetting all about what she has seen here? Indeed, would you not all be better off if you did the same?"

With that, he eased himself gingerly from his smarting side onto his back, sighed deeply and closed his eyes. "My heart is heavy, my head is pounding, my leg is on fire, and my whole body feels trampled by a herd of water buffalo. I will sleep now."

He could feel them all staring at him, and his mind swam with their almost palpable disbelief that he had given up the fight with Haru-Re so easily.

He was so damn tired of always having to be strong! To be the leader. Always having to think of everyone's happiness but his own. Always at war. Always waiting, waiting, waiting for Set-Sutekh to return to this world and take over the rule of his own *per netjer,* as was meant to be. Always so accursedly lonely.

"Stay with him," he heard Rhys quietly urge Josslyn, his voice filled with concern.

"No," Seth said from behind his closed lids. He dipped a spill of anger from the well of frustration within him. "Since Josslyn seems to be more influential with Haru-Re than any of us, I want her to go to him. Find out what he intends for Khepesh."

"Me?" Josslyn exclaimed in consternation. "But I—"

"Tell Lord Rhys when you have Haru-Re's answer," Seth cut her protest off with the curt order. "He and I will decide what's to be done with the *shemsu*. Everyone else is to leave me in peace. From now on I'll see no one but him."

There was absolute silence for several seconds.

"Very well," Josslyn said, hurt tingeing her voice. "If that's what you wish."

"It is," Seth said, without looking at her.

And when they were gone, with an incoherent sound of misery, he released his iron-willed control and let the feelings of anguish rush over him, filling his body with more pain and desolation than he'd ever felt in his life.

For his god.

For his people.

For himself.

But most of all, for the love that could have blessed his life with happiness.

A love that now would never be.

Chapter 18

"He didn't mean it," Gillian said as the three of them sat in the salon of the rooms that she and Rhys shared, to which they'd been brought after being dismissed by Seth. Haru-Re had refused to speak with any of them, and had also denied them permission to seek out Nephtys. Exhausted, Josslyn had then given in to her sister's urging and taken a long nap. Or tried to, anyway. Mostly she'd just stared at the ceiling in a vain attempt at blocking out Seth's rejection. Having finished a light meal, Gillian and Rhys were now attempting to cheer her up.

It wasn't working.

"Like hell he didn't," Joss responded. "You heard him. I obviously mean nothing to him." So much for that bogus proposal. Good thing she'd had no intention of accepting it.

Her sister sent her a sympathetic look, then understanding dawned, widening her eyes. "My God. You're in love with him!"

"Don't be ridiculous," Joss refuted, but her sister knew her too well to be fooled. She might not have fallen as far as love, but she was definitely falling.

"Oh, sis."

"He's ill," Rhys said sympathetically. "He's humiliated and feeling defeated. Give him time to come to terms with what's happening. He'll come around."

Him? What about *her?* What was *she* supposed to do? She'd been thrown into this world against her will! Her few belongings were back at Khepesh—including her money and her passport—and here at Petru she was clearly expected to live in the quarters of a man who never wanted to see her again. Her position was untenable, and her heart was aching as it never had before.

"He can have all the time in the world," Joss said stiffly, battling the hurt and humiliation. She'd sleep on a cot in the kitchen before crawling back to him!

Damn it all! She'd given that man more of herself in a day than she'd ever given anyone else in her entire life. And what did he do? Send her straight into the dangerous grasp of another man. She'd thought they'd turned a corner. She'd thought he'd started to like her as much as she liked him. He'd recited poetry for her, for crying out loud!

"What does he want from me?" she gritted out. "To offer myself to Haru-Re, this time in exchange for *his* freedom instead of my sisters? Because look how well *that* turned out for all of us."

"I'm sure he didn't intend his orders to be taken that way," Gillian said.

"Good, because it's not gonna happen," Joss said heatedly. "I don't want anything to do with Haru-Re. Don't want to talk to him. Don't even want to be in the same room with him. The guy gives me the serious creeps."

"Join the club," Gillian said with a shiver, rubbing her arms. "Aside from the fact that Nephtys would have a fit."

"Trust me, she's got nothing to worry about. Ray doesn't want me, and I sure as hell don't want him."

Not in this lifetime.

"That's not what Seth wants, either," Rhys said confidently.

"He likes you, Joss," Gillian assured her. "A lot. Before he met you he was convinced he wouldn't want you as a consort. But I've watched his face when he looks at you. He's falling for you, sis. Big time."

"Give me a break."

"I agree with Gillian," Rhys said. "I've known Seth for a long time. He's just plain not himself right now." He shook his head. "He is not one to lie down in defeat like a knocked-out boxer. Not while he has a single breath of fight left in his body. Believe me, all of this is the poison talking. Hell, that poison may even have been bespelled to deliberately cause these negative feelings."

Josslyn jetted out an unwilling sigh, wanting so much to believe them. She didn't want to feel this bad about his hurtful rejection. About him. Didn't want it to matter so much. So why did it?

"If you say so."

"I know it's not easy," Rhys said, "but we should do as he asks for now. Nephtys had just sent word that we can come to her now. You must ask her to go with you to Haru-Re. Try and learn what he intends for us. I don't dare speak to him yet. After showing my concern for Seth-Aziz, I'm sure he considers me a traitor to Petru."

Joss looked at her sister in appeal. "You know the situation far better than I do, Jelly Bean. Tell me what you think I should do."

Sitting next to her, Gillian slipped her arms around her and gave her a long hug. "Trust Rhys's judgment, sis. If anyone can steer through these treacherous waters, it's him."

Joss drew in a steadying breath and nodded. "Okay. I'll do it, then. For you and Rhys, and the other immortals who were so kind to me at Khepesh."

"What do you think will happen to us?" Gillian asked Rhys anxiously. "To the *shemsu* of Khepesh?"

"God only knows," he said.

The thought terrified Joss. What would she do if Ray told her Khepesh and everything in it was to be destroyed, as Seth feared, with the *shemsu* of Set-Sutekh—including Rhys—scattered to the winds and the rituals that renewed their immortality to be halted forever? What would become of them?

And most frightening of all… What would become of Seth?

She shouldn't care. After all, he obviously didn't care what happened to her.

But she did. She cared desperately.

The terrible image of a wickedly curved blade slicing

through Seth's neck stole through her mind, making her want to cry out in protest.

She shook off the awful visual. That *wasn't* going to happen. It couldn't.

Suddenly, a commotion erupted in the great hall that led to the residential wing where they were. Shouting and people running, the sound of metal clanging.

Alarm surged through her. "Now what?"

"Wait here," Rhys said. "I'll go see."

"No way," Joss and Gillian said in unison. "We're coming with you."

Rhys frowned, but nodded, and they slipped cautiously out of the rooms and into the corridor, running swiftly in the direction of the great hall. Chaos greeted them.

Rhys grabbed Joss's arm, along with Gillian's, and dragged them behind a giant flowering plant in a nearby alcove. "Stay out of sight. I've been expecting this," he said.

"What's going on?" Gillian asked anxiously.

"Shahin and his warriors must have been spotted getting ready to attack Petru."

"To rescue Seth!" Joss said breathlessly. "Thank God."

"And you," Rhys said. "They won't leave without you either, Josslyn."

"Me?" Joss asked, astounded. "But I'm—"

"You are their leader's prophesied consort," he said somberly. "And Nephtys has foreseen that you are destined to save Khepesh."

"What? That's insane. What could I possibly—"

But she was never able to finish the question. A troop of tall warriors ran past the alcove, their boots tramping in unison like the thundering beat of drums. They wore golden tunics and greaves, with golden Uraeus circlets around their heads, huge curved swords at their sides and grimly determined looks on their faces. There were women as well as men, just as frightening. Some shifted from their human forms as they ran, changing to falcons, panthers, desert wolves and an array of other animals.

Joss, Gillian and Rhys shrank farther behind the sheltering foliage of their hiding place. Rhys twirled his fingers in a motion around them.

"A spell of protection," Gillian whispered. "So they don't find us."

By the time the guards had passed, Joss's heart was thundering nearly as loudly as their receding boots. Fear clawed through her in cold talons. She didn't even want to imagine the coming battle.

She thought of Gemma and the devastation her sister would feel if any harm came to Shahin while rescuing Seth.

"I need to find Nephtys," she whispered urgently as they cautiously emerged. "Someone has to stop this madness!"

Rhys glanced at her. "I'm not disagreeing. But this madness has been going on for a long, long time, Lady Josslyn. How do you propose to stop it?"

"I don't know," she said as determination firmed her resolve. "But someone sure as hell has to try."

My lord!

Seth's eyes sprang open at the urgent hail. He glanced around, expecting to see that Sheikh Shahin had somehow been able to sneak into Petru and his room.

His captain wasn't there. But he must be close, to use the magic of their connection.

Seth opened his mind and reached out to him. *Shahin, what is it? Where are you?*

His answer was swift. *The warriors of Khepesh are approaching Petru, ready to do battle. Can you escape to join us?*

At the request, Seth felt a wave of apathy roll over him, thick and heavy, like Nile mud. What was the point of escape? Or of doing battle?

Shahin, have your warriors turn back. Save yourselves. Don't let the shemsu *perish for naught. The war for supremacy is over, my friend. We have lost, once and for all.*

Shahin's retort came sharp and swift. *Turn back? Are you mad? We haven't even engaged in battle yet!*

Seth scowled. *That is an order!* his mind shouted.

Don't be an ass, my lord! By the staff of Osiris! Haru-Re must have bespelled you to speak like this.

Shock hit Seth squarely in the chest, both at the rudeness of his captain and by the traitorous suggestion that his mind and will had been compromised. The insolence of the man!

He raked both hands through his hair. The sheikh was a meddling old woman! Bespelled? *Seth-Aziz?* The thought was patently absurd! He was a demigod! Much too powerful for such an insidious magical—

Good god.

A sudden dark doubt flew across the periphery of Seth's mind.

Or…was it possible? Could Shahin be right?

No. Not a chance.

And yet, all at once something did not feel quite right about his overly pessimistic attitude. Not when looked at logically. Even in the bleakest days of his past, days that had inspired the poem that still spoke so eloquently of despair, even then he'd been moved to action—if only to end his life.

But then again, this was not a situation he'd faced before. Who was to say it wasn't normal for a vanquished and defeated man to become morose and indifferent?

Shahin's thoughts pleaded with him. *Shift out of the spell, my lord, and come to us. Khepesh needs her leader!*

The captain was wrong. Nothing would save them now. Nothing. And there wasn't a thing Seth could do about it.

But Shahin's urging was strong. And...when it came right down to it, what harm would it do to shift? The poison in Seth's blood would actually dissipate faster, he knew, although he had ignored that fact in favor of... well, feeling sorry for himself.

He blinked. And sighed. Fine. He'd shift, just to prove Shahin wrong.

Still, Seth had to force himself to climb down from the comfortable bed, arguing with his infernal *ba* the whole way.

Though it went against the warning that screamed from every cell of his mind, he said the spell and shifted his body into that of an ordinary tomcat.

And in doing so, he saved himself.

The instant he shifted, the effects of the poison evaporated from his blood and his belly, and the all-encompassing fog of self-pity lifted from his mind.

It was like the blinding of the sun suddenly being extinguished.

His mind snapped to attention, immediately horrified at the resigned pessimism that had permeated his whole being just seconds before.

Damn the eyes of Osiris!

Shahin had been right!

The priestess must have stirred a spell of mental defeat into her arrow poison, along with the painful physical sickness that it had spread through the bones and tissues of his body. The elixir she'd given him had dulled the excruciating pain but had done nothing to counter the disturbing fatalism that had taken over his mind and turned him into a mewling coward. And he had felt sorry for the bitch, having to serve Haru-Re!

Thank Isis Shahin had pushed him into shifting.

More furious than ever, Seth sent his thoughts spinning to Shahin. *I'm on my way. Tell me your plans.*

As he listened to his captain, Seth keenly felt the powerful, roiling energy of the sheikh and his army of Khepesh warriors as they approached Petru. Undoubtedly, the enemy felt it, as well.

Luckily, there was something he could do about that.

Seth summoned a burst of power and called out to his element, summoning a massive wave of chaos and focusing it on the inhabitants of Petru, throwing the *shemsu* of Re-Horakhti into a tailspin of confusion and giving Shahin the chance to get his warriors into position around the palace.

And then, Seth shifted once more. He would have vastly preferred to change into Mihos Rukem and go through the halls of the palace on a rampage, snapping off the heads of Ray's guards with his mighty teeth and jaws. But that would have been pushing his luck.

This time he shifted to a dragonfly, another of his favorite forms. Haru-Re was given to more dramatic figures. He'd been known to shift into huge and fantastical creatures and mythical beasts, a feat of fairly amazing magic. But Seth preferred more natural *ba* forms.

Thus, as a dragonfly, he flew quickly through the halls, unnoticed in the chaos. He saw that his element had been called just in time. The forces of Petru had been mobilizing, rushing to their assigned battle stations to defend the palace against Shahin's attack. With the chaos that had erupted, it would take them ages to reorganize and put up an effective defense, let alone mount an offensive attack to defeat the Khepesh forces.

Seth thought briefly of making a detour to collect Rhys, but decided against it. Lord Rhys had chosen an elegant but impractical Set-animal—a black stallion. There was no way he could make it out of the palace unseen.

Besides, Seth needed Rhys here to protect Josslyn— which his former master steward would do with his life. Of that Seth had no doubt. Rhys had been his best friend for more than a century and knew him better than anyone, save Nephtys. Rhys would not have missed seeing Seth's true feelings for the oldest Haliday sister, despite the necessity he'd felt to reject and distance himself from her. Seth's growing feelings of love and respect for Josslyn had even shone through the miasma of his spell-induced depression. Rhys would know he must do anything required to protect her.

But thinking of Josslyn, Seth could not help himself. Before he left, he desperately needed to see her one last time. Just in case he wasn't granted the opportunity again. And he had to know that she and the others were safe. They would not be affected by his element of chaos, but that didn't mean they weren't in danger from Haru-Re or his warrior guards.

On gossamer wings he flew straight through the palace to Rhys and Gillian's quarters, where he assumed they'd taken her.

She wasn't there.

No one was. The rooms were empty.

His heartbeat sped. Where had she gone? Had Ray taken her as a hostage against the coming battle?

Shahin's voice cut through his worry. *My lord, where are you? The army awaits your arrival. We mustn't delay much longer to keep our advantage.*

Seth groaned inwardly. *I'm on my way. Five minutes.*

He had to find her!

He shot through the grand corridors, where a tumult of disorder still reigned, and on to the palace temple where Nephtys's quarters would be located. He did a hurried search and again found no one in their rooms. The priestesses and acolytes of Re-Horakhti were all in the inner courtyard running around like wild-women, feeling the bite of his chaos and the disturbing energy of his armies gathering outside the walls.

At last he found Nephtys.

She was kneeling quietly before a large scrying bowl,

peering into the water with a look of utter concentration. He circled her head twice to get her attention. She finally looked up. He stopped to hover like a tiny helicopter in front of her face. He didn't have time to shift back and forth to speak to her. He just wanted her to understand what was happening.

After the briefest moment of puzzlement at the sudden appearance of a dragonfly in her room, her brow cleared and she smiled.

"Seth!" She raised her hand and he alighted for three heartbeats on her upturned palm. "Oh, thank the goddess! I knew you'd come back to yourself," she said in a hushed, joyful voice. "Go now. Escape this place before Ray discovers you've gone! Somehow I'll get Josslyn to you at Khepesh. I promise."

He let out a silent curse. Nephtys seemed utterly clueless to the danger that surrounded her!

How had his sister not felt the electric tension in the air and the impending clash of armies? How did she not sense the life-and-death battle that loomed on the horizon, which must surely spell the final end to either Ray or himself?

He swiftly cast a spell to allow his voice to be heard by her. "Nephtys! We are on the brink of war! You must protect yourself!"

Her face refused to cloud. She lifted her hand and spoke softly to him, her eyes dancing with a happiness that was surely destined to turn to profound grief in just a few short hours. "It's okay. Ray told me he loves me! I am to be his true wife, the high priestess of Petru. Oh, *hadu,* I'm so happy! And I swear I'll get your Josslyn to you soon, so you can feel the same joy in your heart as I."

Stunned, all Seth's heart could feel at that news was profound distress.

"You don't understand! I am on my way to join with the warriors of Khepesh, to—" He halted. He could not say it aloud. To tell her that he would do everything in his power to kill Haru-Re in the coming fight.

Though, it wasn't at all certain that he would succeed….

If Seth were to die, what would happen to Josslyn? If he and Shahin and Rhys were all killed, and she was left with no one to defend her against the harsh despotism of Haru-Re, would Nephtys still honor her promise to protect her?

And what if Seth did succeed in killing Haru-Re? Nephtys had carried her bitter need for revenge against her perceived betrayer for five thousand years before this sudden reversal. If, come morning, the man she had never stopped loving was dead, would she feel a need to retaliate against the brother who'd killed him, taking it out on the woman Seth had so unwillingly come to love?

My lord. Shahin's voice reached out to him urgently. *We are about to ride.*

Damnation!

"Find Josslyn," Seth ordered Nephtys. "Get out of Petru and hide yourselves somewhere safe until the outcome of this battle is decided. Please, my sister. I would not have either of you come to harm."

"No!" Nephtys said in alarm. "You mustn't fight!

There is no need for this war now! Ray has changed. He'll listen to me, I swear!"

Seth let out a string of oaths. How could she be so damn naïve? Haru-Re was a man obsessed, and nothing less than total domination over Khepesh would satisfy him.

Seth-Aziz! My lord! The enemy is gathering to charge. You must come now or be left behind!

He didn't have time for arguing with Nephtys!

And he still hadn't found Josslyn, curse the blood of Sekhmet! There was nothing for it. He must trust Rhys to take care of her.

"Nephtys, I beg you, find Josslyn and flee this place," he urged. "Before it's too late." Then he regretfully took wing and flew out through the open window.

"*Hadu,* come back! Don't do this!" Nephtys's voice shouted after him. "He loves me! *He loves me!*"

With his sister's desperate admonishments ringing in his ears, Seth shot past the garden, soaring over the outer wall of Petru and out into the vast burning desert where his faithful followers awaited him.

I'm here, Seth told Shahin as he approached the host.

Silently he recited the incantation to turn his dragonfly body back to human. Without slowing, he conjured a massive warhorse the color of midnight to carry him into the ranks of his men. Robing himself in the magical black tunic and breeches and flowing scarlet *bisht* of the high priest of Khepesh, he wanted to look every inch the powerful demigod of Set-Sutekh, God of Darkness and Lord of Chaos, Ruler of the Hot Winds and Guardian of the Night Sky as he galloped into the heart of his army.

At long last, he would fight the final battle for supremacy between darkness and light in the land of Egypt.

And Seth-Aziz intended to win.

Chapter 19

The sun was just setting as the Khepesh warriors of
Set-Sutekh drew their rearing mounts into long ranks
along the western horizon on the dunes above the palace
of Petru.

Fingers of the blackest blackness stretched greedily
over their silver-helmeted heads, painting over the ever-
darkening indigo sky as though reaching out to snuff
the remnants of light that still glowed over the palace of
their enemy. It was like the hand of the god squeezing
the life from his rival, sending the earth below to float
unconscious into the calm tranquility of perpetual
night.

Were they to prevail in the coming battle, Seth-Aziz
wondered if that would really have happened—perpetual
darkness—had the ancient gods still made Earth their
abode. Somehow, he doubted even winning this endless
war in the name of Set-Sutekh would turn the light to

dark. Not now, living as they all were in the age of technology, logic and one God.

Was that blasphemy?

As Set-Sutekh's high priest, charged with keeping the rituals of the *per netjer* alive and well in Egypt down through the ages, Seth had never before doubted the god he had served so faithfully for so long. Indeed, he did not doubt him now.

Darkness and chaos were the great rulers of the universe. How could anyone dispute that? In the absence of all else, of any kind of control or imposition of an outside force or order, darkness and chaos prevailed. Always.

Seth loved the darkness, reveled in its mystery, wrapped himself in its anonymity, was comforted by its constancy.

Chaos, however, was a more difficult taskmaster. Seth had a deep, instinctive need to control the chaos of life on earth. To outward appearances, Khepesh might give the illusion of anarchy, its *shemsu* free to do anything they wanted, pursue any lifestyle they wished, so long as they served the god in the way they had promised when joining the *per netjer*. But in fact, Seth-Aziz ruled the palace with an iron hand. He did not tolerate any behavior that fell outside their long-established—albeit very liberal—set of rules.

No. Not blasphemy. Not at all.

Egypt had always been a land of contradictions. Of duality. Of opposites. She embraced them. As did Seth-Aziz.

As a native of this land, those things had never bothered him. Nor the *shemsu* he ruled. Those immortals who'd not been born here had chosen this place and this life, often because of those very qualities. Many worshipped other gods, or believed in the One. It mattered not, for darkness and chaos were part of them all. All but the force of pure light they had come to battle.

But Seth wondered now, for the very first time, what would happen to this world when this war was over and a single side—one dark, one light—had claimed victory over the other. Would one aspect come to dominate the world, plunging it into a time of monochromatic political ideals and imposed philosophical conformity? Was that really a good thing?

It was a dilemma to ponder.

He was roused from his thoughts by the approach of a pair of riders. In the falling light of dusk, he couldn't see their features.

Unlike Petru's camel-mounted army, Seth and Shahin's warriors had chosen to go into battle on horseback. Their conjured warhorses were huge and powerful, black as obsidian with glowing red eyes, muscles rippling under their glistening coats, tails flicking, nostrils snorting and hooves prancing in anticipation of the coming action. Magical glyphs and symbols of their god adorned their hides, drawn in shining silver paint that reflected the beams of the moon, making them glow like ancient ghostly apparitions, which he supposed they were.

When the riders approached, he saw the front man was Shahin. The captain galloped up to Seth, lifting his gloved hand in greeting.

Seth returned the salute, and they grasped each other's arms in a warrior's clasp of brotherhood and good luck. Seth saw that the other rider still shadowed Shahin, the smaller horse prancing at Shahin's side in excitement. To his shock, he realized the second rider was Gemma Haliday, dressed as the rest of the *shemsu,* both male and female, in black tunics and loose Bedouin trousers. She gripped a lethal sword in her fist, her expression conveying that she meant business.

Still stunned, Seth looked from her to Shahin. "Is this wise?" he asked, loathe to question the presence of anyone who wished to fight for Khepesh. But if she were to fall in battle, Josslyn would never forgive him, regardless of the outcome.

"I stand by my man, and my lord Seth-Aziz," she said, her back straight and her eyes shiny.

"But you are mortal," he reminded her. "You could so easily die."

Her lower lip trembled. "The fate of Shahin and Khepesh is my own. I've no wish to live without him."

Seth's heart swelled, and for the first time in a long, long time he felt a true stab of envy, for his captain and the devotion he had found in this woman's love. How he longed for a love as true and pure!

You are a very lucky man, my friend.

Though Shahin gave no outward sign, Seth felt his friend's soul overflow with love. *Don't think I am unaware of that, my lord.*

To Gemma, Seth said aloud, "Your loyalty does you proud, Gemma Haliday. I fervently hope I can return the favor one day."

Just then, against the setting sun, another two riders galloped up, their stallions snorting and lathered from a run. Seth recognized them at once. It was Lord Rhys. And with him—

"Gillian!" Gemma cried out, joy mingled with dismay.

"Gem," Gillian returned with a brave but tremulous smile. "Thought I'd find you here."

The two sisters hugged fiercely, tears brimming onto their lashes.

"Oh, Jelly Bean, it's too dangerous!" her sister said, dread and concern running rampant in the words. "You shouldn't have come!"

Gillian swallowed. "And let you have this adventure all by yourself? Not a chance." Only the slight quavering of the young woman's voice betrayed her fear.

Seth's heart was humbled by the faith he was witnessing. Not just in each other and their chosen men, but in him and Khepesh, too. Neither woman had had to show up here to do battle on this day. He would not have blamed them for a single second for staying away.

He turned to Rhys and gave his best friend a smile that made his soul ache. Past the growing lump in his throat, he said, "My loyal Englishman, come to watch my back as always."

Rhys returned his smile, his eyes touched by a century of steadfast friendship. "I am your humble servant, my lord."

Seth answered as he had a thousand times before. "You are neither servant nor particularly humble, Lord Rhys, yet it pleases me to hear you say so." He clasped his master steward's arm as he had his captain's and added, "It pleases me even more to have you by my side on this final day of reckoning."

"Try and keep me away," the Englishman returned somberly. And as if reading Seth's unspoken fears, he said, "Lady Josslyn is safe, my lord. The Lady Nephtys came to fetch her and said she'd seen you. That you had instructed her to keep Josslyn safe from harm."

Seth nodded with a measure of relief. Still, an un-bidden trickle of foreboding seeped through his bones. He trusted his sister. He did. She had never let him down. Not once in over five-thousand years. But…if Haru-Re forced her to make a choice, with whom would Nephtys throw in her lot? Her adopted brother or the only man she had ever truly loved? Seth feared he knew the answer.

Would Josslyn be caught in the crossfire?

Pain razored through his chest.

And at last he understood the truth.

Seeing Gemma and Gillian's devotion to his two friends, and their loyalty to a world in which they had only recently landed and embraced as their new home, Seth knew what was desperately missing from his life.

He loved Josslyn. He didn't ever want to lose her.

He'd been a fool to reject her and send her away. She would have been as true a companion and soul mate as her sisters had proven to be to Shahin and Rhys. Given half a chance, Josslyn Haliday would have been here, right by his side, sword in hand. He knew that as surely as he now knew he didn't want to live on this earth without her, either.

He prayed to the gods that he would survive this day and have the chance to tell her so and beg her forgiveness.

He thought uneasily of her, left on her own in the palace of his enemy with no protector but a priestess with mixed loyalties and unable to do magic on her own. He sent a powerful guardian spell hurtling toward her and hoped it would penetrate the warded walls of Petru.

Then he lifted his hand and swirled a double spell of protection around her two brave sisters, weaving them together with the invisible shields he felt Shahin and Rhys had already cast around them. The magic would not save the women from killing sword blows in the coming fight, but the combined protection was strong and would cause stray slices to glance harmlessly off them. He prayed it would be enough to keep them both alive.

The oranges and reds of the dying sun threw ribbons of vivid color against the darkening backdrop of the night sky. There were no stars out yet, just a kaleidoscope of the ever-changing palette of sunset over the desert.

It was a beautiful thing to behold.

If one must die, it should be on a night like this.

And Seth was ready to die if he must. Haru-Re's tyranny aside, he could not live in a world of perpetual light even if only in metaphor. He would go mad if there were no shadows to step into when he needed a place to disappear. No endless void of black space with which to fill the universe of his imagination. No mysterious night in which to feed the banquet of his senses.

"It is time, my lord," Shahin said, gesturing to the walls of Petru, where scores of golden warriors swarmed like huge glowing fireflies in the light of sunset, lining up, brandishing weapons, preparing for their attack. It would take at least fifteen minutes of hard riding from their gathering point to reach the palace walls. Shahin had waited until the last gasp of the waning sun, for the symbolic effect, and for the practical advantage of the glare in their enemies' eyes. "By the time we get there it will be full darkness."

Darkness was their world. They would take every advantage they could get.

Seth nodded. Together, the five of them—Seth-Aziz, Sheikh Shahin, Lord Rhys Kilpatrick, and Gemma and Gillian Haliday—cantered their mounts to the front of the ranks of Khepesh warriors.

Seth's majestic stallion reared up and pawed the air, claiming his place as the alpha in the order of the magical beasts, somehow knowing it was the natural place of his master.

There was a hum of tension in the air, thick and electric. The drugging, spicy smell of preternatural energy wafted on the breeze that teased above the army as from a field of opium poppies in full blossom. Magical power ebbed and flowed from the *shemsu* in rivers of energy, raising the hairs on even Seth's arms and buzzing through his brain like a horde of locusts. He'd never felt the like in all his days.

The warrior guardians of Khepesh were as committed as he.

Tonight it was all or nothing.

Live, and rule the whole world.

Or lose, and perish from the earth forever.

At his nod, Sheikh Shahin gave a signal, and as one the *shemsu* raised their scimitars. They all looked to Seth-Aziz.

Pride swelled his chest to bursting.

"All praise to Set-Sutekh!" he shouted, raising his own weapon above his head. "We fight!"

"For the glory of good!" the men shouted back as one.

With a heart filled with love for his people, but scant hope for a future, Seth-Aziz gave his final order. *"To the death!"*

The men let out a roar of approval. The horses reared, eyes wild.

The last sliver of the sun went down behind them.

And the immortal followers of Set-Sutekh charged toward the stronghold of the enemy, prepared to meet their destiny.

Chapter 20

"We must hurry!"

Nephtys urged Josslyn to move faster. They were practically running up the narrow stairs, but Haru-Re was waiting for her. Ray had summoned Nephtys to the highest parapet that jutted from the top of Petru's enclosure wall, where he was said to be pacing and shouting orders to the commanders of his vast legion of followers. He'd asked Nephtys to bring the other woman to him before the battle was engaged, and sent one of his guards to accompany them—for their protection, he'd said. She didn't want to believe it was to ensure she obeyed. Not after the exquisite afternoon they'd shared.

She was still floating. Because today he'd made love to her for the very first time.

Oh, they'd had sex before. Lots of times. And he'd fucked her plenty, too. But never before today had they made love together. Sweet, lingering, heart-rendingly emotional love.

"I love you, Nephtys," he'd whispered softly in her ear when they'd lain in each other's arms afterward. "I want you to be mine forever."

And she knew he'd meant it, because he hadn't pierced her flesh with his fangs nor drank of her blood. Instead, he'd punctured a small hole in the underside of his wrist and fed her with drops of his own blood, to cool the addiction for him that raged within her.

Even now she felt intoxicated by it. Euphoric.

His.

But in the air she also felt the distant pounding of a thousand hooves. Were the warriors of Khepesh already on the move?

"Nephtys, slow down!" Josslyn called, breathing hard as they clambered up the endless circular granite staircase inside the soaring tower, plastering themselves against the cold, rounded walls every few minutes to let more warriors go past. "You're killing me!"

Nephtys shot a sharp glance down at her. "I'd never hurt you, Josslyn. I hope you know that. I couldn't. My brother loves you."

The mortal woman blinked up at her and then halted at a landing to bend over and catch her breath. "I think you've gotten faulty information somewhere. Seth wants nothing to do with me."

Nephtys fought to control the other feeling that was nearly drowning her: *fear*...for Seth's safety. For his very life. Seth-Aziz had neglected to tell her the battle he'd spoken of was to take place *today!* She could feel the army's approach, felt the roiling presence of Shahin's warriors practically outside the walls, charging in for combat, and she was terrified. Why had Seth done this? She'd *told* him she could convince Haru-Re to leave Khepesh in peace, now that she had claimed his heart! Why hadn't Seth *believed* her? All she'd needed was a little more time!

Josslyn was still breathing hard, so Nephtys stirred the air with her fingers and sent it to fill her lungs and said, "Trust me, men are clueless idiots. This I know."

Her brother's lover straightened, testing her breathing. "Wow. How did you do that?" She shook her head. "Never mind. Look, you won't get an argument from me about men being clueless. But you're wrong about Seth. He's made it pretty clear—"

"Yes, yes." Nephtys waved a hand impatiently. They had to *move!* "My brother is stubborn as a donkey and likes to think he's in charge of everything around him, including his emotions. But as you and I both know so well, emotions are impossible to govern. They are what they are, and the goddess help us if we try to ignore them or pretend they don't exist."

"Sometimes one doesn't have a choice," the other woman muttered.

Nephtys turned and hurried up the last few steps, anxious to reach Haru-Re before he gave the order to charge out to meet the Khepesh army, and Josslyn followed.

"You love him, too," Nephtys said approvingly. She heard Josslyn exhale but otherwise remain silent. No denial. Good. That would help. She'd been desperately formulating a plan to try to stop what was happening.

Josslyn was the cornerstone. Having her cooperation was key.

They reached the top of the parapet, and her worst fears were realized.

Ray stood like a masthead upon the narrow battlement, stalking back and forth, peering out over the vast, undulating desert toward a sliver of sun that hovered on the western horizon. Against the shrinking arc of molten brilliance, the black slash of her brother's army rode, resplendent, mounted on the backs of massive black stallions, galloping hard in ranks three deep across the golden dunes.

Though still in the far distance, they were advancing quickly. And they were glorious! The sight made her shiver in both awe and terror.

As Haru-Re watched them come, a deep scowl was etched on his handsome face. *He* gave her shivers, too.

She could feel his preternatural energy sizzle and pop with his anger. The air around him glittered with sparks, and when he tipped his head back and raked his fingers through his hair, shimmering streamers of fire leapt around his head like a halo of golden snakes.

Sweet Isis, even in such a precarious situation, the man made her knees weak. His body had the perfection of a demigod, his mind was as sharp as his vampire fangs, his strength terrible and his power awesome.

She yearned to belong to him in every way, with a craving that filled every pore of her body with need, every beat of her heart with love.

And yet, she could not let him hurt her brother.

Outside the walls, the vast army of Petru had

assembled, the warriors riding a host of ghost camels so numerous it was impossible to see the ground below.

Here, on the battlements, scores of men and women ran to and fro carrying longbows and shouting to one another to get into position. If she didn't know better, she'd think Seth's element still held sway over the palace. But Ray had long since smashed through the spell of chaos and shattered it.

Thinking of Ray's immense powers, and the vastness of the army he had gathered, her heart quailed. Seth and his comparative handful of men didn't stand a chance!

Ray spotted her and Josslyn, and a brief smile curved his mouth as he turned his head to follow their progress along the rampart. She hurried toward him, followed by the other woman and their trusty guard.

When she finally reached Ray, he caught her up by the waist and lifted her to meet his lips. *"Meruati,"* he murmured, kissing her. "You've come to me."

"Of course," she returned, kissing him back, passion sweeping through her. Being held in his arms was like floating on clouds of joy. "Did you doubt it?"

He just smiled, then glanced at Josslyn. The smile faded, and he spoke to her. "It seems your faithless consort has deserted you to my tender care," he said with no small satisfaction ringing in his voice.

Josslyn's gaze went in dismay from the galloping warriors of Khepesh to the eager armies of Petru gathering below and back to Haru-Re. "If you mean Seth-Aziz, I am not his consort," she said. "And I wasn't deserted. I chose to stay here in Petru."

Ray's brow rose. "Indeed?"

"My parents live here. Although I still haven't been

allowed to see them," she added, the words tinged with accusation. "Why not?"

"First I must be convinced of your loyalty," he responded, his expression turning hard. He gestured toward Seth's advancing army. "Your sister, it appears, is not to be trusted. Can you blame me for suspecting you?"

Josslyn's face faltered and she glanced anxiously back at the galloping warriors. "What are you talking about?"

With a small motion, Ray conjured a spyglass and handed it to her. "Take a look at the group of riders leading the charge. Recognize anyone?"

She did, and gasped in horror. "No! What are they *doing?*"

Nephtys swiped the glass from her and peered through it. "Blessed Isis," she said in dismay. Both of Josslyn's sisters as well as Lord Rhys were riding stallions next to Seth and Shahin, black robes flying in the wind like raven wings, weapons flashing and glinting in the dying light.

"Ray! You must stop this!" she cried, dropping the instrument and grasping his arms. "This isn't necessary!"

"Oh, but it is," he refuted, a gleam of impending victory glowing in his eyes. "This is the moment I've awaited for five millennia. Finally I have you at my side, and now I shall have all the world bowing at my feet, mine alone, to rule over as I wish."

She shook her head. "No," she breathed. "You mustn't do this. You can't!"

"On the contrary, I can, and I will," he growled.

"Please! You mustn't hurt my brother!"

He just laughed. He snapped his fingers, pointed at her and Josslyn, and gave the command she'd dreaded in her heart.

"Seize them!"

Chapter 21

Instantly four of Haru-Re's warriors surrounded Joss and Nephtys, grasping their arms so they couldn't escape.

Joss struggled against their steely hold. "No! Damn it, let go of me!"

Fear gripped her nearly as hard as the men did.

Coming up here had been a *huge* mistake. She glanced down at the quickly advancing army of Khepesh, and her heart pounded out of control. She should never have trusted Haru-Re. And she wasn't so sure about Nephtys, either.

"Ray!" Nephtys cried, pulling at her arms, betrayal flaying her expression. "What is this? Tell them to let me go!"

"Meruati," Haru-Re said soothingly, coming over to Nephtys and gently putting his hand against her cheek. He kissed her and said, "It's all right. It's just for show.

I would never let my men harm you, you must know
that. But play along with me now. If Seth-Aziz thinks
his sister and his chosen consort are both in mortal
danger, he will surrender without a fight. No one will
be hurt or killed."

Oh, please.

Despite her quaking limbs, Joss barely resisted
snorting. Surely, Nephtys wasn't falling for that load?
She might be in love, but she wasn't stupid.

"I am *not* Seth's chosen consort!" Joss yelled at him
as a distraction, to give the priestess a chance to get hold
of herself and think straight. Besides, she was really
getting tired of everyone saying that. Were they all deaf
and blind? "Seth-Aziz doesn't give a damn about me,
so your plan won't work!"

He spared her a narrowed glance. "That's not what
I've heard. But even if it's true, your sisters will hardly
let him sacrifice you."

Oh, God. Her pulse took off at a tear. For a second
she'd forgotten Gemma and Gillian were with Seth. But
Ray's assessment was correct. Her sisters would cut off
Seth's head themselves before letting anything happen
to her.

"You're wrong," she bluffed, but even to herself the
statement lacked conviction. She looked to Nephtys for
aid. If they were going to get out of this, it would have
to be through her influence.

Nephtys gazed at Haru-Re with an expression so
wounded that Joss thought his heart must be made of
stone. "I can't believe you're doing this," the priestess
lamented, tears welling in her eyes. "You said you love

me. You said you want to make me the happiest woman in the history of time!"

The hardness of his face shifted, and with a sigh he signaled her captors to let her go. His voice softened as he took her hands and kissed her knuckles. "I do, my only heart. I want to lay the world at your feet. To give you the bright sun and the two horizons and all the goodness that enlightenment brings. But you have to see, to do that I must claim victory over Khepesh and Seth-Aziz."

"Why?" Joss demanded desperately, when it looked like Nephtys might cave at his pretty promises. "You already have all that. What does eliminating Khepesh do for you, other than satisfy your insatiable greed for power?"

Fury swept over Ray's features. Lightning flashed overhead, lighting up the darkening sky over the palace. "By the love of Horus, you are insolent!"

The grip of his warriors tightened.

He slashed up a hand and boomed, "Hold her up so her lover can see what he risks with this attack!"

She screamed in terror as his men obeyed, lifting her high over the upper parapet. They were at least three stories above the ground, of which a narrow band around the foot of the wall was covered with large, sharp rocks that had been arranged in colorful, beautiful patterns. But from her perspective they looked positively lethal. No doubt even immortals who fell onto their jagged points would be smashed beyond healing.

Oh, God!

She wanted to twist and jerk herself free, but one

slip of her captors' fingers and she would bounce off the wall and plunge to an instant, horrible death.

She stifled another scream when they thrust her far out over the wall's edge, and a circle of brightness appeared around her as though she were lit up by a floodlight. She held her breath, praying for her life.

She knew Seth must have heard her screams through their blood connection and could feel her abject fear. As proof, the gait of his stallion faltered and he wheeled about, peering up and yelling to those around him. His muscular horse reared and pawed the air as he reined it in and stared straight up at her across the thousand yards of desert that still separated them.

The warriors charging at full tilt behind him wheeled their mounts away in confusion to avoid mowing him down. Against the fast-dimming orange and yellow of the sunset's last glow, she could see Shahin's silhouette gallop along the front line, shouting orders so the army slowed and eventually came to a chaotic standstill.

Sweet Jesus.

Joss forced herself not to look down. Told herself not to search out her sisters in the distant turmoil. But it was impossible. They were much closer now, and she saw clearly when Gillian and Gemma converged on Seth and started to argue and gesticulate at her and then him. He didn't appear to answer, didn't even seem to hear them, just continued to stare up at her hanging there like a Christmas angel as his stallion reared and chomped at its bit to start the charge again.

Seth wasn't the only one being yelled at. Behind her, she heard Nephtys argue with Ray.

"—barbaric! I will not go along with this savagery!

I never believed the awful things they said about you, always thought you were a good man beneath it all, but now I—"

"Enough of this!" Ray shouted. Joss cringed as bolts of lightning flashed through the sky above, now darkened nearly to black. "Your brother can go straight to the fires of Hades! *He* is the one attacking *me*, in case you missed noticing!"

"Because you've been threatening Khepesh for weeks! *And* you took Seth prisoner!" she argued back just as vehemently. "He probably thought you were going to execute him and burn his palace to the ground!"

There was a silent pause, and Joss wished like hell she could turn around and see what was happening. But when she heard Nephtys gasp, it wasn't hard to guess.

"Blessed Hathor!" Nephtys cried. "You *were* going to kill him! Oh, Ray, you promised me you'd back away from this horrible feud if I consented to wed right away!"

"I'll back away when that viper of a brother of yours is nailed into his fancy coffin," he shot back. *"Permanently!"*

Joss heard Nephtys gasp even louder. "And what about Josslyn?" The priestess's question wavered with anguish. "Do you plan to execute her, too? To let your minions drop her from this parapet to her death?"

Omigod. Dread swamped over Joss, and an unbidden sound of dismay escaped her throat. Did Nephtys *have* to bring that up? She squeezed her eyes shut against the burning tears that threatened to break loose.

"Killing the daughter of one of my immortals is the last thing I want to do," Ray clipped out. "But Josslyn

Haliday's fate is now firmly in the hands of Seth-Aziz."

In a strangled tone, Nephtys protested, "No. I won't let you. If you do this awful thing, Ray, I swear I'll—"

"You are mine now!" he barked at her. *"And you will do as I say!"*

Joss heard Nephtys swallow audibly. "So that's how it is. I thought you were willing to change, for me, Ray. To stop this never-ending madness, because you love me," she said, in almost a whisper. "But I can see now I was wrong. So very wrong."

"Nephtys—" he began impatiently.

But he never got the chance to finish.

Because Nephtys went calmly to the edge of the battlement and stepped up onto the parapet next to Joss. The priestess smiled sadly at her and whispered, "I'm so sorry."

And then she jumped.

Chapter 22

"Noooo!"

Seth could not stifle the anguished roar that erupted from him as his sister stepped over the side of Petru palace wall and started to fall toward the earth. His heart screamed, tortured, because he could never get there in time to save her.

Even so, he lunged from his saddle, shifting before he hit the ground. He changed to an eagle, flying as swift as an arrow toward her. Perhaps he could—

But before he reached her, a huge, scaly monster with giant wings swooped under her falling body and caught her on its back.

Haru-Re had shifted into a golden dragon just in time to save Nephtys.

Swallowing down his thundering heart from his throat, Seth's eagle flew close and circled the beast to make sure his sister was all right.

She was quietly weeping and clinging to the dragon's neck as Haru-Re winged her back up to the top of the rampart…where Seth saw that Josslyn was finally being hauled back in over the parapet by the bastard warriors who'd held her over the edge.

Fury the likes of which he'd never known burst through him. By the *gods,* he would avenge this outrage!

Suddenly he saw that Josslyn was not tracking Haru-Re and Nephtys's progress through the sky, but his own…the only person of the dozens gathered on the ramparts whose eyes were on the lone bird of prey rather than the dramatic rescue. Did she know the circling eagle was Seth?

He swooped closer.

Josslyn's face was a portrait of worry as she shook her head at him and frantically tried to wave him off.

He didn't think so.

As the dragon landed on the battlement with its precious burden, Seth spun down after them and shifted. He landed on his feet in front of Josslyn, his back to her and his sword gripped in his hand, ready to cut anyone to ribbons who tried to come between them.

With a roar, he unleashed his element. Chaos descended on the warriors of Petru, both on the high ramparts and those beyond the wall of the palace. Their camels broke ranks and started to run amok, spitting and bucking off their riders, who scurried back into the palace in a jumble of confusion.

In the middle of it all, unaffected, Seth and Haru-Re squared off. Nephtys was still weeping, an arm held up defensively across her face as the dragon stood on its hind legs and gathered her in with its wing. Flame poured from its mouth, licking at the sphere of protection that Seth had thrown up around himself and Josslyn. He could feel her behind him, hands shakily gripping his tunic, fingers digging into the flesh of his arms.

The air was electric with dark power. It roiled and churned around them, whipping up in a hot, foreboding breeze that burned at his skin.

Seth wanted to grab Nephtys away from the beast that was Haru-Re and flee with her and Josslyn back to Khepesh and safety. But he couldn't reach his sister. Not tucked as she was under the wing of the fire-breathing monster. Not without leaving Josslyn open to harm.

And he would not risk Josslyn.

Nor would he leave Nephtys.

Haru-Re raised up and roared back, fire bursting forth from his mouth, preternatural energy spraying from every shiny scale on his huge body. *He must kill the beast.* Seth summoned every ounce of strength he possessed and every last vestige of magical power and lifted his sword high above his head.

He may die this night, but by the balls of Mithra he would take Haru-Re with him!

They each took a step toward the other, faces set in masks of hatred. He started to swing his sword.

"Stop!" Josslyn's authoritative command cut through the night air, for the second time startling both Seth and Haru-Re into halting in their tracks.

She shoved around him and stood with her fists bunched on her hips, staring the two of them down like the very image of Isis.

"Are you both *insane?* Why? Why are you doing this?" she demanded.

He and Haru-Re glared at each other for a split second, then swung their gazes to the mortal woman who had dared to interfere.

By the *gods,* it would take a thousand years to list all the reasons for the eternal battle between Seth and Haru-Re. Between Khepesh and Petru. Between darkness and light.

And yet, as he thought about them, each of those infinite reasons slowly withered and paled in Seth's mind, leaving but a single one: the fact that Haru-Re was threatening the two women Seth loved more than life itself.

Standing here today, expecting to die, *ready* to die, he realized there was only one thing that mattered in this world.

Love.

Everything else was meaningless.

"Get behind me, woman," he ordered Josslyn, suddenly terrified he would lose her at the exact moment he finally understood what Nephtys had been telling him all along.

Josslyn Haliday is your soul mate.

"No," she said, stubborn to the last.

Sekhmet's teeth! He wanted to grab her and—

Nephtys wriggled out from under Haru-Re's dragon wing and ran over to Josslyn. They wrapped their arms around each other and stood their ground, united against him and Haru-Re.

"Josslyn's right," Nephtys said tearfully. "You are both so blind! I can't stand this!"

With a swirl of golden scales, Haru-Re shifted back to his human form. But instead of the fire-breathing fury Seth had expected to see on the face of his enemy, he saw only bewilderment and dismay as Ray turned toward Nephtys.

"Why did you do it, *meruati?* Why in the name of the gods did you jump like that?"

Her eyes filled, and she looked miserable. "Because I can't stand by and watch the two men I love kill each other! I would rather die than to have to choose one of you over the other."

Her words stabbed at Seth's heart. Hadn't he just thought exactly the same thing about her and Josslyn?

"What would you have us do?" Ray demanded hoarsely. Seth frowned, wondering where this was coming from.

Josslyn's shoulders squared. "Make peace," she said, the words echoing loudly across the battlement.

"Now it's *you* who's insane," Ray ground out, more like himself, casting a sidelong glance at Seth. Then Ray looked back at Nephtys and beckoned to her. "Come to me, my heart. Please. I need you with me."

She shook her head. "I'm sorry. I can't. Not unless I know things will be different between you and my brother."

"But I don't see how that's possible!" Ray said, spilling frustrated sparks from his fingertips.

"I'm told," Josslyn interjected, "that you two are the last of the vampire demigods. That once there were dozens of you, and hundreds of *peru netjeru* flourishing in Egypt. Thousands of *shemsu* keeping the ancient rituals. Now they're all gone. Only Khepesh and Petru are left. Do either of you really want to be the last one standing in this twilight of the gods?"

"Of course!" Haru-Re said in bafflement, obviously not getting the nuance of what she was saying. "Who wouldn't want to be the sole ruler of the immortal world?"

"Me," Seth answered with a tired sigh. Frankly, he didn't care either way. He just wanted the followers of Set-Sutekh to be left to live as they wished, with no interference from the outside world and no fears of their home being attacked or taken over by a megalomaniac demigod.

Haru-Re frowned at him. "I don't believe you."

Seth shrugged. "It's true. I am bone-weary of this eternal struggle for dominion. I miss the friends who have been taken. I despair of the old gods ever returning, and I yearn to spend the rest of my nights puzzling the meaning of life, wrapped in the arms of my beloved."

He glanced at Josslyn, who was listening with parted lips and a look of hopeful wonder shining in her eyes. She swallowed and turned back to Ray. "You see? You've been fighting all this time for something that is now freely offered for a word of conciliation."

Ray's gaze sought Nephtys and hesitated a long moment. As though he understood the import of his response to his future with her.

"This…this is what I've wanted for as long as I can remember. To be the sole demigod left on earth. To have the power and magic of this world at my fingertips. To be the ruler of all the immortals and spread the golden light of dawn throughout the land."

"Yes," Nephtys said wistfully. "I knew that."

"But," he continued, "I would give it all up, *meruati*, if that is your wish. You are more important to me than any possession or promise of power. I don't want to lose you a second time. I couldn't bear it. Please say you'll come back to me."

Seth could see the heart of his sister melt completely. "Do you mean it?"

"With all my heart."

"Then I will. Oh, Ray, I will."

"And by the crown of Horus, please Nephtys, swear you'll never, ever jump from a place higher than two feet again."

A slow smile curved her lips. "My sweetest love, I knew you'd catch me. I know you'll always catch me, Ray."

The Guardian of the Sun looked stunned. "That's a hell of a lot of trust to have in a man like me."

"Yes," she said softly. "It is."

Chapter 23

The two armies were recalled, and at dawn the next morning a joint Great Council meeting was convened, where Joss's plan was to be argued by the leaders of Khepesh and Petru.

It seemed like a no-brainer to her. But then again, she was the new kid on the block. Her sisters, however, agreed with her, so she was pretty sure it was a good plan. Gillian and Gemma sat in the audience with their men, lending moral support as Joss explained her solution to the somewhat stunned—and very suspicious—councils of the two *peru netjeru*.

"Set-Sutekh is the God of Darkness and Lord of the Night Sky," Josslyn said after a few words of greeting and introduction. "Re-Horakhti is Lord of Light and God of the Sun."

"Everyone already knows all that," one particularly cantankerous old goat pointed out immediately.

"So then the answer is obvious," she continued undaunted. "Rule jointly. Khepesh shall be masters of the night, and Petru will reign during the day." She smiled. It was so easy. That they hadn't put this in place themselves about four thousand years ago was flabbergasting.

Still, every member of both councils frowned.

"That's it?" one asked, to head shakes and murmurs from the rest. "*That's* your answer?"

"In all its simplicity. Really, what more is needed?" She knew there were issues to be solved, but really, people. Share or die. Didn't they see that?

The cantankerous goat rose to his feet. "Ridiculous. This addresses nothing," he pronounced, starting to leave.

Gemma, the cultural anthropologist and born mediator, prompted her with a nod from the back of the room.

"Naturally," Joss continued, "the Great Councils will have to hammer out the details, so everything is divided fairly between you. That is an immense responsibility, which will take all the intelligence and skill of both councils to accomplish."

The old man halted and turned.

She smiled again. "But I am sure that won't be a problem. The main thing tonight is that you all agree that the hostilities must end."

"Why?" the old man demanded, reminding her a little too much of herself. Always asking why. Never just accepting what was right in front of her face.

"There is good reason for our strife," he said hotly.

"The followers of the sun will never bow down to the darkness! It is unnatural!"

Not that she thought you should just meekly accept anything handed to you. But sometimes, when appropriate, you had to take some things on faith…or go crazy.

This whole bizarre world was a case in point.

An unruly discussion erupted among the councils and the audience about what it would mean to them personally, and about the nature of light and dark, and about whether one's preference denoted good or evil in the world, and if it said something about one's inner soul to choose to serve the shadow world versus the supposed state of enlightenment.

Not that the leader of Petru seemed terribly enlightened to her. The supposed "Guardians of Darkness" seemed far more tolerant and open-minded.

But she let them all talk. She trusted they'd come to the same conclusion she had: If they continued on their present path, they were surely all doomed to perish in the struggle, because neither would give in.

She glanced over at Seth, who occupied the larger of two ornate silver thrones placed on the western side of the grand audience chamber where the meeting was being held. She sat in the smaller one. It felt a bit weird, a bit frightening, to find herself in such an exalted position, but Nephtys had insisted. Nephtys herself sat on one of two golden thrones on the eastern side of the room, next to Haru-Re.

Seth was watching Joss in return, pride beaming from his eyes. His intense regard made her squirm a little.

Seeing it, he offered her his hand. She gratefully took it, needing the reassurance of his touch.

She loved the strength she felt in his long fingers, in the thick brush of power that purled over her skin from his fingertips. She also loved his square-jawed face and aristocratic nose, his flashing black eyes and his imposing body. He wasn't picture-perfect handsome, but God, was he ever sexy. Her insides did summersaults and her toes curled just looking at him.

Let alone the shivers he gave her as they lay together in the intimacy of his bed.

Memories flooded through her of the few times they'd spent in each other's arms. Lord, how she loved being with him!

He'd taken her again last night.

After the harrowing experience on the walls of Petru, he hadn't let her out of his sight. His personal guard had come to collect them, and to her relief, Seth had swung her up behind him on his huge black stallion for the ride back to Khepesh. She'd clung to his waist, comforted by his familiar masculine scent, absorbing his calm strength through their physical contact and the emotions of his steady compassion through the blood magic they shared.

He'd fed her. He'd bathed her. And then he'd taken her to his bed and made love to her.

She'd loved every minute she'd spent with him. Holding him. Feeling him. Taking him deep within her body.

How had this drowning emotion happened to her so quickly? So completely?

Was she bespelled? Were her profound feelings for

Seth the result of the magic of his vampire bite, as he'd said?

She didn't think so. Nephtys had told her how it felt to have the blood addiction. The hot cravings. The aching, sizzling, agonizing need that coursed through a woman's blood at the very thought of the vampire's sharp fangs.

But that's not what Josslyn felt. The stinging kiss of the vampire was not what she craved when she thought of Seth-Aziz. No, her cravings were of a much more personal nature. The cravings of a woman for a man, and all he offered for her intimate delight and enjoyment. Cravings every mortal woman had for the man she loved.

His bare chest. His sculpted lips. His long, thick cock.

Fangs were just icing on the cake.

As if reading her mind—and perhaps he was—Seth gave her a slow, lazy smile, crinkling the corners of his eyes and sending heat quivering through her body.

His lips quirked slightly and his brow rose a mere fraction of a millimeter. In invitation?

She felt her cheeks grow warm. And certain other parts of her body, as well. She sent him an answering smile, just as subtle. Just as telling. Just as much an invitation.

She shouldn't. She knew he didn't really want her. After his daring defense of her on the ramparts of Petru, she'd expected some kind of acknowledgment of their relationship. At least a simple statement of his feelings for her. Not necessarily a declaration of love— though that would certainly have been welcome. Just...

something. Something verbal, rather than the physical intimacy he'd showered her with since that harrowing episode.

Admittedly, they hadn't been alone together for more than a few hours since then. He'd been caught up in a whirlwind of activity and meetings with the other leaders of Khepesh, always in a crowd. But he'd insisted she accompany him wherever they went, keeping her close by his side.

Still, he hadn't brought up the future. Nor had the Great Council, despite his previous warnings of their plans for her. Apparently they'd changed their minds about her.

Unfortunately, Seth hadn't. He obviously felt protective, and enjoyed making love with her. But she knew he would break her heart into a million pieces when the day came and he finally let her go.

Right now she didn't care. She was basking in the wellspring of his attentions, and she would not give up that feeling for anything.

No, not even to protect her fragile heart.

But it hurt, that he didn't want her for more than this. It hurt like crazy.

With a deep breath, she turned back to the arguing councils, keeping his hand in hers, loathe to let him go.

From across the room Nephtys caught her eye and sent her a beaming smile and a wink. Damn, she really wished she would stop doing that! Joss was sure her cheeks were as crimson as the embroidered sash Seth wore over his black robes.

Nephtys couldn't be more wrong about their relationship!

As they'd all walked into the audience hall earlier, the priestess had suddenly halted and scanned the room—the furnishings, the thrones, the councils and onlookers as they sat cross-legged on the floor on the thick Persian carpets. She'd broken out in a huge grin and spun to Joss and Seth and exclaimed, "This is it! My vision! It's come true!" And then she'd hugged them both, along with a puzzled Haru-Re for good measure. She'd been sending Joss meaningful smiles ever since.

Yeah. The whole vision thing made Josslyn acutely uncomfortable.

Seth had not commented one way or another. Not surprising. He still hadn't brought up the future, hadn't as much as uttered the word *consort* or even *lover* since dismissing her so coolly two days ago.

Obviously his feelings had thawed. Or rather, heated. Considerably. *Physically.* But that didn't mean he wanted to make their arrangement permanent. As in *eternity* permanent.

Hell, okay, Joss didn't know if *she* wanted it permanent, either. She'd known Seth-Aziz, for what, three days? Four?

Regardless of her current feelings for him, because they could change—just look at the 180 Nephtys had done with Ray!—would it not be totally nuts, not to mention scary as hell, to commit to an eternity with a man after so short a time? Eternity was a long, long time.

But it was clear from Nephtys's face that the priestess expected her to do just that.

To be perfectly honest, Joss's own reckless heart wanted to jump over that cliff without looking down. But her mind? Much more cautious. Her mind remembered the view from the top of Petru's wall....

And yet, despite the way he'd avoided any mention of the future, every time she looked at Seth she felt... God, she felt more cherished, more secure, more alive with wonderful possibilities than she'd ever felt before in her life. She wanted to dive into his meltingly dark eyes and lose herself in them forever and ever.

Irrational, terrifying, but there you go. Josslyn Haliday was stone cold in love with the man.

And how scary was *that?*

The noise level pulled her attention back to the audience chamber with a jolt. The shouting had increased as the debate heated.

They were going round and round. It seemed like most of the leaders of both camps agreed with her obvious solution to the political dilemma and wanted to avoid total annihilation for one of the palaces, and possibly for all the *shemsu*. But some of the most vocal debaters were still not convinced their side shouldn't claim a total victory, and damn the consequences.

Desperately needing an outlet for her pent-up feelings of frustration over Seth, she felt herself grow impatient. Did they not see how this would benefit everyone concerned?

Wanting it just to be over, when there was a pause in the argument Josslyn pulled her hand from Seth's and stood.

"You're all speaking of politics and war," she said over the din, "of territories lost and gained, of hoarded assets, of filching followers, of secret rituals and stolen magic, of the problems of sovereignty and identity. But there's one thing you haven't talked about," she said to the debaters. "The most important thing of all."

A hush fell over the room in waves, and all eyes turned to her.

"Tell us, Lady Josslyn. What could be left?"

She blinked at the use of the title she'd never get used to and cleared her throat. "The point you're missing is, the world needs *both* of you. The dark *and* the light. What would we mortals do without the cool darkness of night or the dark shadows hidden deep in our psyches? And how could anyone live without the blessings and the fruit of the sun or the enlightenment of knowledge gained? We might prefer one way of living over the other, but we could never exist without both in all our lives."

Slowly, murmurs of assent could be heard.

"I don't pretend to know anything about your world, really," she continued. "But I do know mine has lost so much experience and wisdom that can never be regained, because we mortals so often choose to destroy what we don't understand. Don't make the same mistake. The powers of the universe have designed this planet with the contrasts of day and night, darkness and light, order and chaos. Who are we, whether mortal or immortal, to tell the universe it's wrong?"

There was a moment of silence as her words were digested.

Amidst an undulating sea of nods, a vote was called for, and at long last the momentous decision came to be made to merge the forces of light and darkness into one powerful union that would rule the earth together.

The last two to voice their votes were Seth-Aziz and Haru-Re.

When his turn came, Seth rose regally to his feet and said, "Lady Josslyn has spoken wisely. I, for one, agree with her and am honored to throw in my lot with those who have chosen peace between our peoples." He lifted his gaze across the chamber. "Furthermore, to prove my seriousness and pledge my sincerity to the cause, I hereby give my official blessing to the marriage of my sister, the Priestess Nephtys, to Haru-Re, High Priest of Petru."

A few gasps mingled with cheers of approval.

At this, Haru-Re also rose, to a shower of felicitations. "I, too, vote for peace, not war." He smiled at Nephtys and beckoned her to rise with him. "As does my future consort, Nephtys, my truest love. With our coming union, we hope to forge a true and lasting friendship between the palaces of Petru and Khepesh, and in so doing keep alive the rituals for both our gods, indeed all the ancient lore, for many millennia to come."

He sought out Joss with his gaze. "And to prove *my* sincerity, I hereby bequeath a secret which because of my selfishness I have held closely guarded." He glanced at Nephtys. "I now wish to share it and put to right some of the mistakes I've made in the past." His bride-to-be nodded and smiled.

There was a stirring in the crowd. Joss wondered what the secret could be. The last one he'd revealed— the ancient dream spell discovered in his library—had been huge.

"Many centuries ago," he said, "I uncovered a papyrus in the archive taken from the defeated *per netjer* of Sekhmet."

A chill went down Joss's spine. The very temple where she and her sisters had been working when all this had started! She couldn't help but wonder if the powerful goddess had a hand in the events of the past month...

"In the writings," Ray went on, "I discovered one of great import, containing a secret hidden long ago by the first immortal high priestess of that temple." Everyone held their breath. "In it was revealed the way to reverse the spell that turns human to *shabti*."

Joss jumped to her feet, clapping her hands to her mouth in shock. Was it true?

In the audience, she heard Gemma gasp. Gillian, too, cried out with a joyous sound, then burst into tears as Joss turned to seek their gazes in disbelief. Shahin stood frozen, utterly stunned, staring at Haru-Re. Joss knew from Gemma that his own mother had been serving Haru-Re as a *shabti* for over three hundred years.

As one, they all turned to Nephtys for confirmation. She nodded, her eyes filling with tears when she saw how moved they all were by the news. Could it really be so?

"How?" Joss managed to tear her focus back to Haru-Re and ask. "How is it done?"

"It's almost too easy," Ray said. "The *shabti* must only be removed from the *per netjer*. That's all. Just like the spell that preserves our immortality, without the monthly rituals of renewal, the *shabti* spell simply unravels and dissolves, restoring the person to their former self, their consciousness and their will. Afterward, they can pick up their life as though the interruption never took place. Other than the time displacement, of course."

Nephtys expression turned to one of comprehension. "So *that's* why you were always so bent on retrieving *shabtis* who escaped the palace," she murmured.

Haru-Re nodded gravely. "At first it was because I didn't want to lose their services. But after a while, I realized how terrible it would be to awaken from what you think is an afternoon nap, only to find yourself living in another century, or even a different millennium. I wished to spare them that horror, at least."

Joss thought about that. It was true, she supposed. Romantic time-travel novels aside, it would be pretty awful to wake up a hundred, or a thousand, years in the future. But still…

Thank God in heaven the victims would all be freed now.

Including her own mother.

She gazed at Haru-Re with new respect. This truly showed how much he had changed. Or perhaps, Nephtys had been right all along, and he just needed encouragement to allow the natural goodness within him to emerge. She'd like to think so.

Happiness glowed from deep within her as she exchanged joyful looks with Gillian and Gemma and a still-stunned Shahin.

Joss hadn't seen her parents yet, but now…oh, now she had such wonderful news to share with her father! Isobelle Haliday was alive and would once again be the vibrant, loving, beautiful woman Joss remembered from her childhood!

There was no better gift in the world.

Seth's arm slipped around her shoulders in a warm embrace. She looked up and he tenderly kissed her brow.

"I believe your work here is done, my love." He tipped up her chin with a knuckle and smiled. "And now perhaps you'd fancy a visit to Petru with your sisters? This time under more pleasant circumstances, I would hope."

If the man hadn't already captured her heart completely, this loving, considerate invitation would have done it for sure.

Josslyn's heart was gone. Utterly and absolutely lost to this amazing man. And there was nothing she could do about it.

Or wanted to.

She rose up on her toes, kissed his lips and whispered, "Seth-Aziz, you are truly the most wonderful man in the world."

Chapter 24

When it came right down to it, Seth had no idea how to deal with his love for Josslyn.

He'd been a demigod for five millennia, a high priest for longer than that, all the while a respected leader of his tight-knit underground community, steering the destinies of the immortals with power and authority through good times and bad, through thick and thin.

He'd never been at a total loss before.

Never in such a quandary as to his *own* destiny.

Not until he'd met the stubborn, wise, unpredictable, loyal, mouthy and inordinately tempting Josslyn Haliday.

He wanted her. He wanted her in the worst way. He wanted her in the best way.

He wanted her in *all* ways.

She seemed to want him. Physically, at least. She seemed to like him. A lot. She smiled when she saw him, her face lighting up with pleasure. She melted into him when he held her close. She came to him eagerly when he beckoned. Came for him with abandon when he touched her. Hadn't she just said, not three hours ago, that he was the most wonderful man in the world?

He was terrified of making a mistake. He was so bad at this! All he wanted was a clue. But when he tried to probe her feelings, through their blood connection, no matter how delicately and subtly he searched for some indication of how she really felt about him, she'd managed to keep her emotions so carefully guarded, so tightly shut away, that he'd been unable to decipher them.

Even as they'd shared his bed for a few hours last night, as she'd given him her body so completely, her heart had been impossible to weigh.

Was it because he'd acted like such a bastard before, blaming her for things she'd had no part in, sending her away when she'd offered herself to him so selflessly and without guile? Telling her that love had nothing to do with his wanting her as his consort. What a thoughtless, cruel thing to say to a woman!

He had to tread delicately now. He didn't want to scare her off by coming on too strong again. He'd nearly succeeded last time in a bad way. What a fool he'd been! By the feather of Thoth, he regretted his unthinking actions! His closed mind. His lack of feeling.

He wanted to beg her forgiveness. Desperately. To show her he'd finally come to his senses. But he could think of no gift worthy of her to made amends. Even Haru-Re had given her something far more precious than anything Seth could summon up to present her.

He glanced over at the woman who occupied his every waking thought, to where she and her sisters were speaking animatedly with their father. Josslyn was dressed in a loose-flowing silken gown that glided sensually over her body while emphasizing her lovely curves. The dress was robin's-egg blue, an uncommon shade for a Khepesh woman, who tended to wear darker, jewel-like colors, but it looked beautiful with her luxuriant blond hair and pale skin, so he didn't begrudge her the slip into the tones of Petru. She was gorgeous today, and glowing from the reunion with her parents.

They were all sitting on the grass in the garden behind the temple of Re-Horakhti at Petru, he and Rhys off to one side by the sacred, fragrant lily-filled pool, Shahin sitting quietly with his silent mother, lost in thought.

Josslyn was holding her own mother's hand, a shadow of sadness tracing over her pretty features whenever she looked at her.

It couldn't be easy for any of them to see the woman who'd birthed and raised them languish in such a hollow state. But at least it would be over soon. Trevor Haliday was already speculating on how and when he could carry his wife away from Petru, so the wicked spell would fade away and his beloved wife could emerge from the empty shell she'd been living in for the past twenty years.

"You can take her to my home in North Carolina," Gemma was saying to her father. "Live in my apartment until she's better. Then come back to us here, where we can all be together." Gemma reached out to take Shahin's hand between her palms and kissed it. He smiled at her, but his eyes were seeing something far away, in the distant past.

"I should come with you," Josslyn said to her father, jolting Seth to attention. "I can—"

Seth shook his head and interrupted firmly, "No. We talked about this, Josslyn. You can't leave Khepesh."

"But you said I could!" she countered.

"After you've joined the *shemsu*," he returned.

"Then let me do it right away. I'll—"

"*And* after a good number of years have passed," he cut in. "There are many things to learn about your new powers before you can go out into the world again."

"Then I won't join at all. It won't be a factor."

Just *once* he wished she would simply accept his commands without arguing! Gillian and Gemma were the same way, according to Rhys and Shahin's complaints. It must be some kind of blasted family curse.

"Not possible," he stated categorically. "You *will* join."

And why was she so transparently anxious to leave Khepesh…to leave *him?* How could she not see that she belonged here? That she belonged to him?

Didn't she understand that he would never, could never, let her go? Not in a million years, and even that would be too soon? Not after she'd shared his bed and listened to his dreams of a peaceful, prosperous future, filled with happiness. Didn't *she* know she was the main reason for that happiness?

"You can't possibly think I'd betray the *per netjer?*" she persisted. "I think I've proven my loyalty!"

He jetted out a breath of irritation. He had no intention

of discussing this in front of the others. "You'll stay here because I wish it," he told her, possibly a bit more sharply than intended.

Still. *He* was the high priest here. The reigning demigod. She was a mere initiate, not even of the *shemsu* yet—even if Nephtys had big plans to teach her the ways of the temple and make her a priestess like herself, trained to hold and preserve the secret of immortality. *That* was far in the future.

For now she must obey him!

Josslyn scowled fiercely, but to his annoyance, the others were trying hard to hide impertinent smiles. Rhys was actually grinning, the scorpion. Even Shahin was shaking his head at him, a sardonic slant to his mouth.

"What?" Seth demanded of them all.

Trevor Haliday's brows flicked as he looked from one daughter to the next, ending with his oldest. He drilled a look at Seth while saying to her, "Sweetie, we can talk more about this tomorrow. I think Seth-Aziz has something he wants to discuss with you now. Isn't that right, my lord?"

"Yes. I do," Seth said, rising from the grass with as much dignity and authority as he could muster. He held out his hand to her. It was time he showed her the way of things.

"Come with me, *heret-ibi*. Please," he added when her scowl deepened.

Her mouth thinned, but she took his offered hand and let him help her up. Who said there were no more miracles?

He crooked his arm and calmly waited until she reluctantly took it.

Small favors.

"Seth, I—"

"Shush," he admonished. "You'll have your chance to say anything you wish when we get where we're going."

"And where is that?" she asked.

"You'll see."

He could almost hear her debate with herself over whether or not to object. To forestall further argument, at the edge of the garden he shifted to Mihos Rukem. He knew she loved his favorite Set-animal, and if anything could make her forget her displeasure with him, it was the Black Lion of Egypt.

He nudged her with his muzzle, urging her to lift the hem of her gown and climb onto his back.

"It'll be ruined!" she said.

Like he cared. He could conjure her a thousand dresses in the blink of an eye. He let out a few clicks of a growl and pushed his nose under the hem, raising it several inches up her legs.

A tactical error.

His sensitive nose could smell the scent of their earlier lovemaking on her, despite the shower they'd shared after awakening this morning. He breathed in deeply and felt his balls grow hard and heavy. His growl deepened as he traced a lingering path up her calf with his nose, and higher still, pulling a gasp of scandal from her when his intent became clear.

She swatted at him. "Stop!" she hissed in embarrassment. "My father is watching!"

With an inward chuckle, he nudged her again, and this time she quickly clambered onto his back.

She rode him like a queen, head high, holding fistfuls of his black mane to keep her balance, the gown fluttering about her bare legs and feet as he trotted toward the front gate of Petru. The pathway parted before them like the Red Sea, as the *shemsu* of Re-Horakhti backed away to look on in admiration.

The Golden Portal yawned open, and he leapt forward, once again running with the desert wind. He felt Josslyn relax against his neck, the muscles of her body melding with his in the loping run, as they did when they were making love.

He felt completely, blissfully free and wild. And he loved having her with him.

He wanted her here forever.

His huge paws ate up the miles between Petru and Khepesh, bringing them quickly to his destination....

His own tomb.

Chapter 25

Josslyn recognized the place at once.

It was definitely the same place she'd seen Rhys carry off her sister Gillian last month. And also where she'd later met Nephtys on that fateful afternoon.

God, had it only been four days ago?

Joss clung to the fur of the huge black-and-tan lion that was Seth, as he trotted up the steep incline of the *gebel,* heading toward the familiar narrow eye in the rock. Behind it lay the tomb, with its square, plain-hewn antechamber…and the mysterious secret door that Nephtys had insisted Joss not unlock. Instead, the priestess had spirited her away to the tunnel entrance that had led her deep underground, to the Great Western Gate of Khepesh.

And to a fate she never could have imagined.

Mihos Rukem slipped through the keyhole opening in the *gebel* and came to a halt. She slid off his back.

Had he brought her here to show her the secret of the mysterious Ptolemaic door? Or perhaps another unexpected change of fate awaited her....

She shivered, a spill of foreboding cascading down her spine.

"What are we doing here?" she asked nervously.

Not that a lion could answer.

"Josslyn," Seth's deep voice said from behind her.

She spun. The sunlight barely penetrated the tomb's antechamber, and her eyes hadn't yet gotten used to the dimness. Dressed in his Bedouin robes, Seth's tall, impressive form was a solid black silhouette backlit by radiating beams of silver light. A wave of power rolled over her, the last of the energy from his shift. The man truly was magnificent. She sucked in a breath, unable to resist his regal appeal.

"I have something to show you," he said, his voice low and smooth.

Those six words never failed to send shivers of desire coursing through her, for they always came just before he stripped her naked and led her into some amazing new erotic experience that left her breathless and wanting more. *Much* more.

"Okay," she whispered.

He tipped his head and a corner of his lip curved up. "Always so willing."

"Is that a bad thing?" she asked, suddenly unsure if he thought she was—

"No, it's a very good thing."

She swallowed. *Thank God.*

Already her body was heating, moistening, preparing itself for him.

He made no move to touch her, though. Didn't strip away her clothes with a quick flick of his hand. Didn't look at her with that hungry, drowning look he gave her when he was thinking of something very, very wicked.

"So…" she said, even more uncertain. "What did you want to show me?"

He took a step toward her, but his gaze went over her shoulder. "My tomb," he said.

A trill of energy brushed over her, feeling like the silken swipe of a cat's tail. Goose bumps blossomed on her skin.

She faltered and glanced around at the bare stone walls, carved in a simple faux block pattern. "Yours?" Then it hit her. "Oh, Seth. You died?"

He inclined his head. "My death was a required part of the ritual that made me vampire. I could not become a demigod without going through it."

A soft sound of horror slipped from her throat. "My God."

"Goddess, actually. Sekhmet, the bitch. She would take her pound of male flesh, one way or another." His shadowed smile held no humor.

"How…?" she asked, a horrified kind of curiosity getting the better of her. She was, after all, a scientist at heart. She'd heard rumors of Sekhmet's association with blood and vampires, but had never heard definitive proof before now.

"I was bled to death."

Jesus. "Good Lord. Was it awful?" she asked.

"As I recall, it was…unpleasant."

She regarded him for a moment and tried to imagine

what it must have been like for him. Trading his life for untold power and immortality—but at such a price. "Was it worth it?"

The humorless smile reappeared. "Ask me again tomorrow."

She wasn't sure what that meant. But before she could pursue it, he slipped past her and moved his hand over the two stone blocks that marked the edges of the secret door, using his energy to trip the metal lever cleverly hidden in the seam between them.

At once, a low rumble started, deep in the bowels of the tomb. Inch by slow inch, a square section of rock started to slide backward. When it stopped, there was an opening large enough for a person to crawl through.

Oh. My. God.

"Frightened?" he asked.

"You're kidding, right?"

In the darkness, he tunneled the fingers of one hand gently through her hair. "Josslyn," he murmured, his voice silken, "you will never have anything to fear. Come what may, I will always protect you."

She swallowed. That sounded almost like...

No, she must be imagining the unspoken vow in his words, of a future together.

He pulled her mouth to his and kissed her. As though sealing his promise.

"Seth—" she murmured. She needed to know.

But he laid his thumb over her lips. "Go through the door, into the tomb, Josslyn."

Her pulse jumped and her hands started to tremble.

Something was going on. Something she didn't understand. "You're scaring me."

"No need," he said. "Remember, I'm here to protect you. Besides, it's not dangerous."

"Then why all the mystery?"

"What happened to my intrepid archaeologist? Now go."

She nibbled on her lip. She didn't know why she was so nervous. She'd been in hundreds of tombs before. Hell, she'd napped in them. With mummies as roommates. But she felt something, a kind of tingling on the nape of her neck. He seemed a little too...anxious. Or something.

"Tell me what's inside first."

"By the *gods* you are exasperating! Inscriptions. Nothing more. Now get in there before I put you over my knee and—"

"Okay! I'm going."

She took a deep breath, dropped to her hands and knees and crawled through the opening. Seth followed close behind her. When they rose, he made an arc with his hand and several torches sprang to life, filling the chamber with light.

She gasped in amazement.

He hadn't lied. The four stone walls were filled floor to ceiling with precisely chiseled, gorgeously painted Old Kingdom scenes and inscriptions.

"Oh, Seth!" she breathed, spinning around to look at it all. "They're exquisite!"

Her eyes were immediately drawn to the main funerary scene on the focal wall opposite the entry door. It showed the tall, nearly life-sized, distinctive figure of Khepesh's half-man half-mythical jackal-like patron god, Set-Sutekh, accepting gifts and adulation from the slightly smaller figure of his high priest. There was a name inscribed next to him, but Joss would have known that handsome, aristocratic profile anywhere.

"That's you!" she said.

He nodded. "A rather good likeness, I thought."

She stared at the portrait, and a strange, creepy feeling of wonder shivered through her at the thought that he had been frozen in that pose paying homage to his god for five-thousand years—yet she was standing here now, right next to the man himself.

"Wow," she whispered.

She stepped back to take in the whole elaborate scene. Fanning off to either side of Seth and flowing around all four walls of the antechamber were scores of smaller figures, men and women, some standing, some kneeling respectfully on their heels, some dancing or playing instruments. There were birds and flowers and a multitude of animals. All doing honor to Seth-Aziz and bringing offerings to the god.

"It's magical," she said, completely enchanted. "They seem almost…alive. Like every one of them could step right off the wall and come to life."

All at once she noticed two figures near the end of the line of supplicants, a man and a woman. The man sported a very un-Egyptian mustache, and the woman was blond.

Joss gasped in recognition. "That's Gillian and Rhys!"

Seth smiled and pointed to another couple, farther up within the revelers. "Yes. And here's Shahin and Gemma."

"Oh!" She shot him a look, then turned back to the

painting. And suddenly she understood. "These people on the walls, they're the *shemsu* of Khepesh, aren't they? You've put them all here, so their names will be kept alive forever, never to be forgotten."

Again he nodded, this time somewhat wistfully. "I come out here sometimes, to look at their faces. To remember the friends we've lost over the years and wonder who might be the next to go. Ponder who will take their places. If anyone will…"

And she was sure he took every passing personally to heart. She could see it in his face, the loneliness of loss and the burden of responsibility.

"Surely, now that there's peace with Petru, things will be better."

"I pray you are right."

He was such a compassionate leader; such a good person.

She couldn't help falling in love with him a little bit more.

She laid her head against his shoulder, and he put his arm around her. For several long minutes they looked at the many faces in the painting. "It's amazing how the artist could fit everyone in. How many *shemsu* are there altogether?"

"I'm not sure. I suppose I should count them one day. Three or four hundred, I should think."

"Wow."

"There's someone missing, though," he said. "Here." He gestured to a slim, empty spot just to the side of his own figure.

"Really? Who?"

"You."

She whipped her head around to look at him, hope blossoming in her heart. "Me?"

He smiled down at her. "That blank space is meant for my true wife and consort. Honestly, I've despaired of ever filling it."

She blinked. "Oh?"

"But I was thinking I'd like to put your image there, if you'll let me."

Her lips parted, her heart racing. "Truly?" she whispered.

"Truly," he assured her. "I love you, Josslyn."

Her soul took flight and sang with joy. Finally! "Oh, Seth, I love you, too. With all my heart."

He kissed her then, long and deep, and his magical energy wrapped her in an enveloping spill of sizzling warmth and shivering power. She knew she would always be safe and protected while she was in his arms. And always, always loved.

"Will you let your name be carved next to mine, and always be my beloved wife and honored consort, to be by my side through all eternity?"

"Yes, oh, yes," she whispered, and held him close, her heart overflowing with happiness. And she knew for certain that an eternity would not be nearly long enough to show the world how much she loved this amazing man.

Chapter 26

One year later...

Seth-Aziz, high priest of Set-Sutekh, vampire demigod and leader of the *shemsu* of Khepesh, walked through the stately portal to the luxurious Khepesh Palace temple and was immediately swallowed up by the *shemsu* who crowded the huge courtyard. Already it was a crush, and the Ritual for Eternal Life was not to start for another hour.

The women's gowns rustled with diaphanous silks and elegant satins, their every expanse of exposed skin sparkling with precious jewels. Most of the men wore traditional tunics and trousers, but layered them with exquisite robes of every color and pattern benefitting their positions as Keepers of the Ancient Ways.

The Khepesh temple courtyards were also resplendent, adorned by thousands of fragrant flower garlands and twinkling with the light of ten thousand scented candles. The high arched ceiling looked especially dazzling tonight. Or perhaps it was just the stars in his eyes. Seth had never been happier. Gone forever was the man who'd wondered over his existence and the reason for his being.

One woman had changed all that. And tonight she would become his forever.

Thank goodness he'd arrived early. Everyone was turning to greet him and give their blessings and well wishes. Seth wanted to take his time and speak with each one of his followers, to feel the pulse of energy swirling through the temple and absorb the awesome power that his people were gifting him with on this joyful and momentous occasion.

It wouldn't do to be late to the ritual that would make his wife immortal.

Apparently, he wasn't the only one to think so. A long while later, as he entered the temple's Courtyard of the Sacred Pool, he saw that Rhys and Shahin were already waiting for him. It wasn't quite as crowded in there, and his brothers-in-law were standing at the edge of the sacred basin of Set-Sutekh, gazing at the delicate magical bridge that had been conjured over the pool for the ceremony, and looking as nervous as two gazelles peering into a lion's den.

Tonight, their wives would be granted eternal life, as well.

To Seth's pleasant surprise, a third man paced back and forth between the pool and the portal to the inner sanctum. Trevor Haliday, their wives' father. Seth greeted him first out of respect, though he was the lowest ranking of the three men. Indeed, he wasn't even immortal any longer…though he would always be counted as one of the *shemsu*.

"Lord Trevor," Seth said warmly, clasping his hand between his. "I'm so happy you made it in time for the ceremony. Your daughters will be thrilled you're here." He glanced around. "And where is your lovely wife?"

Haliday's eyes softened. "With the girls, helping them get ready."

Trevor and Isobelle Haliday had just today arrived back in Egypt from an extended stay in North Carolina, where Isobelle had slowly returned to herself and caught up with the world after living in a vacuum for twenty years. Haru-Re had been correct, being excluded from the renewal rituals had thankfully released the magical hold on her mind, but the *shabti* spell was a powerful one, and it had taken many months to complete the process.

Trevor Haliday hadn't wanted to return to Egypt too soon, and even now Seth could feel the man's almost palpable worry that simply being here at Khepesh would cause his wife to disappear again into oblivion. Praise the gods, that did not seem likely. Isobelle was as bright and charming as a woman could be and showed no signs of regression.

All three sisters had been moved to tears at the reunion with their mother, despite the fact that they'd all been in constant touch with both their parents via phone and email, thanks to the modern technology Rhys had installed at his desert estate aboveground.

"Are you sure you won't change your mind?" Seth now asked his father-in-law. "There's still time for you both to be added to the ceremony." Being away from Khepesh had allowed Isobelle to recover, but as expected, the same absence had caused Trevor to lose his immortality.

Lord Trevor shook his head. "Very kind, but no. My wife and I have decided to remain mortal for now. I must say, it's damned disconcerting being nearly the same age as one's offspring." He lifted a shoulder with a smile. "Perhaps one day in the future, when we achieve the proper parental age difference…"

Seth laughed, though with a note of sadness. He genuinely liked the man, and adored Isobelle. He was sorry his in-laws had chosen to live among the mortals, and Josslyn had been more than distraught at the news. "I hope you will very soon," Seth said. "You've raised some amazing daughters who are destined to be exalted among the *shemsu*. It goes without saying that their parents will always be welcome and honored in Khepesh. No doubt Petru, as well."

"Why, of course you are both welcome at Petru! Anytime at all."

Haru-Re's hearty voice drew Seth's attention to a group of gold-clad *shemsu* that had just entered the courtyard. Ray joined Seth and Trevor.

Seth had to admit, the high priest of the Sun God had become almost cloyingly cheerful since taking Nephtys as his official consort. There'd been a special glow over the palace of Petru that could be seen nearly to Khepesh. However, Seth didn't begrudge him. Not in the least. Over the past year, the two leaders had spoken often, and come to agreement on most things. He'd even go so far as to say they'd become tentative friends. It was good to have someone with whom to share the weighty responsibilities of ruling the immortals and maintaining the rituals of the old ways. Finally there was someone who truly understood the philosophical burden he'd thought he alone had felt all those years.

"My lord Haru-Re," Seth greeted him formally with a bow. "It is good to see you."

Ray returned the greeting, then smiled broadly. "So. The big day."

"At long last," Seth allowed with an equally sincere smile. "Nephtys is preparing the women now."

"Who would have thought, after all the years as bitter enemies, it would end like this between us," Ray said, his bright eyes crinkling. "Peace, prosperity and so in love it almost hurts."

Seth chuckled. "Speak for yourself. I feel wonderful."

Especially after the long hours of lovemaking he and Josslyn had shared together earlier. Afterward, they had lain in each other's arms and talked about the future. His plans for the united *shemsu,* her plans for becoming a priestess like Nephtys.

They'd spoken of having children…something he had never dared wish for before. Gemma had discovered a papyrus in the library of Sekhmet containing a spell that could, for a short while, restore a vampire's seed to potency. There was no guarantee it would work, but his heart was still singing over the possibility of one day soon holding his own child in his arms. Gillian and Gemma were also making similar plans, and of course Rhys and Shahin did not have the impediment of being dead. So, at the very least, Seth would be an uncle. He grinned at the thought of spoiling his nieces and nephews rotten.

To be surrounded by a large, extended family of his

own, with joyous youthful voices and pattering feet, would make him the happiest man on earth.

Haru-Re slapped him on the back. "Ah, my friend, I sense the direction of your thoughts. I will have my librarian send over a spell I found among the scrolls of the temple of Min to increase a man's virility."

Seth gave an embarrassed laugh. "Am I so easy to read?" he asked wryly.

"When it comes to love," Ray returned with a wink, "we men wear our hearts on our sleeves. It is a good thing, I think, when honestly felt."

"Yes," Seth agreed. "A very good thing."

Just then the flames burning in the torch-sconces lowered, and the light in the courtyard dimmed. By now the chamber was filled to capacity, the *shemsu* surrounding the sacred pool and forming a semicircle around the portal to the inner sanctum, the holy of holies, where the ceremony was to take place. Slowly a reverent silence fell upon the crowd.

It was time.

Rhys and Shahin joined him, and the three men made their way through the hushed darkness to their assigned places at the center of the bridge above the sacred pool, where they would await their women.

The courtyard was now dark as the blackest night, pierced only by the sparkle of thousands of tiny candles lining the bridge that led over the sacred pool, and a million diamonds glittering from the ceiling overhead.

From all around, soft music started to play. It was the welcoming chant of the immortals accompanied by the ethereal instruments of the spheres, the music of the ancient Universe greeting the new arrivals to the fold of the *shemsu*. Seth could feel the preternatural energy, the swell of magical power that filled the room. It swirled and grew, until it was almost a living, breathing thing, joining each person to the other in a cosmic union of immortal souls.

Then the stately temple portals swung slowly open, and the procession began.

Lit up from above by the glow of magical moonbeams, Nephtys walked slowly down the jasmine-strewn path that opened up through the center of the swaying throng of immortals. Behind her walked the three sisters, arm in arm.

In the center was Josslyn.

His wife.

Seth's breath caught in his throat. Ray was right. Seth loved her so much it hurt. His heart ached with the pure joy of knowing she was his. And would be his for the rest of time.

She was so beautiful. Her blond hair was like the glitter of stars, her lithe body dressed in a gossamer gown of the most delicate silver color imaginable. Like her sisters, her eyes were made up in the manner of the ancients, rimmed with black liner and smuged with kohl, looking dark and sultry as Isis herself. She looked exotic and sensual and deliciously tempting.

He could feel her heart beating, fast and anxious.

Next to him, Shahin and Rhys stirred, equally struck by their own women's beauty.

By the gods, Shahin's awe-filled thoughts drifted into Seth's head. *Are we not the luckiest men in the world?*

"By any measure," Seth murmured. "We are truly blessed."

Rhys nodded with a smile of agreement. "Indeed we are."

Nephtys stepped onto the bridge and a swell of energy washed over the sacred pool, raising a pineapple-and-spice fragrance from the large pink water lilies that floated on the pond below. Seth held out his hands to her as she approached.

"My sister. I greet you, Priestess of Set-Sutekh, God of the Moon and Lord of the Night Sky, and now of Re-Horakhti, God of the Sun and Lord of all the Days. Nephtys, Guardian of the Sacred Ritual of Immortal Life, I ask you on this night to grant your favor upon our three supplicants, Josslyn, Gemma and Gillian Haliday."

"My brother, Seth-Aziz, High Priest of Set-Sutekh and Lord of Khepesh, I answer your call and proceed to the sacred altar to perform the secret ritual to transform mortal to immortal and grant these women the powers of the *shemsu.*"

The three men stepped aside to let her pass. Then Seth turned to Josslyn. It was the most sacred, solemn ceremony in the world of the *per netjer,* but he couldn't help the smile that leaped onto his face.

"Heret-ibi," he whispered. "Josslyn, my only heart."

"My lord," she whispered, the joy on her face shining for all to see. She did a deep curtsey, as was expected for the ceremony. And then she took his arm, and he led her across the bridge and down to the threshold of the inner sanctum, the holy of holies. The cave-dark chamber was alive with the glitter of a forest of tiny candles. The sweet spice of incense and ambergris and a thousand flowers wafted from four of the six sacred side altars.

The central altar was his own obsidian sarcophagus, inside of which he slept each month for three nights surrounding the full moon. It was clear of any sacrifice or decoration, as were the two altars that flanked it. They were reserved for the ceremony.

He and Josslyn waited at the portal for her sisters to join her, led by Rhys and Shahin. When they did, each man kissed his woman and stepped back.

Seth's heart thundered. The ritual was not dangerous, but it was momentous. And it would change his life forever.

A hush fell over the crowd as Josslyn, Gemma and Gillian moved into the inner sanctum, where Nephtys stood at the foot of his gleaming black sarcophagus. She, too, looked lovely, arrayed in her narrow, pleated priestess gown of shimmering silver, her youthful eyes shining with solemn excitement. She greeted each of the women. The tableau they presented was unique and beautiful, and eerily familiar to Seth. It could have been carved and painted on the walls of the most luxurious of the ancient pharaoh's tombs.

"You are the chosen of the god," Nephtys sang the sacred chant, her voice echoing through the courtyards of the temple like the sweet tones of a bell ringing. "Come and join the *per netjer* of the Ancients. Be with us, and help to keep our names alive forever in the mouth of the Universe!"

The *shemsu* also began to chant, an eerie, dissonant harmony, that sent shivers of power spilling through the bodies of everyone there. Seth closed his eyes and drank in their power and their magical energy, filling himself with the love of his people for himself and his bride. They loved her nearly as much as he did.

He had made the right choice. She was everything that had been missing from his life.

She was his soul mate.

One by one, Nephtys bade the sisters lie down on the three central altars in preparation for the ritual. Josslyn's gaze sought his. He could feel the tremulous fear and cautious jubilation running through his own body, as well as hers. Their connection was strong, and getting stronger every day.

As was their love.

Sweet Isis, how he loved her!

He nodded, and her shoulders notched down a fraction, trusting him. She climbed on top of his sarcophagus and lay back on its smooth, cool surface. Her sisters did the same on the two flanking altars.

Then Nephtys turned her back to the crowd and began the sacred ritual chant over them, the words of which she alone knew. It took forever it seemed. Or perhaps it was just Seth's impatience that made it seem so. The priestess chanted, the *shemsu* sang and Seth's heart raced.

And then, at last, it was over.

His wife and her sisters sat up, blinking. Again, Josslyn's gaze sought his. She smiled, and he felt an overwhelming rush of love spill through him. Her love and his, mingled together as one, coursed through both their bodies. And their souls.

"I love you," she mouthed.

His eyes swam with happiness. And he whispered back, "I love you, too."

Epilogue

It was nearly sunrise.

Isobelle Haliday lifted her face to the warm glow emanating from the eastern horizon, and smiled. Contentment wrapped itself around her body like a beautiful hand-stitched quilt.

It was good to be alive. So very good.

She slid from her mount, a spirited palomino mare, her soft-booted feet touching the hard ground of the Egyptian *gebel*. She felt an instant connection with the earth below, as old as time and solid as the love she held for her three beloved daughters.

In the indigo sky above, an elegant black hawk soared in circles, and on her shoulder a dragonfly had alighted, cheerfully iridescent in the gathering dawn, the flutter of its wings as quick as the blink of an eye.

Isobelle laughed merrily when the dragonfly took off and buzzed around the mare's nose, making it shake its head and sneeze. Some things would never change. Thank God! She still couldn't believe she had missed twenty years of her precious daughters' lives. She aimed to make up for every last minute.

"Now, now, you two," she admonished, but the words were filled with affection and laughter. Laughter that burst out loud when the hawk dropped from the sky, did an awkward pirouette and transformed into her middle daughter, Gemma…who promptly landed on her butt on the ground.

"Ow!" Gemma cried with a chagrined frown.

"The landing could use some work," her oldest, Josslyn, said drily from behind them, straightening her gown after her more dignified shift.

"Just you wait," Gemma returned, climbing to her feet and brushing herself off. "It's only the first day. Pretty soon I'll be eating bugs like you for breakfast."

Isobelle wrinkled her nose. "I most certainly hope not!" She, Josslyn and Gemma turned to the mare and waited expectantly.

It shook its head, its golden mane flying.

"Come on, Jelly Bean," Joss said with a grin. "No chickening out. You gotta do it sometime. Better in front of those who love you."

After a moment, the horse reared up hesitantly, and with a shimmer of darkness, transformed into Gillian.

Who promptly also landed on the ground. "Crap," she muttered.

But nothing could dampen their infectious grins and joyous group hug the four women shared as they came together on the top of the steep cliffs.

"Hurry, the sun is rising!" Isobelle exclaimed.

It was such a special day. The first day of her daughters' immortal lives. And the first full day she had been reunited with her children since coming out of her long mental slumber. A good day, indeed.

It was time they gave thanks for the many blessings the Universe had granted them. Second chances were so rare.

"We're doing this old school," she announced, and pulled an icy bottle of champagne from the shoulder bag she'd carried from Khepesh. She opened it with a pop to a chorus of cheers and excited clapping from the girls.

The frothy liquid poured out onto the dry ground and disappeared into it as though the spirits of the earth were lapping it up. Which, she figured they were. How else could you explain the fantastical, wonderful things that had befallen her beloved family here in this mystical place?

Her girls—all amazing women now—laughed as they passed the bottle around between them, each taking a bubbly drink from it in turn. When it came to Isobelle, her eyes filled with tears.

She raised the bottle. "To my beautiful, beautiful daughters," she said, her heart swelling with the immense love only a mother could feel. To think she had nearly lost the chance to know them! "May all your days be filled with untold happiness and an abundance of love. I love you so very much."

She swallowed the effervescent champagne past the enormous lump in her throat.

"Oh, Mom," Josslyn said, her voice choked with emotion. "It's so good to have you back with us. You have no idea how much you were missed."

"Oh," Isobelle said, her tears brimming over along with her heart. "I think I do."

With their arms around each other and their faces wet with tears of joy, they all turned to face the rising sun.

The start of a new day.

The start of a new world.

A new beginning for all of them.

And when the darkness came at sunset, the nighttime would embrace them, too, along with the husbands they loved, and their lives would be complete. Just as the Universe intended.

From the western edge of the *gebel* came the swift crunch of approaching footsteps.

Speak of the devil. "They're here," Isobelle said with a broad smile.

How lucky they were to have such faithful and true partners to share the joys and sorrows of life! To nurture and care for them and protect them from all harm, come what may.

The four handsome men crested the rise, their long black robes flying in the wind behind them like wings of fate—Trevor, Rhys, Shahin and Seth.

"Our men," Josslyn said, happiness overflowing in her voice, and lifted her arms to embrace her husband.

"Yes," Isobelle said. Their big new family for all to share and love, forever after.

Isobelle gazed up at the man who had proven so true of heart, and whom she so adored, then at the husbands of her beloved daughters, and her heart rejoiced.

And she knew, at last, they'd found home.

* * * * *

Harlequin

nocturne™

COMING NEXT MONTH

Available February 22, 2011

HNCNM0211

REQUEST YOUR FREE BOOKS!

2 FREE NOVELS PLUS 2 FREE GIFTS!

n o c t u r n e™

Dramatic and Sensual Tales of Paranormal Romance.

YES! Please send me 2 FREE Harlequin® Nocturne™ novels and my 2 FREE gifts (gifts are worth about $10). After receiving them, if I don't wish to receive any more books, I can return the shipping statement marked "cancel." If I don't cancel, I will receive 4 brand-new novels every other month and be billed just $4.47 per book in the U.S. or $4.99 per book in Canada. That's a saving of at least 15% off the cover price! It's quite a bargain! Shipping and handling is just 50¢ per book in the U.S. and 75¢ per book in Canada.* I understand that accepting the 2 free books and gifts places me under no obligation to buy anything. I can always return a shipment and cancel at any time. Even if I never buy another book, the two free books and gifts are mine to keep forever.

200/338 HDN FC5T

Name	(PLEASE PRINT)	
Address		Apt. #
City	State/Prov.	Zip/Postal Code

Signature (if under 18, a parent or guardian must sign)

Mail to the Reader Service:
IN U.S.A.: P.O. Box 1867, Buffalo, NY 14240-1867
IN CANADA: P.O. Box 609, Fort Erie, Ontario L2A 5X3

Not valid for current subscribers to Harlequin Nocturne books.

Want to try two free books from another line?
Call 1-800-873-8635 or visit www.ReaderService.com.

* Terms and prices subject to change without notice. Prices do not include applicable taxes. Sales tax applicable in N.Y. Canadian residents will be charged applicable taxes. Offer not valid in Quebec. This offer is limited to one order per household. All orders subject to credit approval. Credit or debit balances in a customer's account(s) may be offset by any other outstanding balance owed by or to the customer. Please allow 4 to 6 weeks for delivery. Offer available while quantities last.

Your Privacy—The Reader Service is committed to protecting your privacy. Our Privacy Policy is available online at www.ReaderService.com or upon request from the Reader Service.

We make a portion of our mailing list available to reputable third parties that offer products we believe may interest you. If you prefer that we not exchange your name with third parties, or if you wish to clarify or modify your communication preferences, please visit us at www.ReaderService.com/consumerschoice or write to us at Reader Service Preference Service, P.O. Box 9062, Buffalo, NY 14269. Include your complete name and address.

HN11

USA TODAY *bestselling author Lynne Graham*
is back with a thrilling new trilogy
SECRETLY PREGNANT, CONVENIENTLY WED

Three heroines must marry alpha males to keep
their dreams…but Alejandro, Angelo and Cesario
are not about to be tamed!

Book 1—JEMIMA'S SECRET
Available March 2011 from Harlequin Presents®.

JEMIMA yanked open a drawer in the sideboard to find
Alfie's birth certificate. Her son was her husband's child.
It was a question of telling the truth whether she liked it or
not. She extended the certificate to Alejandro.

"This has to be nonsense," Alejandro asserted.

"Well, if you can find some other way of explaining how
I managed to give birth by that date and Alfie not be yours,
I'd like to hear it," Jemima challenged.

Alejandro glanced up, golden eyes bright as blades and
as dangerous. "All this proves is that you must still have
been pregnant when you walked out on our marriage. It
does not automatically follow that the child is mine."

"'I know it doesn't suit you to hear this news now and I
really didn't want to tell you. But I can't lie to you about it.
Someday Alfie may want to look you up and get acquainted."

"If what you have just told me is the truth, if that little
boy does prove to be mine, it was vindictive and extremely
selfish of you to leave me in ignorance!"

Jemima paled. "When I left you, I had no idea that I was
still pregnant."

"Two years is a long period of time, yet you made no
attempt to inform me that I might be a father. I will want
DNA tests to confirm your claim before I make any deci-

sion about what I want to do."

"Do as you like," she told him curtly. "*I* know who Alfie's father is and there has never been any doubt of his identity."

"I will make arrangements for the tests to be carried out and I will see you again when the result is available," Alejandro drawled with lashings of dark Spanish masculine reserve.

"I'll contact a solicitor and start the divorce," Jemima proffered in turn.

Alejandro's eyes narrowed in a piercing scrutiny that made her uncomfortable. "It would be foolish to do anything before we have that DNA result."

"I disagree," Jemima flashed back. "I should have applied for a divorce the minute I left you!"

Alejandro quirked an ebony brow. "And why didn't you?"

Jemima dealt him a fulminating glance but said nothing, merely moving past him to open her front door in a blunt invitation for him to leave.

"I'll be in touch," he delivered on the doorstep.

What is Alejandro's next move? Perhaps rekindling their marriage is the only solution! But will Jemima agree?

Find out in Lynne Graham's
exciting new romance
JEMIMA'S SECRET

Available March 2011
from Harlequin Presents®.

Start your Best Body today with these top 3 nutrition tips!

1. SHOP THE PERIMETER OF THE GROCERY STORE: The good stuff— fruits, veggies, lean proteins and dairy—always line the outer edges of the store. When you veer into the center aisles, you enter the temptation zone, where the unhealthy foods live.

2. WATCH PORTION SIZES: Most portion sizes in restaurants are nearly twice the size of a true serving and at home, it's easy to "clean your plate." Use these easy serving guidelines:
- Protein: the palm of your hand
- Grains or Fruit: a cup of your hand
- Veggies: the palm of two open hands

3. USE THE RAINBOW RULE FOR PRODUCE: Your produce drawers should be filled with every color of fruits and vegetables. The greater the variety, the more vitamins and other nutrients you add to your diet.

Find these and many more helpful tips in

YOUR BEST BODY NOW
by
TOSCA RENO
WITH STACY BAKER

Bestselling Author of
THE EAT-CLEAN DIET

Available wherever books are sold!